"I regre[...]
throug[...]
"I can o[...]
job."

"I've lost everything." She looked at the store's disarray in despair.

"You haven't." Ben wanted to grip her upper arms and make her meet his eyes, but knew better. "You have supporters. People will realize you would never have stolen that money. Just... give them time."

"I can't afford to give them time," Nadia said drily. "And...do I want people who condemned me without a second thought to become good customers? They would have to pretend, and I'd have to pretend..." She shook her head. "I can't stay in Byrum, not after this. And I'll never dare call the police again, I know that."

"Nadia—"

She took a step back. "You've worn out your welcome."

He hesitated, but recognized he couldn't make this better. Not now, maybe not ever.

He dipped his head. "Things will look better tomorrow."

She didn't dignify that with a response.

When he walked out, she immediately locked the door behind him.

Dear Reader,

The story that became *Her Amish Protectors* sneaked up on me while I was writing *Plain Refuge*. First I became intrigued by a character, then by an idea.

Ben Slater came to life only because Daniel, the hero in *Plain Refuge*, needed a friend, someone he connected with on a deep level. Thus we got Ben, who had inexplicably left an urban police department in New Jersey to take a job as chief of a small-town department in rural Missouri. The "why" didn't matter in *Plain Refuge*, but it began to bug me. I'd created the guy. Why *would* he do something like that?

And then there was the quilt auction. I chaired a large charity auction (benefiting a no-kill animal shelter) for fifteen years. It was a *huge* amount of work. The week leading up to the auction was insane. Auction day, I started with setup first thing in the morning and kept going through wrap-up at eleven o'clock or so at night. Then the drive home, and I'd topple into bed, so exhausted I slept like the dead for twelve hours. And here's the thing: someone had to take all that money home. Of course, that was me. It always made me just a teeny bit nervous to keep it from Saturday night through Monday morning. What I had in a box in the bedroom were mostly credit-card slips. But the Amish deal primarily in cash, so the proceeds of the quilt auction...are a temptation!

Janice

USA TODAY Bestselling Author

JANICE KAY JOHNSON

—

Her Amish Protectors

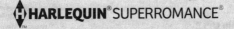

Recycling programs
for this product may
not exist in your area.

ISBN-13: 978-0-373-64029-4

Her Amish Protectors

Printed in U.S.A.

www.Harlequin.com

An author of more than ninety books for children and adults (seventy-five for Harlequin), **Janice Kay Johnson** writes about love and family—about the way generations connect and the power our earliest experiences have on us throughout life. A *USA TODAY* bestselling author and an eight-time finalist for a Romance Writers of America RITA® Award, she won a RITA® Award in 2008 for her Harlequin Superromance novel *Snowbound*. A former librarian, Janice raised two daughters in a small town north of Seattle, Washington.

Books by Janice Kay Johnson

HARLEQUIN SUPERROMANCE

Plain Refuge
A Mother's Claim

Brothers, Strangers

The Baby He Wanted
The Closer He Gets

Because of a Girl
The Baby Agenda
Bone Deep
Finding Her Dad
All That Remains
Making Her Way Home
No Matter What
A Hometown Boy

Anything for Her
Where It May Lead
From This Day On
One Frosty Night
More Than Neighbors
To Love a Cop

Two Daughters

Yesterday's Gone
In Hope's Shadow

The Mysteries of Angel Butte

Bringing Maddie Home
Everywhere She Goes
All a Man Is
Cop by Her Side
This Good Man

Visit the Author Profile page at Harlequin.com for more titles.

PROLOGUE

HEARING *HIM* TALKING on the phone behind her, she risked opening her eyes a slit. Her best friend still looked back at her with the shock and vacancy of death, a line of blood drying where it had trickled from her mouth. Without moving, she could see only Colin's legs and feet where he lay sprawled on creamy plush carpet. Carpet splashed with scarlet splotches, as was the glass-topped coffee table. Keenan, now...

His fingers twitched. His shoulders rose and fell slightly with a breath. In. Out.

Her terror swelled. If his father saw any hint of life, he'd pump another bullet into his eight-year-old son. He thought they were all dead—Paige, eleven-year-old Colin, Keenan and the baby of the family, six-year-old Molly.

And Paige's friend, who had happened to drop by this evening with a book of quilt patterns that Paige had wanted to look through. Wrong time, wrong place.

Except, she'd managed to inch over when Damon's back was turned so that she could shield

Molly's small body. Molly was breathing. Damon couldn't be allowed to see. Once she'd laid a hand over the little girl's mouth to stifle a moan.

She ached to whisper reassurance to Keenan, who wasn't within reach. To beg him to stay absolutely still.

Every breath was agony, searing pain flaring from her abdomen. Blood had spurted when the bullet struck and she had gone down with that first shot. She vaguely remembered hearing Colin's terrified scream. Damon had turned away to shoot his son and forgotten her. Probably, she thought dully, her wound would be fatal. But she desperately wanted Molly and Keenan to live. All three of them might survive if the police stormed the house soon.

There'd been a bullhorn earlier, before Damon answered his cell phone. That could have been fifteen minutes ago, or two hours ago. She floated in a dreamlike state. Only the pain anchored her here.

No. Not only pain. Molly and Keenan.

It took an enormous effort to comprehend what Damon was saying.

"Hell, no, I'm not going to let that bitch talk to you! If you don't quit asking, that's it. Do you hear me?" The savagely angry voice bore little resemblance to the smooth baritone she knew from phone calls and the times Paige had invited her to dinner with her family.

Pause. "They're with their mother. No, I'm not going to upset them by putting them on the phone, either."

They're dead or dying. Paige is dead. Please, please. We need you.

Time drifted. Occasionally, she heard him talking.

"I lose my job and she's going to *leave* me?"

Molly was still breathing. Keenan…she wasn't sure.

Whoever was on the phone with Damon listened, sympathized, gave him all the time he wanted to air his furious grievances.

While we die.

She quit listening, quit peeking at a dying boy. She let herself float away.

CHAPTER ONE

"Now, we both know you want that quilt." The auctioneer had strolled down the aisle between folding chairs until he was only a few feet from one of the two bidders on a spectacular Album quilt. "And for a cause this important, you can spend a little extra. Isn't that right?" He thrust the microphone toward the woman next to the man holding the bid card.

She giggled.

Nadia Markovic held her breath. She'd put in a huge amount of work to make tonight's charity auction at Brevitt House happen, and it was paying off beyond her wildest dreams. The ballroom in this restored pre–Civil War house was packed, and bidding had been lively on the least-coveted quilts, intense on the stars of the evening. Watching from beside the temporary stage, she felt giddy. Profound relief had struck when the trickle of first arrivals had appeared two hours earlier then had gathered strength, until her current ebullience made her wonder if she'd bob gently toward the ceiling any minute.

"We're at twenty-eight hundred dollars right now," the auctioneer coaxed. "What do you say to twenty-nine hundred?"

The poor guy glanced at the woman, sighed and raised his bid card again.

The crowd roared.

The other bidder's number shot up.

The silver-haired auctioneer, lean in his tuxedo and possessing a deep, powerful voice, looked around at the crowd. "Three thousand dollars, all for the victims of the recent tornadoes!"

This time, he couldn't persuade the second bidder to go on. He declared the Album quilt sold to the gentleman holding bid number 203.

Sturdy, middle-aged Katie-Ann Chupp, the Amish woman who had been Nadia's assistant chair, exclaimed, "Three thousand dollars! Colleen will be so glad."

Colleen Hoefling was a superb quilter. Standing at the back of the room and smiling at what was presumably congratulations from others clustered in her vicinity, she did look pleased, but not surprised. Nadia had recently sold another of Colleen's quilts through her shop, that one in the classic Checkers and Rails pattern, for $2,800.

As the bidding began for a lap-size Sunshine and Shadows quilt, Nadia found herself trying to add up what they'd already earned but failed. She should have made notes in the catalog—

A woman in the ballroom doorway signaled for her, and Nadia slipped out to the foyer where the reception and cashiers' tables had been set up. The auction software program being used tonight was new to all of them. Nadia had entered the original information—the quilts, estimated values and the names and addresses of all registered bidders—which made her the de facto expert.

A woman who had won the bidding on two quilts was trying to check out, but her name didn't appear on the computer. Realizing the woman was an unexpected walk-in, Nadia added her to the software, took her payment, then printed a receipt.

"Quite an event you've put on," the woman said, smiling. "I don't really *need* any more quilts, but one of those April tornadoes missed us by less than a mile. Could have hit our house."

Nadia thanked her again, realizing anew that she'd hardly had to sell the cause to the people who lived in northern Missouri. They saw the devastation, year after year.

The good news was that at least a third of tonight's attendees had come from outside Missouri, either as a way to help or because they were passionate collectors excited by the mix of antique and new quilts being offered tonight. The Amish-made were among the most prized.

Nadia added the check to the gray metal lockbox. At her suggestion, they'd offered an express pay option, but surprisingly few auctiongoers had taken advantage of it. At charity events she'd helped with in Colorado, hardly anyone had paid cash. Here, apparently people were used to the fact that few Amish businesses accepted credit cards. The piles of actual cash already in the lockbox, much of it from the earlier sales tables, bemused her. It awakened something a tiny bit greedy, too. She itched to start counting the bills, even though the software would supply totals.

Able to hear furious bidding on a queen-size quilt from an elderly Amish woman, Ruth Graber, Nadia lifted her head. She expected this one to surpass the $3,000 that had been the evening's high so far. The Carpenter's Square pattern was intriguing but not complex; it was the elaborate hand quilting with incredibly tiny stitches that made this one stand out.

"Do you mind covering for me while I race to the bathroom?" one of the volunteer cashiers asked.

Nadia smiled. "No, I'll be glad to sit down for a minute." With a sigh, she sank into the chair behind one of the three networked laptop computers, not so sure she'd be able to get up again.

Of course, she'd have to make herself. Closing out and cleaning up after the auction would be a job in itself, all those display racks to be dismantled, chairs to be folded and stacked onto the rolling carts, the vast ballroom to be swept. It had to be pristine by morning. This gorgeous historic home was open to the public from 9:00 a.m. until 4:00 p.m. daily except Sundays. Tomorrow was Saturday.

She couldn't crash until she got home, however late that turned out to be. Lucky adrenaline was still carrying her.

The cause was what mattered, of course—she'd seen for herself some of the devastation left in the paths of giant twisters. She had hoped, too, that her willingness to take on organizing the event would help earn her a place in this town that was her new home.

And, okay, she was selfish enough to also hope that the success would bring in more business to A Stitch in Time, the fabric and quilt shop she had bought and was updating. If the quilters in Henness County adopted her and came first to her store both for their fabric *and* to offer their quilts on consignment, she would survive financially. Otherwise...she'd gone out way too far on a brittle limb when she moved to the county seat of Byrum in a part of the country she'd never been until she decided she needed to begin a new life.

She had quickly discovered the local Amish kept a distance from everyone else—the *Englischers*—that was difficult to erase. Their goal was to live apart from the world, to keep themselves separate.

But Nadia felt she was making friends among them now, Katie-Ann being one.

Just then, Rachel Schwartz appeared, hurrying from the direction of the bathrooms. She was another Amish woman Nadia counted as a friend. When she saw Nadia, she headed toward her instead of the ballroom door. Tonight she wore a calf-length lilac dress and apron of a slightly darker shade as well as the gauzy white *kapp* that distinguished Amish women.

"Have they gotten to Ruth's quilt yet?"

"They're bidding on it right now," Nadia said.

A swell of applause coming from the ballroom made her realize she'd missed hearing a total for Ruth's quilt. But the cashier beside her leaned closer. "Thirty-five hundred dollars! Boy, I wish I had that kind of money to throw around."

Nadia laughed. "I'm with you, but what a blessing so many people who do showed up tonight."

Rachel beamed. "*Ja!* Didn't we tell you? Trust in God, you should."

Her Amish volunteers had all insisted that any endeavor was in God's hands. They *hadn't* insisted the night would therefore be a success, which was quite different. They'd all worked hard on making tonight happen, but they were unwilling to worry about the outcome. If a thunderstorm struck so that the auctiongoers stayed home, that would be God's will. A person couldn't be expected to understand His purpose, only to accept that He *had* a purpose.

No thunderstorm, thank goodness.

But Nadia only smiled. "You did tell me."

Rachel rushed toward the ballroom, brushing against a man who happened to be strolling out at just that minute.

He drew Nadia's immediate attention, in part because of his elegant dark suit, a contrast to what everyone else was wearing tonight. The Amish, of course, wore their usual garb. Otherwise, most of the people who'd come to bid or volunteer were dressed casually, some in khakis, some even in jeans.

Along with being beautifully dressed—although he'd skipped the tie, leaving his crisp white shirt open at the neck—this guy personified tall, dark and handsome. His every move suggested leashed power. From a distance, his eyes appeared black, but as he approached she saw that they were a deep, espresso brown. And those eyes missed nothing. Nadia had caught occasional glimpses of him all evening, strolling or holding up a wall with one of those broad shoulders. His gaze swept the crowd ceaselessly.

She had yet to meet him, but another volunteer had identified him when she asked. Byrum police chief Ben Slater was a Northerner, Jennifer Bronske had murmured, as if the fact was scandalous. From New Jersey. No one knew why he'd sought the job here or accepted it when it was offered.

Apparently, Chief Slater felt an event of this size and importance demanded his watchful presence. Or else he was suspicious of all the outsiders. Who knew? She hadn't had so much as a shoplifter in her store, but he might have been conditioned to expect the worst.

His dark eyes met hers for the first time. It felt like an electrical shock, raising the tiny hairs on her arms. Nadia couldn't imagine why she'd responded that way. His expression was so guarded, she didn't have the slightest idea what he was thinking as he walked toward her.

She was peripherally aware she wasn't the only one transfixed by his approach. The other two cashiers were staring, too, although she couldn't tear her own gaze from him long enough to tell if they were admiring a gorgeous male specimen, or frozen the way a small mammal is when a predator locks onto it. Nadia wasn't even sure which *she* felt.

He stopped on the other side of the table from her, his lips curved but his eyes remained watchful. And he held out a hand. "Ms. Markovic, we haven't met. I'm Ben Slater, chief of the Byrum police department."

She focused on that hand, long-fingered and powerful enough to crush a man's throat—and she knew what her reaction meant. That was a spike of fear she'd felt. When she made herself accept his handshake and looked into his eyes again, she saw a flicker that told her he hadn't liked whatever he'd seen on her face.

"Chief Slater. Several people have pointed you out," she said pleasantly, suppressing her completely irrational response. The antipathy she felt toward law enforcement officers was one thing, this something else altogether. Although she had to wonder if he wore a holster beneath that perfectly fitted jacket. The sight of a handgun could send a shudder of remembered pain and terror through her. "Thank you for coming tonight. I don't suppose you're planning to bid on one of those quilts, are you?"

She was pretty sure he was amused now. "As beautiful as they are," he said, in a velvet deep voice, "I'm afraid I can't bring myself to spend thousands of dollars on a bed covering."

"They're more than that," she protested. "They're works of art."

"I won't argue." His smile was devastating in a lean, beautiful face. "Unfortunately, I don't spend thousands of dollars for wall art, either."

"A Philistine," she teased, even as she marveled at her daring.

He laughed. "I'd call myself a man who lives on a modest paycheck."

She heaved a sigh. "Oh, well. I guess you're excused, then."

"What about you? I didn't see you bidding, either."

This time, she made a face. "I can't afford what the quilts are going for, either. I do own several beautiful ones already, though." She hesitated. "Actually, I'm a quilter. I donated one of the lap-size quilts that already sold. That was all I had time to do, what with getting a business up and running."

"The fabric store."

"That's right."

"Not someplace I'm likely to shop."

She chuckled. No, he would be wildly out of place amidst the riot of color and femininity in her store.

But then she had an odd thought. The previous owner of her building had died in a fall. She'd heard a rumor that the police suspected the elderly woman had been pushed down the stairs, but rumors had a way of sprouting from the smallest of seeds. Still, even when an accident resulted in a death, the police responded, didn't they?

"You must have been in my building before."

His gaze became opaque. "I have."

"Did you...know Mrs. Jefferson?"

"No. I was new on the job when she died." One

side of his mouth tipped up. "And, you know, she did run a fabric store. As we've established, not my kind of place."

Nadia smiled again, but it took a bit of an effort. When she heard the rumor, she'd seriously considered backing out of the sale. She'd have been within her rights, if there was any real reason to believe Mrs. Jefferson had been murdered. That was the kind of information the Realtor should have disclosed immediately. But then she'd told herself not to be an idiot. The location was perfect for her business, and she loved the idea of being able to live upstairs from it. What, did she think no one had ever died in the town of Byrum?

But she heard herself say, "I came here thinking this was a peaceful community. Learning about Mrs. Jefferson's death really disturbed me."

More thunderous applause from the ballroom had the police chief glancing over his shoulder, but his dark gaze returned to her. "No place is completely peaceful, Ms. Markovic. Humanity being what it is."

"I know that." Wait. Was he *confirming* that awful rumor?

No, he was speaking in generalities, of course. And, no, she absolutely would *not* ask him what he thought about the elderly woman's death. Since she went up and down those stairs several times a day, the last thing she needed was to obsess about the older woman who had plummeted to her death on them.

Or to think about how intimately *she* had seen death.

Nadia was rescued from trying to think of something pleasant to say by renewed excitement from the ballroom. Even the police chief looked around. Nadia noticed the third cashier hovering, the one whose seat she was occupying. A stream of people started out of the ballroom, so she stood and said, "Looks like it's time to go to work."

Chief Slater had stepped back, but was waiting when Nadia came around the table. "Pleasure to meet you," he said.

She forced a smile and lied. "Likewise. Except I hope I never need to call you."

"There are other reasons for two people to talk," he murmured, nodded—and walked away.

INTRIGUING WOMAN, BEN REFLECTED, as he stood at the back of the ballroom and watched the last few quilts be auctioned for staggering prices.

Sexy woman, too. Hair as dark as his, white, white skin that would give her trouble in the hot Missouri sun and haunting eyes he'd label as hazel, inadequate as the word was to describe the seemingly shifting colors: green, gold, whiskey brown. And lush curves. The woman was built. Breasts that would more than fill his large hands, tiny waist, womanly hips and long legs that weren't sticks. Scrawny women had never done it for him.

For just a second, he'd thought she returned his interest. But something else had darkened her eyes. Wariness? Okay, he was a cop. Some people reacted that way to him, although usually they had a guilty conscience. She didn't look like the type.

He frowned. He wasn't so sure what he'd seen *was* wariness. She'd almost looked…afraid.

The minute the thought crossed Ben's mind, he knew it was right. She'd moved here because she'd believed the community to be peaceful, which suggested wherever she'd come from wasn't. Still, you'd think if she'd been the victim of a crime, law enforcement presence tonight would have reassured her.

For a moment, he didn't see the still-full ballroom, the auctioneer, the spotters. He saw only her face, gently rounded rather than model beautiful. And he saw that flare in her eyes, and knew whatever she'd felt had been for *him*, not what he represented. Or, at least, not only what he represented.

He grimaced. Maybe he bore an unfortunate resemblance to some scumbag who'd beaten her. Mugged her. Stalked her. Or what if she'd had an ex who'd been a cop *and* violent?

Bad luck. What Ben would like to do was drop by the fabric store and persuade Ms. Nadia Markovic to take a break for a cup of coffee. But scaring women...that wasn't a feeling he enjoyed. He'd keep his distance, at least for now.

He abruptly refocused on the stage, because Nadia had taken the microphone and was thanking everyone for coming and letting them know how much money had been raised. Over $100,000 just from the auction, plus an additional $20,000 from the sale hall open today, where many more quilts had been available as well as other textile arts. A drop in the bucket compared to the need, but a nice sum of money nonetheless.

"And, finally," she said, "we all owe thanks to the artists who donated the work of thousands of hours, their skill and their vision, to help people whose lives were devastated by nature's fury."

The applause was long and heartfelt. Ben joined in, watching as Nadia made her way from the stage and through the crowd, stopping to exchange a few words here, a hug there. She was glowing. Nothing like the way she'd shut down at the sight of him.

Even so, he hung around until the end, thinking about how much money was stashed in that metal box behind the cashiers. He couldn't shake the big-city mentality. Hard to picture anyone here trying to snatch it—but better safe than sorry.

He clenched his teeth. That had been one of

his mother's favorite sayings. She had, once upon a time, been firm in her belief she could keep her family safe by adequate precautions. Until the day she found out shit happens to everyone.

Keeping that in mind, he stepped outside and waited in the darkness beneath some ancient oak trees until he saw Nadia Markovic safely in her car and on her way.

THE FOURTH STAIR *always* creaked, and it always made her start. Which was silly. Older buildings made noises. Nadia had had an inspection done before she bought this one, and there wasn't a thing wrong with the structure. Yet the creak made her think of clanking chains, moans and movement seen out of the corner of her eye.

Had the stair creaked before Mrs. Jefferson's fatal fall? Nadia wrinkled her nose at her own gothic imagination. Only then she got to wondering if the police had noticed that one step creaked. Because nobody could sneak up those stairs—unless they knew to skip that step. Or the person hadn't bothered, because he or she was expected, even welcome. Either way, it suggested the killer wasn't a stranger.

She rolled her eyes as she set the money box on the dresser in her bedroom. If Mrs. Jefferson had the TV on, she wouldn't have heard anyone coming. Or she could have been in the bathroom, or maybe she was going a little deaf. No one had said.

Or, oh, gee, she'd stumbled at the head of the stairs and fallen. There was a concept. A neighbor had said that the poor woman had suffered from osteoporosis. Tiny, she had become stooped with a growing hunch. She should have moved to an apartment or house where she didn't have to deal with stairs.

And Nadia did *not* want to think about tragedy of any kind, not tonight. If she hadn't encountered Ben Slater, she wouldn't have felt nervous for a minute going upstairs in her own home.

While she was at it, she'd refrain from so much as thinking about him, too. She'd forget that odd moment of fear, or her surprising physical response to the man. Instead, she'd let herself enjoy satisfaction and even a teeny bit of triumph, because tonight they'd exceeded their original goal by a good margin. She could hardly wait to deposit the money in the bank tomorrow morning.

Normally, she didn't like to have money lying around. She made regular deposits to limit how much cash she had on hand in the store. But whatever Chief Slater said, Byrum seemed to be a peaceful small town. She read the local paper, and most of the crimes mentioned in it were trivial or had to do with teenagers or the weekend crowd at bars.

Nadia had locked up as soon as she was inside, checking and rechecking both the building's front and back doors as well as the one at the foot of the staircase leading to her apartment.

Worrying came naturally to her, and the tendency had worsened drastically after— Nope, not gonna think about that, either.

Instead, she removed her heels and sighed with relief. Most people hadn't had to dress up at all, the event having been advertised as Missouri summer casual, but since she'd opened the evening and closed it, she'd felt obligated to wear a favorite silk dress with cap sleeves while hoping it wasn't obvious her legs were bare.

She took a cool shower, brushed her teeth and went to bed wearing only panties and a cotton camisole. She threw even the top sheet aside. The small air-conditioning unit in the window helped, but she usually turned it off at some point during the night. It didn't just hum, it rattled, which was really annoying.

Maybe *that's* why Mrs. Jefferson didn't hear someone coming up the stairs.

Nadia groaned, but even as exhausted as she was, it was bound to wake her up later. Replacing it was on her wish list.

So, as she often did, she basked in the scant flow of chilly air until her eyelids grew heavy, then forced herself to crawl out of bed and turn off the air conditioner. Tonight, not even a sultry ninety degrees would keep her awake.

THE SCREECH OF the alarm jolted Nadia to enough consciousness to slap the button to shut it off. Then she moaned and buried her face in the pillow. Why hadn't she planned to close the shop today?

Dumb question. Saturday was her busiest day in a typical week, and she bet lots of people would stop by just to share the excitement generated by last night's event. Plus, she needed to slip out before noon to deposit the money, since the bank's Saturday hours were so limited.

"Ugh." Her eyelids felt as if they were glued shut, or maybe weighted down with a thin coating of cement. She *had* crashed last night. Unfortunately, her body wasn't ready to reboot.

Another cool, or even icy-cold, shower would help, she decided. She just had to get up and make it that far.

With a whimper, she rolled out of bed. It only took a minute to gather clothes. Heading for the bathroom, she tried to decide why her entire body ached. Yes, she'd worked hard yesterday doing setup, and she'd been on her feet for hours on end, but she wasn't in *that* bad shape.

Nadia had gotten all the way into the bathroom before her brain stuttered. *No, no. I just didn't see because I wasn't* looking.

So she set the neat pile of clothes on the countertop, then very slowly turned around. Through the open bathroom door, she could see her dresser. She could even see her reflection in the beveled mirror above the antique chest of drawers.

She just didn't see the money box.

CHAPTER TWO

HAVING SLEPT POORLY last night, Ben was not happy when his phone rang while he was in the bathroom trying to scrape off the whiskers he'd grown since he last shaved at approximately 6:00 p.m. yesterday. He glared at himself in the mirror and groped for the phone. Half his face still covered with foam, he snapped, "Yeah?"

"Um…Chief?"

Recognizing the voice, he sighed. "Sergeant. Sorry. What's up?"

"Ah, just had a call I thought you'd want to know about. Since you said you were going to that event last night."

Tension crawled up his spine. "The quilt auction."

"Yeah. The lady who organized it says somebody stole the money. She's next thing to hysterical."

How in hell…? "I know where she lives. I'll be there in fifteen minutes."

Incredulity and worry spinning in his head, he finished shaving, got dressed and went out the door without his usual second cup of coffee. In front of her building, he parked directly behind a squad car.

After he rapped lightly on the door that had a closed sign and no one came, he went in. An astonishing array of colors filled the space. Rows and rows of fabric on bolts flowed naturally from one shade to another, while quilts hung on every wall. At the rear was a door leading into another space that had been a storeroom in the past, but he knew Ms. Markovic was offering classes now, so maybe she'd converted it. The store was a whole lot more appealing than it had been the last time he'd been here, after Mrs. Jefferson's death.

To his right, a wide doorway opened to a hall that gave access to a restroom for customers, ending at a back door. He was all too familiar with the layout, including the oddly shaped closet beneath the staircase. Ben stopped long enough now to examine the lock on the apartment door.

Voices came from above as he mounted the stairs. One step still creaked, resulting in abrupt silence above. Sure enough, Officer Grumbach appeared at the head of the staircase.

"Chief." He looked relieved.

Ben nodded a greeting and entered the apartment.

Nadia sat in an easy chair, arms crossed and held tight to her body. Her mass of dark hair was loose and unbrushed. She wore a stretchy

camisole with no bra beneath—he had to make a
conscious effort not to let his gaze drop to those
generous breasts—and what looked like thin
sweatpants. Her face was pinched, even paler
than last night. And her eyes fixed on him, un-
blinking.

He sat on the coffee table right in front of her.
"Okay," he said in a deliberately gentle voice,
"tell me what happened."

"I don't know what happened!" she cried.
"Like I've told *him* over and over."

Hovering by the doorway, the young red-
headed officer flushed.

"Let's put it another way," Ben said. "I saw
you drive out of the parking lot last night."

Her eyes widened. "You were still there?"

"I was. That was an awful lot of money you
had."

Her teeth chattered. "It never occurred to any
of us that something like this could happen."

"Now I wish I'd escorted you home, too," he
said.

Nadia shook her head. "I got home fine. I had
the box. I thought of hiding it downstairs, but I
decided to keep it close by instead. So I put it on
the dresser in my bedroom."

He went very still, not liking the implication.

Officer Grumbach cleared his throat. "When
I checked, the back door was unlocked. And Ms.

Markovic says the door at the foot of the stairs was unlocked this morning, too."

"But I checked both last night!" Nadia's voice rose. "I locked my apartment door and verified that I had. I did!"

Unable to help himself, Ben reached out and laid a hand over hers, now writhing in her lap. She froze, took a couple of deep breaths and continued in a quieter voice, "I worried a little, because I always do, but how could anyone get in?"

He frowned. "Are you a heavy sleeper?"

"Not usually, but I don't think I've ever in my life been as tired as I was when I got home last night."

"That's understandable." He took his hand back. "So you were locked up tight last night. The money box was sitting on your dresser when you fell asleep."

"I had to have slept more deeply than usual. I never even got up to use the bathroom. I turned my air conditioner off because it's so noisy, but for once it might not have bothered me. If not for my alarm, I wouldn't have woken up when I did. I was still tired."

He nodded his understanding. He gave passing thought to whether she could have been drugged, but her eyes were clear, she was unlikely to have been drinking anything during cleanup at the end of the evening, and he'd heard from more than one person that she'd been at the mansion from the beginning of setup early in the morning to the very end, at close to eleven. She had to have been dead on her feet.

Her teeth closed on her lower lip, the eyes that met his desperate. "Without the air conditioner, it was hot up here."

An upstairs apartment like this would be, even though it was still early summer.

"All I had on was this—" she plucked at her camisole "—and panties. I didn't even have a sheet over me."

Horror to match hers filled him. No, she hadn't been raped, but she'd been violated anyway.

"He—" her voice shook, and she swallowed "—he could have stood there and looked at me. And I never knew it." She went back to trying to hug herself.

"Officer Grumbach, please go find Ms. Markovic a sweater or sweatshirt."

He nodded and disappeared into her bedroom. She didn't even seem to notice until Grumbach handed her a zip-front, hooded sweatshirt. After a moment, she put it on and hunched inside it.

"This morning?" he nudged.

She accepted the cue. "This morning, I got up, grabbed clothes and started into the bathroom. That's when I realized the box was gone. I *knew* where I'd left it, but I ran around searching anyway. I don't know what I was thinking. That I sleepwalked? Hallucinated last night? Anyway, I searched this whole damn place, then I ran down to my car to make sure I didn't leave it on the seat. I parked in front last night," she added.

"That was smart." He nodded his approval. "Do you lock the car?" Not everyone in Henness County did. Law enforcement kept busy enough, but the crime rate per capita was substantially lower in what was usually a peaceful town and rural surroundings than it had been in urban Camden, New Jersey.

"I always do. And it was still locked, so I knew—" She gulped to a stop.

Ben straightened, careful not to let her see what he was thinking. Because there were two possibilities here, and the most obvious was that she was lying through her teeth. If so, she was one hell of a liar, but he didn't know her well. Nobody in these parts did. The first thing he'd do when he got to the station was run a thorough search on Nadia Markovic's background.

Possibility two was that somebody had somehow unlocked two doors without leaving a scratch or making a lot of noise—because however sound her sleep, Ben was betting she'd have woken if she heard a strange sound right there in her apartment—and walked out with the money. And if that was the case…odds were good the thief had been a participant or volunteer at the auction. Who else would know who had the money?

What would have happened if she had awakened to see someone looming in her bedroom? Had the thief been prepared to kill if necessary?

A question he didn't need to ask himself until he eliminated the possibility that she had either planned the entire event with the intention of profiting from it, or had succumbed to temptation at some point and decided to keep the money.

"Have you had anything to eat or drink yet this morning?" he asked abruptly.

Comprehension was a little slow coming. "No. No." She shook her head. "I couldn't eat."

"You can," he said firmly. "Let's go in the kitchen, and I can at least pour you a cup of coffee."

"Tea. I drink tea."

"Tea it is." He rose and held out a hand. Just like last night, she stared at his hand for a split second longer than would be usual before taking it. He boosted her to her feet. "Officer Grumbach, I think you can go back to patrol now." On a twinge of memory, Ben glanced at her. "Unless you'd be more comfortable not being alone with me, Ms. Markovic."

"What? Oh, no. That's fine." She summoned a weak smile for the young officer. "Thank you. I'm sorry I yelled at you."

"You were understandably upset, ma'am." Grumbach nodded and departed in what Ben suspected was more relief. He was a new hire, barely experienced enough to be out on his own. He'd done fine, though; Ben made a mental note to tell him so.

Nadia wanted to make her own tea, but he persuaded her to sit and let him do it. Waiting for the water to boil, he investigated her refrigerator and cupboards, finally settling on a croissant he heated in the microwave before splitting it open and slapping on raspberry jam from a local Amish woman. He recognized the label. He added extra sugar to the tea before setting the cup in front of her, then the croissant.

Under his stern gaze, she did eat and sipped at her English breakfast tea. Finally, she admitted to feeling better.

"Then let's talk." He pulled a small notebook from his pocket. He thought being recorded might stifle her. "Who knew you were taking the proceeds home?" he asked bluntly.

She blinked. "I can't imagine…"

He cocked an eyebrow. "But the thief had to know."

"Oh, dear God," Nadia whispered. She stared into space for a minute. "Well, Katie-Ann Chupp, of course. Julie Baird, Karen Llewellyn, probably Rachel Schwartz."

Two Amish, two *Englischers*. Even he'd come to divide his citizenry that way. From what he'd learned since moving to Byrum, it would be a cold day in hell before either of the warmhearted Amish women would so much as give a passing thought to stealing, never mind carrying out a heist like this. They'd have no need. If either woman's family was struggling financially, all they'd have to do was ask for help, and it would pour forth. That's how the Amish worked; they took care of each other. On the other hand, he knew both the other women, at least in passing, and felt reasonably sure neither made a likely suspect, either. Julie Baird's husband was a doctor, Karen's a representative for a farm equipment company. Still, he noted all four names.

Nadia reeled off a few more, then admitted that anyone helping with cleanup might have heard or guessed that she would be taking the money.

Yes, it would have been logical to suppose the event chair would deal with the evening's take, which could widen the suspect pool considerably. But would somebody really break in to look for the cash box without being 100 percent certain Nadia had taken it home? Ben didn't think so.

Of course, that somebody could have been lurking outside to see who carried the box out, and even though Ben had been watching for just that eventuality, landscaping around the historic mansion included a lot of dark bushes and trees.

"Did you see anyone around last evening who wasn't involved with the auction?" he asked.

Her forehead crinkled. "I don't think… Only Mr. Warren, wanting to be sure everything was going smoothly. He left after I promised to lock up and then return the keys sometime today, but I bet he went by after we were gone last night to make sure I had."

Ben would bet the same. Lyle Warren, head of the historical society that maintained and showed the house, was anal to an extreme. He fussed.

"Anybody ask questions about the money?" Ben asked.

She stared at him. "Well…of course they did."

"No, I was thinking about interest in how much cash you had versus checks or credit card slips."

Nadia moaned, and he didn't blame her. Once word got out, people would have to contact their credit card companies, maybe wait for new cards, put a stop on checks. Those among them with a strong conscience would then reimburse the auction committee, meaning the total sum wasn't lost. But if the thief made use of credit card numbers or altered and cashed checks, everyone would be pissed, whether the credit card companies and banks took the loss or not.

Unfortunately, some inks were easy to "wash" from a check, allowing the thief to change the recipient's name and even the amount the check was made out for. Depending on what info the auction cashiers had written down, checks could be an aid to identity theft, too.

And anyone who had not just a credit card number, but also the expiration date, name on the card and the code from the back was home free to spend up to the limit.

When she finally answered, he could tell her thoughts had gone a different direction.

"Nobody asked," she said, her voice thin. "I think…most of them are so used to transactions with the Amish being primarily cash, nothing about the evening would surprise them. You know? But every time I opened the box, I was surprised. I mean, there were *wads* of money. So many of the sellers during the day were Amish, I bet three-fourths or more of that twenty thousand dollars was cash. And last night… I'll have to find out, but even if it was only half…"

In other words, somebody might have gotten his or her hands on between sixty and seventy thousand dollars in cash. Even if the thief didn't make use of the credit card numbers, the loss was substantial, even cataclysmic.

"Have you told anyone yet?"

She shuddered. "No."

He decided to ease into the personal stuff. "Will you tell me why you moved here, Ms. Markovic?"

That had her staring. "What does that have to do with anything?"

Was she really that obtuse? He studied her face and couldn't decide.

"I'm wondering whether you left behind somebody who dislikes you enough to want to do you a bad turn, and profit from it, too."

"Oh. You mean an ex-husband or something?"

"A stalker, anyone who feels wronged by you."

She started to shake her head again.

"Have you ever taken out a restraining order?"

"No. Never."

"Were you married?"

"No."

"Have you ever been in a relationship that ended badly?"

"No. Really."

He rolled his shoulders. "That takes us back to my original question. Why did you move and why here? And where did you come from?"

"Colorado Springs. I grew up in Colorado, even stayed there for college."

Big change, Ben mused, to leave a town of half a million residents at the foot of the Rockies for Byrum, with its flat terrain and 3,809 residents. He'd guess Colorado Springs to be politically liberal, too, while this part of Missouri was anything but. Of course, he was one to talk, coming from the urban jungle of Camden, New Jersey.

Nadia drew a deep breath. "I wanted— I

needed—" The words seemed to be hitting a blockade.

Once again, he reached across the table and took her hand, which felt damn cold in his, considering the air temperature.

"I was running away," she whispered.

SHE COULDN'T HAVE just said, *I needed a change*? But, no, the down-deep truth had slipped out. Nadia wanted to bury her face in her hands. Except one of hers was engulfed in his big, warm, comforting hand.

"From my family," she added hastily. Like that helped. There was no getting out of this now, even if her past couldn't possibly have anything to do with the money being stolen.

"I...had something traumatic happen. I couldn't get past it. I thought making a change would help."

The intensity in his dark eyes made it hard to look away. "You wanted a peaceful small town."

"Yes."

"Surely there are nice small towns in Colorado."

His speculative tone unnerved her. Evading the question wouldn't be smart. "I wanted to get farther away from home. Everyone I knew either babied me, or they kept thinking of *fun* things we could do. And I know they were trying to cheer me up, but..."

"If I do some research, would I find out what happened?"

Had he even noticed his thumb was circling in her palm, which was way more sensitive than she'd ever realized?

"Probably," Nadia said. "But it really didn't have anything to do with this. I mean, the money."

He didn't say anything, just watched her. Why had she opened her big mouth?

She bent her head and looked at the tabletop. "It was a domestic violence thing I got caught up in by chance."

"Not your family."

"No. And…I have to tell you, I really hate to talk about it." Even trying to get *out* of talking about it caused the memories to rush over her, still shockingly vivid, colored in blood.

He saw more than he should, because his hand tightened. Or maybe it was because in his job he saw the horrifying aftermath of similar scenes. On a swelling of remembered bitterness, she wondered whether he would have made the same decisions those cops had.

"Will you give me the bare bones anyway?"

"You don't need to hear this," she said stubbornly.

He waited, his eyes never leaving her face.

"I stopped by a friend's house." Oh, heavens—she was going to do this. "I'd obviously arrived at a tense moment. My friend—Paige—tried to hustle me out, but too late. Her husband had gone to get his gun. He shot all three kids, me and Paige. I…pretended to be dead. It was, um…"

Ben Slater made a low, guttural sound. The next thing she knew, he'd circled the table and crouched beside her chair. So close. He laid a hand on her back. Nadia was shocked by how much she wanted his arms around her, to bury her face against his neck, but she made herself stay where she was, focused on the grain of the oak table.

"Did anyone but you survive?"

"Their daughter. She was six. She's seven now." The little girl's recovery was the only spark of hope emerging from the horror. "Otherwise… even he killed himself at the end."

Ben breathed a profanity. "How badly were you injured?"

"I was lucky." She touched the spot where she knew the scar was on her abdomen. "The bullet came at an angle and missed everything important. I bled enough that I guess my acting was believable." She even managed a sort of smile.

"How long ago was this?"

"A year and a half. It left me really jumpy, and I had bad dreams. And, like I said, my friends and family were driving me nuts. Plus, I'd been teaching quilting classes and selling my own quilts, but also working for the assessor's office. My dream was to have my own store. Property values and rents are lower here, so I could swing it with what I'd saved. And interest in quilts is high anywhere the Amish live." She might very well lose her store now. The reminder was chilling. If people didn't think she'd stolen the money herself, they'd see her as careless.

Not just *people*. Chief Slater. Of course he had to suspect her! Nadia couldn't believe she hadn't realized that sooner. He didn't think someone from her past had pursued her here to Byrum; he needed to investigate her, and she'd just given him a jump start.

So much for wanting to sink into the safety of his embrace.

Her spine stiffened and she felt his hand drop from her back. "As I said, what happened is irrelevant."

A flicker in his eyes told her he'd noted her withdrawal. He rose and looked down at her. "To the heist? Probably. But in other ways? Of course it isn't."

Pulled by the power of that velvety voice, roughened now, she couldn't help but look at him. His eyes were nearly black, the bones in his face prominent, his mouth tight.

She swallowed a lump in her throat, and waited.

"Aren't there a couple of other apartments on this block?"

He was thinking someone might have been

awake to see an intruder. She wished that was possible.

"The one next door is empty right now. The florist went out of business."

He frowned. "Right."

"I heard a group of Amish furniture makers may have taken the lease. I hope so."

"It would work well with your business," he agreed. "And we don't want vacancies downtown."

"No. The next closest apartment is above the barbershop."

Slater grimaced. "Lester Orton."

Mr. Orton had to be eighty years old. He seemed to cut hair fine, and must handle the stairs to his apartment, but he was going deaf and she'd noticed his lights went out every evening by nine o'clock at the very latest.

"There are several upstairs apartments across the street, too, but it was my back door that was unlocked. Even if one of those neighbors had been looking out the window, they couldn't have seen anything."

"Unless he was using a flashlight."

"Yes, but that wouldn't tell you anything."

He did the neutral cop expression well, but she was already shaking her head.

"That's not true. It would...*corroborate* my story, wouldn't it? Isn't that the word police always use?"

"It is, and yes, it would." No discernible emotion there.

Nadia would have liked to resent his suspicion, his ability to shift from cool questions to compassion and back again. Maybe he'd held her hand because he was basically a nice man who really had felt for her. More likely, he'd been trying to make her believe they had a connection. Which was deceitful, but...he was doing his job. She couldn't dislike him for that.

He went back to his seat, and they looked at each other, him appraising her, Nadia gazing coolly back.

Finally she asked, "What should I do now?"

He hesitated. "I think you need to start letting your committee members know what happened. I'll be talking to them, too. One of them may have noticed someone expressing unexpected curiosity about the event, or someone hanging around who shouldn't have been there." He paused. "Do you have a list of attendees?"

"I can pull up a report from the software on people who preregistered and the walk-ins who made a purchase." She closed her eyes. "I need to let them know, too, don't I?"

"Certainly the ones who wrote checks or paid by credit card. They'll need to put stops on those payments. I'm guessing most of them will then make a new payment, so you won't be out the entire amount." The lines in his forehead deepened.

"Ask them to let us know if their card number is run or their check already cashed, too."

"Isn't that awfully hard to do?"

"You mean the checks? Yeah, it's tougher than it used to be," he agreed. "I doubt that will happen. Credit card numbers...you know what a big business stealing those has turned into. Even so, my suspicion is that the thief was solely after the cash."

As much as two-thirds of the money so many people had worked hard to raise for victims who needed it desperately.

Well, the only cowardly thing she'd done in her life was pack up and set out across country to start over. She wouldn't add another now. *Shower,* she told herself, *get dressed and begin.*

Slater asked if there had been walk-ins who hadn't made a purchase, and she could only say, "I assume so, but I have no way of knowing. Also...most people came in pairs." Spouses were one thing, but some bidders had probably brought a friend instead.

He gave her his email address so that she could send him a list of attendees and the contact info. Even then, he wasn't done. He asked if she'd changed the locks since buying the building— no—and suggested she have it done immediately.

He gave her one last penetrating look with those disconcertingly dark eyes and said, "Think, Ms. Markovic. This wasn't a stranger. He or she had to know not only who had the money, but how to get into your apartment without making a sound. He could have had a penlight—probably did—but it's also possible our thief already knew the layout."

He also asked her to walk him to the foot of the stairs and lock behind him. Which, like replacing the locks, was closing the barn door after the horses were out... Except, what if last night's intruder had been thinking about *her*, and decided to come back?

Alone, Nadia scuttled upstairs to an apartment that no longer felt like a refuge.

CHAPTER THREE

NADIA HAD BEEN to the Bairds' house several times, because Julie had hosted some auction committee planning sessions. Sprawling and open, it was the fanciest house in town except possibly for a couple of the huge nineteenth-century mansions. The interior was light and airy, the colors all pastels. Nadia had noticed before that Julie only purchased quilts in soft colors. She was currently taking a beginner-level class, having decided to take up quilting herself, and—no surprise—she'd chosen a creamy yellow fabric as centerpiece, to be accented with paler creams and delicate pinks.

Not much older than Nadia's thirty-two, Julie was an attractive, slender woman with a shining cap of blond hair. Nadia had wondered if she went to a salon in Saint Louis or Kansas City. No other women around here had hair as skillfully cut.

Leading Nadia to the living room, Julie said, "I'll have Mary bring us iced tea. Or would you prefer lemonade?" Mary Gingerich was a young

Amish woman who kept the house spotless and served as maid when Julie had guests.

"Oh, thank you, but no. I can only stay a minute," Nadia said, smiling apologetically. The smile probably looked as forced as it felt. "I... have something I need to tell you."

Looking concerned, Julie faced her. "What is it?"

Nadia blurted it out, just as she had half an hour ago to Katie-Ann. "The money from last night was stolen."

Julie stared, comprehension coming slowly. "What?" She gave her head a small shake. "How?"

Fingernails biting into her palms, Nadia told her.

"You've informed the police."

"Yes, of course. I called 911 as soon as I discovered the money box was gone. Sheriff Slater seems to be taking charge of the investigation himself."

"And what does he say?" Julie sounded...cool. She hadn't suggested Nadia sit down.

"He'll be talking to everyone working on the auction. I'm sure you'll hear from him. He's interested in who might have been hanging around without an obvious reason, and whether anyone was asking questions about the evening's proceeds."

Her perfectly arched eyebrows rose. "You mean, about who was taking charge of the money?"

"Yes, or seeming curious about how much of it was cash versus checks and credit card slips."

"I see." The pause was a little too long. "I don't really know what to say. I'm certainly... shocked."

And she wasn't going to be supportive, Nadia could tell that already. "I'm devastated," Nadia said frankly. "I don't know what I can do other than help Chief Slater to the best of my ability."

"Perhaps you should consider making some financial recompense," Julie said, her voice having chilled even more.

"Julie, I'm a small-business owner. I have no cushion that would allow me to do anything like that." Feeling the burn in her cheeks, Nadia said, "I must be going. I need to tell everyone who was on the committee what happened in person."

"I appreciate you doing that. I'll walk you to the door."

In other words, if she didn't hustle, the door would slap her in the butt. She had no doubt that the moment she was gone Julie would start calling everyone but the Amish volunteers, who didn't have telephones. Nadia thought of asking her to wait, but keeping herself together was a strain already. She said, "Goodbye," without adding her usual, *See you Wednesday for the class*. Somehow, she felt sure Julie Baird would have an excuse for dropping out. Or she might not even bother with one.

Nadia drove half a mile from the Baird home, which was on landscaped acreage on the outskirts of Byrum, before she pulled over, set the emergency brake and closed her eyes. She had known—feared—that some people might react like that, but Katie-Ann's warmth and sympathy had given her hope that these women she had started to think were friends would believe in her. She wanted to go home, climb into bed and pull the covers over her head.

The image startled and dismayed her. This wasn't close to the worst thing that had happened to her. Nobody was threatening to hurt or kill her. This was all about shame and her sense of responsibility. *So suck it up*, she told herself.

Her appointment with the locksmith wasn't until four. She still had time, and she had to do this.

Karen Llewellyn next, then… Nadia made a mental list of who she needed to see and in what order, talked herself through some slow, deep breathing, then put the car back into gear.

WHEN LYLE WARREN saw Ben, alarm flared in his eyes. *Now, why would that be?* Ben asked himself, his instincts going on alert.

"Mr. Warren." He held out a hand.

The older man, tall and bony, eyed that hand dubiously before extending his own. Ben was reminded of Nadia Markovic doing the same last night. The shake was brief. Lyle said, "I'm surprised to see you here, Chief Slater. What can I do for you?"

Ben had first visited the Brevitt mansion, where Warren maintained an office, then tried him at home. At last he'd tracked him down to what he'd been told were the remains of a grist-mill a few miles outside of town. Walking the distance from where he'd had to park, Ben had begun to think he should have waited until Warren returned to town. He'd done some hiking in Upstate New York and New England, but he wasn't much of an outdoorsman, and he'd had the unfortunate experience of encountering poison ivy not long after moving to Missouri. He *thought* that was Virginia creeper growing thick among the trees here, but wasn't positive. It and poison ivy looked too much alike. One of them had three leaves, the other… He couldn't remember. Five? But the answer was irrelevant, since he also didn't remember which was which.

He'd found Lyle Warren prepared for the trek in heavy canvas pants and boots, in contrast to Ben's dressier shoes and slacks. Warren hadn't seemed like the woodsy type.

Now Ben surveyed the ruins. "You're thinking you can do something with this?"

"If we can purchase the property. We could restore the building."

Okay, the brick walls still stood, although Ben

wouldn't have risked leaning on one. Graffiti had been sprayed on a couple of those walls, and when he walked a few feet to peer inside, he saw cigarette butts and discarded condoms. Nice.

"According to records, the original mill on this site was built in eighteen thirty-seven," Lyle said, in his precise way. "It was burned down in the Civil War. This one was erected using the original foundation in eighteen sixty-nine, shut down at one point, then restarted in the eighteen nineties. The steel rollers were, unfortunately, removed during World War II to be melted down. We do have some of the other equipment in storage."

"Huh."

Lyle's mouth tightened, making him look as if he was sucking on a lemon. "This land is owned by Aaron Hershberger, who is Amish. Although he isn't farming this strip, he is reluctant to sell any part of the land. He doesn't want a tourist site right next door, he says."

Ben wasn't about to say so, but he could sympathize. The Amish were tourist attractions themselves. They might take advantage of that fact commercially—their fine furniture, quilts and other products were profitable—but they had to be annoyed by the outright nosiness of visitors who didn't respect personal boundaries. Ben didn't know Hershberger, but he'd noticed the farm as he passed, with dairy cows grazing in a pasture, an extensive orchard, several acres of what Ben thought might be raspberries, neatly tied in rows, and a handsome huge barn with a gambrel roof and stone foundation. If the mill became starred on maps, he'd have a steady stream of cars passing his place and a lot of strangers tramping through these woods. Maybe through his fields, too, in a quest to get an up close look at a "real" Amish farm.

Lyle planted his hands on his hips and gazed yearningly at the crumbling brick walls and burbling creek overhung with maples, sycamore trees, dogwoods and some others Ben didn't recognize. "The fool is too shortsighted to recognize how critical historic preservation is. If we dawdle another five or ten years, this site might be lost to intrusive vegetation and the teenagers who obviously use it for…for…" Apparently, *sex* wasn't a word he was actually willing to speak.

Ben hadn't noticed any drug paraphernalia, only cigarette butts and beer cans, or he would have planned to speak to the Henness County sheriff, Daniel Byler. But what was going on here… Kids would be kids. He'd had sex for the first time himself in a boarded-up house.

Of course, all he'd had to worry about was an unstable transient climbing in the same broken window he had. Here, the mill looked like a great hangout for cottonmouths and rattlesnakes.

"I don't suppose you came out here to look

at the mill," Lyle said, shoving his hands in his pants pockets.

"You're right. I didn't. I need to ask you some questions about yesterday's event."

He frowned. "I was told it went well."

"It did. Very well." Ben barely hesitated. "However, the proceeds were stolen during the night from the volunteer who had taken them home."

Lyle blinked a couple times. "Stolen? But... how?"

"It would appear somebody waltzed into the woman's bedroom and helped him or herself to the money box."

The guy took a step back. "But...why are you talking to *me*?"

Did he receive a salary from the historical society? Ben found himself wondering. Even if he did, the odds were it wasn't much. Did he have family money? Lyle might have the mannerisms of an elderly man, but he wasn't more than mid to late forties. He could be struggling financially, but didn't want to lose his status by quitting the historical society gig. Or...was he passionate enough about his cause to steal to benefit the historical society? Say, to buy this piece of property? Would he be making Aaron Hershberger a new, higher offer soon?

"Because I understand you were in and out last night," Ben said. "I'm compiling a list of who was present, particularly locals, and thought you might be able to add to it."

"Oh." His features slackened briefly in what Ben took for relief. "Well, it's true I've had people remark on how observant I am. I suppose…"

Ben suggested they walk and talk, so they made their way back to the cars. A couple of names did pop up in Lyle's recollections that surprised Ben a little. Lyle was quite sure no one had asked him about the money.

"Why would they? I didn't know anything about it. I don't even know who took it home." He unlocked his car door and opened it, stepping behind it as if to put a barrier between him and Ben.

"I'll bet you could make a good guess," Ben suggested, trying to keep the dryness from his voice. "Observant as you are."

"Well…" Lyle appeared briefly pleased. "I suppose I would have assumed that Ms. Markovic had it. She'd taken responsibility for locking up, you know, which means she was the last out. And she *was* in charge of the whole event."

"You're right. It was Ms. Markovic who was robbed."

His forehead creased. "She wasn't hurt, was she?"

"No. In fact, she never knew she had an intruder until she woke up this morning and found the money gone."

"That's…well, it's dreadful. So much work went into it. I never did hear how much money they raised."

That sounded genuine, although Ben took almost everything with a grain of salt. Which might be one reason his personal life was so lacking.

"Just over a hundred and twenty thousand dollars."

"Oh, my. Oh, my."

"That's one way to put it." Ben gave himself a shake. "I need to be going." He pulled a card out of his shirt pocket and extended it. "Here's my number. If you think of anyone you didn't mention, hear any rumors, please give me a call. It's my hope we can recover this money."

"That would certainly be best," Lyle agreed.

When Ben drove away, Lyle hadn't moved. He still stood beside his car, looking after Ben's marked BPD unit, his thoughts well hidden.

NADIA RETURNED TO her shop midafternoon to find her one full-time employee, Hannah Yoder, answering questions from two women whose clothing and colorful tote bags labeled them as tourists.

Nadia greeted the women and chatted briefly with them before deciding neither was serious about buying a quilt. Truth was, they were probably enjoying interacting with a real Amish person. She excused herself and went upstairs. She ought to leave her purse and go back down, even let Hannah go home, but what if people came into the store because they were excited about the auction? Or, worse, because they'd heard about the missing money and wanted to judge whether she was guilty or innocent for themselves?

All the more reason to hide up here.

With a sigh, she sank into a chair at her table and massaged her forehead and temples, pressing hard to counteract the pain that had been building all day. Her neck hurt, too, as did her shoulders. Tension made her feel as if she'd been stretched on a medieval rack.

She'd talked to—she had to count—nine people today, the ones she felt obligated to tell in person. Mostly volunteers, several quilters and the head of the relief organization that was to have funneled the money to the homeowners and farmers most in need of help.

The four Amish women had, while shocked and dismayed, also seemed genuinely distressed for Nadia. They had, one and all, plied her with sympathy and food.

Bill Jarvis, from the relief organization, had all but reeled, as if she'd struck him. "But...we had such hopes," he said, leaving her almost speechless. With the best intentions in the world, she had let so many people down. Bill didn't seem to blame her, at least, not yet; given a little time, he might circle around to anger.

Of the remaining women Nadia had told, one had been openly sympathetic, one scathing and two on the fence. If those were her odds, she'd be posting an out-of-business sign within a couple of months. Her Amish shoppers might stick with her, but her biggest competition was a nice, Amish-owned fabric store in Hadburg, the next-largest town in the county, and closer to where most members of the faith lived. Many worked in or owned businesses in Byrum, but their ideal was rural living and Nadia knew of only a few who had homes or apartments in town. She wouldn't even want the Amish to entirely abandon the Hadburg store just to support her.

Of course, going out of business was only one option. Another was the possibility of being arrested.

Now she was just being pathetic. How could Chief Slater arrest her? She didn't have the money. Full stop.

So now what? she asked herself drearily.

Help him to the best of her ability, even if the man had disturbed her both times they'd met, although for different reasons. And what she could actually *do* to help was a mystery.

When a knock on the door at the foot of the stairs came, Nadia pushed herself wearily to her feet.

Instead of Hannah, a man stood there patiently waiting. Medium height and thin, he had light brown hair graying at his temples and a face too lined for what she guessed to be his age.

"Ms. Markovic?" he said. "I'm Jim Wilcox." When she apparently looked blank, he tapped the embroidered insignia on his shirt. "Wilcox Lock and Key?"

"Oh! Oh, yes. Thank you for coming."

"You said you had a break-in?"

"Actually, what we suspect is that the intruder had a key."

He frowned. "Well, first thing I'd suggest is that this interior door require a different key than the front and back doors. I put these locks in myself, had to be seven or eight years ago. I suggested the same to Mrs. Jefferson, but she didn't want to be bothered to have to figure out which key went to which door."

"I actually meant to get this lock changed when I first moved in," she admitted, "just because it opens to my private living space. I've had so much else to do, though, and really the only other person who has a key is Hannah Yoder—"

"Who is trustworthy." He nodded. "Even so…"

"Even so," Nadia agreed.

"You want me to replace all three locks."

"Yes."

He backed up a step. "I'll get started, then."

But he didn't keep going. Instead, he cleared his throat. "I hope you weren't home when you had the break-in. I mean, that you weren't hurt or... frightened."

"I slept through it," she said wryly. "But I was scared to death come morning when I realized he'd been *right there*—" She cut herself off with a shudder.

"I'm real sorry, Ms. Markovic." He looked truly distressed, but Nadia had found most people in her new community to be kind. Or, she had until today.

She smiled with difficulty. "Thank you, Mr. Wilcox. I appreciate you coming so quickly."

He bobbed his head awkwardly and retreated, presumably going out to his truck to get the new locks and whatever tools he needed.

Nadia made herself go into the store, where she found a trio of women she knew.

"Is it true?" one of them said right away.

She had to say, "Unfortunately."

FRUSTRATED, BEN DECIDED to go by and talk to Nadia again before he called it a day. She might have learned something, or at least that's what he told himself. The underlying truth was that he wanted to find out how people had reacted to her disclosure. She'd gotten to him this morning, when she had explained why she needed to start over in a new place. He hadn't been able to help thinking about the parallels with his sister in her lengthy recovery from the assault that shattered her life, and hoped everyone Nadia talked to had at least been decent to her.

Online, he hadn't had any trouble finding articles about the horrific episode when she'd been shot. Turned out, she'd given him a very condensed version. It sounded like a real nightmare, and one that had gone on for hours. He also learned that she'd spent those hours using her body to protect the little girl, somehow keeping her quiet after she regained consciousness. Nadia had saved young Molly's life. She was labeled a heroine in news coverage. He'd seen a picture snapped from a distance away of her being brought out of the house on a gurney. The cops and EMTs in the photo all looked grim in a way Ben recognized. The sight of murdered children scarred the most hardened cop. And to know their own father had killed them…

He shook his head in denial, even though he knew better. Fathers, and mothers, too, regularly hurt and killed their own children.

Nadia was closing up when he arrived. She let him in, then turned the sign on the door to Closed. His gaze went to the shiny new dead bolt lock.

"I see Jim has been here."

"Yes. I don't think he charged me enough. He seemed to feel bad about what happened."

"Yeah, he was pretty upset when Mrs. Jefferson died, too."

"He told me he recommended she replace the lock on the apartment door, but she didn't want to be bothered with two different keys."

Ben nodded. "Jim felt guilty that he hadn't insisted."

"Wait." She gaped at him. "Do you actually think someone *killed* her? That she didn't just fall down the stairs?"

"I'm sure she was pushed," he said grimly.

"But…how can you know?"

"Because her head hit the wall a lot higher than it could have if she'd fallen. We found blood and hair in the dent. It took some real force to launch her up instead of down. The ME agrees, too. People who fall bump down the stairs, but her injuries are consistent with the greater force theory."

"Oh, no," she whispered.

He kept a snapshot of Edith Jefferson's body, just as he did one of every other crime victim he'd seen. Crumpled at the foot of the stairs, Edith had appeared shockingly tiny and hideously damaged.

He tried to shake off the picture. "It happened long before you came to town. What happened to her was personal. It had nothing to do with you."

"No, I know, but…" She shivered. "Even if

she'd changed that lock, it might not have made any difference."

"It might not have," he agreed. It stuck in his craw that he hadn't been able to make an arrest. Nothing had been stolen. Nobody seemed to have both motive to kill the old woman and opportunity. He hadn't closed the case, though, and wouldn't. He hoped like hell this current investigation didn't end up in a similar limbo. So far, it wasn't looking good. "So, how'd your day go?" he asked.

She told him, but he had a feeling this was the condensed version, too. Her face was pinched, her luminous eyes clouded. It was especially disturbing because he'd seen her glowing on the stage last night as she thanked everyone. The contrast was painful.

She might have taken the money, he reminded himself, but couldn't quite believe it. Okay, didn't want to believe it.

He threw out names of people he had been told were there last night. Turned out several were playing a behind-the-scenes role or had good reason to be attending. A couple of the names had her shaking her head.

"I don't know any of them. Or, if I've met them, I didn't catch their names."

She didn't invite him up to her apartment, and since he hadn't come up with anything else to ask her, Ben finally said, "I'll bet you haven't eaten today."

Expression mulish, she retorted, "You made me have breakfast, remember?"

"A croissant. Did you stop for lunch?"

Her lips compressed.

"You may not feel like eating," he said quietly, "but you need to make yourself. And take something for that headache."

Nadia stiffened. "How did you know?"

"You have all the signs." He knew he could have massaged some of that pain away, but he couldn't let himself put his hands on her. As the last person to have the money, she remained a suspect.

"You're right." She sagged slightly. "I'll follow your advice. I promise."

He left on that note. On the drive home, he called to let his dispatcher know where he'd be, then made another call to order a pizza for pickup.

Usually by the end of a day, he was sick enough of people to relish a few hours of solitude. Tonight, his house felt strangely lonely when he finally let himself in.

For once, he was glad when his phone rang shortly after he'd cleaned up when he was done eating, and especially when he saw the name displayed. His sister. Odd timing, when she'd been on his mind so much the past few days.

"Lucy."

"Hey," she said. "Did I get you at a good time?"

"Yep. Just had pizza and I was thinking of kicking back and watching some baseball. How are you?" He made the question sound light, but it wasn't. It never was. While he was in college, Lucy, only a year and a half older than him, had been brutally raped and left for dead. The rapist was never identified and arrested. She was the reason Ben had changed his major from prelaw to criminology.

Lucy had remained...fragile. She was gutsy enough to move into an apartment of her own despite their parents' opposition, and she held a job, but to his knowledge she never dated, probably never went out at night, which limited any friendships. She lived a half life, because she could never forget. He saw hints of the same vulnerability in Nadia, but also more strength.

"I'm okay," his sister said now. "But I was thinking."

Ben waited.

"Would you mind if I came for a visit?" she said in a rush.

Traveling was something else she didn't do.

Hiding his surprise, he said, "What, you think I'll say no? I've only been trying to talk you into coming since the day I moved."

"I know. Something happened that shook me up—nothing big, just the usual—" which meant she'd had a panic attack "—and, you know, I've been reading about your part of Missouri. I'd like to see it."

"It's pretty country, but not spectacular."

"I'm curious about the Amish. They sound so gentle."

Ben had his suspicions that behind the facade even the Amish had their share of drunks and spousal and child abuse, but he had to admit that on the whole the ones he'd dealt with were straightforward, good-humored and honest. Their belief in forgiveness was profound. Okay, he still had trouble believing an Amish woman who had suffered what Lucy had could truly forgive her rapist. But then, he was a cynic.

"They seem like good people," he agreed. "Individuals, just like any other group."

"Yes. I just thought…" Lucy hesitated. "I don't know. That Byrum sounds like a nice place. Even…"

Oh, hell. He braced himself. Don't let her say *safe*.

What she did say was almost worse. "Peaceful," she finished.

He remembered what Nadia had said, word for word. *I had something traumatic happen. I couldn't get past it. I thought making a change would help.*

She'd sought peace here, too, and hadn't found it.

"I'm a cop," he said, his voice coming out rough. "They hired me for a reason, Lucy."

"I know, but it's not the same as what you dealt with here, is it?"

The hope in her voice just about killed him.

"No." What could he say but, "When are you coming?"

She *would* be safer here. She'd have him, and nobody would hurt Lucy on his watch.

She never forgot, and neither did he.

CHAPTER FOUR

AT LEAST, WITH today being Sunday, Nadia didn't have to open her store. Too bad she had to spend her day doing something worse than facing the avidly nosy and the angry in person. Instead, she was going to call every single person who'd written a check or used a credit card for a purchase at Friday's event. Karen Llewellyn had offered to help, the reluctance in her voice only part of why Nadia had insisted on handling the entire task herself. The main reason was her sense of responsibility. She'd lost the money. To the extent she could, Nadia vowed to face the unpleasant consequences alone.

She knew a few attendees, and was well aware that some calls would prove more difficult than others. *Difficult* being a euphemism, of course.

Strictly alphabetical was the only way to go, she decided.

With a cup of tea steeping at her elbow, she opened her laptop and began. Her very first call was to the woman she'd added as a walk-in last night, Louise Alsobrook.

"Oh, you poor dear!" was the first thing Ms. Alsobrook exclaimed after Nadia's stiff explanation. "Didn't *somebody* among your volunteers have a safe?"

"Unfortunately, no," Nadia said. "And really… I don't think any of us dreamed of something like this happening. The community has been so supportive. I've been involved with charity events in a larger city before and nobody worried about securing the money until the bank opened."

"Greed can happen anywhere," the woman said practically. "Well, I just looked online, and the charge to my credit card hasn't been presented. I'll ask my credit card company to put a stop on this number and issue a new card. In the meantime, I'll put a check in the mail for the same amount, or even some extra. Because a lot of what's gone must have been cash, wasn't it?"

"Yes, unfortunately. Thank you so much, Ms. Alsobrook," Nadia said fervently. "This is…such a nightmare, and you've been very kind."

"Oh, honey, I know all of you worked so hard. Now, should I send it straight to the aid organization?"

"Yes, please." She asked that Ms. Alsobrook add a note to let Bill Jarvis know that it was a replacement for the stolen credit card slip. He'd agreed to keep track so that the auction organizers knew who had sent money and how much.

"I'll send that check first thing tomorrow," Ms. Alsobrook promised.

Eyes stinging, Nadia ended the call, made a note and allowed herself a few sips of tea before she reached for the phone again.

ARMS CROSSED ATOP the white-painted fence, Ben watched foals with legs too long and spindly for their bodies gamboling in the field as their mothers grazed placidly. Gary Edgerton bred, raised and trained horses destined to be harness racers or to pull an Amish buggy. His wife was the quilt enthusiast, but both had attended the auction and spent a substantial amount.

Having heard approaching footsteps, Ben wasn't surprised when a man's voice came from behind him.

"A lot of money on the hoof."

Ben turned to see Edgerton watching him rather than the mares and foals. "Cute little buggers," Ben commented. "How old are they?"

"A couple weeks old up to three months. The last few broodmares are due any day."

Ben knew next to nothing about horses. He'd never thrown a leg over one in his life, although he'd now ridden in a buggy and had become accustomed to the splats of manure decorating the streets of his town, as well as to the hitching rails as common as they would have been in the nineteenth century.

"Why the age spread?" he asked. "I thought foals were born in spring."

"Mares don't all come into season at the same time. Some breedings don't take, so we have to wait until she's ready again for a second go-around."

Edgerton offered a tour, but Ben asked for a rain check.

"Guess you go at it hard when this much money is missing," the guy remarked.

"Ms. Markovic called?"

"This morning. She and Allison had words."

"And why is that?"

The horseman snorted. "Woman comes out of nowhere, charms her way into taking the lead on the auction, leaves with the money and, oh, oops, reports it stolen the next morning. You're in the wrong job if you're credulous enough to believe crap that smells a lot worse than my manure pile."

From long practice, Ben hid his irritation successfully. "Allison thinks the same?"

"Hell, yes!" Expression bullish, Edgerton glared at Ben. "Slick a scheme as any I've ever heard of."

"She put a lot of money into starting that business," he said mildly. "Sure, Ms. Markovic would walk away with some money, maybe sixty, seventy thousand in cash. But if most people think the same as you and your wife, her business will go under. I don't think she'd come out of it much, if any, ahead."

"Sixty thousand bucks on top of what she recovers by selling the building and the business? That's not a bad take. And then she can move on, pull the same shit somewhere else."

Unwilling to argue the point, because, yes, he was already considering that very scenario, however unlikely he believed it to be, Ben steered him to recollections of Friday. Mrs. Edgerton had attended the quilt sale earlier in the day Friday and spent money there, as well as a larger amount at the evening auction. Edgerton offered the names of a few people who weren't already on Ben's list but sneered at the idea any of them would steal.

"These are folks who have lived around here their whole lives," he insisted, as if that was all Ben needed to know about them.

Choosing not to point out that he'd arrested more than a few longtime residents for crimes ranging from misdemeanor shoplifting to rape and negligent homicide, Ben ascertained that the missus was up at the house and went to talk to her.

She was even sharper-tongued than her husband had been. Ben drove away without having learned anything useful, but with a sour taste in his mouth and a cramp of pity for what Nadia must be experiencing.

There were more people he should talk to, but he was increasingly doubtful that he'd learn anything new. He needed to get a more complete list of volunteers from Nadia... With a grimace, he corrected himself. He should get that list from Julie Baird or Katie-Ann Chupp. Because, much as he disliked the idea, Nadia remained his only potential suspect right now. Katie-Ann—yeah, he could count on her for complete honesty. But this, if memory served him right, was church Sunday for the Amish. With no child missing, no dead body, he couldn't justify bothering her before tomorrow.

BEN HAD WORKED BEFORE with Tricia Mears, the deputy prosecuting attorney who was waiting for him at the station. Thanking her for coming, he escorted her to his office. As soon as he shut the door, she said, "I have your warrant."

He needed to search Nadia's financial records, something that also would have to wait until morning, when banks opened. If she really were a thief, she'd hardly be brazen enough to deposit the money. If she found a secure enough hiding place, she could filter the cash slowly into her finances with no one having a clue.

"You drag a judge out of church to get this signed today?" he asked.

Maybe in her late twenties, tiny and blonde, she grinned. "Wouldn't dare. But I was parked in Judge Greenhaw's driveway when he arrived home after church. He asked if this couldn't have waited, but he didn't seem to really mind. And, like everyone else in town, he already knew about the theft."

"Did he have an opinion, too?" Ben asked drily.

"Hadn't had occasion to meet her, he said, but he understood why you had to look at her first."

"Thanks for getting right on this," Ben said.

Vibrating with energy, she perched on the edge of the seat she'd taken across the desk from him. "Anything else I can do for you?"

"Not yet. What I'd like is to find out where everyone who attended that auction stands financially, but I kind of doubt Greenhaw would go for such a sweeping warrant."

"That's safe to say." She rose to her feet. "Unless you'd like to…well, throw around ideas, I need to show my face at my grandparents' for Sunday dinner."

He waved her off. "Go."

Only a few minutes later, someone knocked on his door. When he called, "Come in," Officer Danny Carroll entered.

In his early thirties, stocky and stolid, Carroll had demonstrated the kind of judgment and work ethic that put him at the top of a short list for promotion. Today, he and Riley Boyd had gone to Nadia's block to speak to the neighbors who hadn't been home yesterday.

Ben leaned back in his desk chair. "Anything?"

"I found one woman, a Laura Kelling, who saw a light in Ms. Markovic's place during the night Friday. She'd gotten up to go to the bathroom, but has no idea what time."

Wonderful. "Overhead light?"

"She was uncertain about that. She lives across the street, but a few doors down. Not a perfect angle. She said the light was diffuse, just a glow coming from somewhere inside, downstairs. She claims it went out while she was watching."

"So something about it caught her eye," Ben said thoughtfully.

"That's my take," Carroll agreed.

"And she couldn't pin down the time at all."

"She went to bed about ten because she needed to be up by six yesterday morning. She admits to getting up at least once, sometimes twice a night."

"Ms. Markovic was home just after midnight. Is it likely this Ms. Kelling would have needed to use the bathroom that quick?"

Officer Carroll shrugged. "Depends when she cut off liquids for the night."

That was true, unfortunately. Ben could imagine a defense attorney trying to persuade a jury that the witness's bladder would have held out longer than two hours and that, therefore, the light she saw had shone inside what should have been a dark building well after Ms. Markovich had gone to sleep.

After which the prosecutor would point out that they had only Ms. Markovic's word for when she turned out the lights and went to sleep, and that it was entirely possible she had gotten out of bed at some point during the night to hide the money in a location the police were unlikely to find in any initial search.

Something he probably should have had done yesterday, he reflected, although he had taken precautions to ensure she couldn't sneak the money out of the building and hide it elsewhere.

"Okay, thanks," Ben said. "Have you spoken to everybody?"

"Yep. Sundays are good that way."

Left alone again, Ben realized he was disappointed. He would have liked incontrovertible evidence to turn up showing that someone besides Nadia had taken the money. And he knew better than to develop feelings for a suspect, far less allow sympathy or any other emotion to influence him. Because of his usual objectivity, he'd been called a cold bastard; no one outside his family having any idea how much rage burned in him for one particular class of criminals. He'd succeeded in hiding it from the people he worked with until the day he came close to crossing a line that would have ended his career and conceivably resulted in jail time.

The hatred for rapists was one explanation for why his blood boiled every time he pictured a man slipping uninvited into Nadia's bedroom, detouring from his main purpose to look his fill.

Statistically, the odds were the thief was a man. In this case, the auction volunteers, who were most likely to know who had the money, were all women except for a few men dragged in to assemble the stage, do some heavy lifting and build quilt display racks. Imagining a woman in Nadia's bedroom instead of a man wasn't a big improvement. Either way, what sense of security she'd gathered around herself after the tragedy would be stolen again.

Unless, of course, nobody else had ever stepped foot in that bedroom, and she knew exactly where the money was.

He wondered whether she'd give permission for a thorough search of her premises.

Ben groaned, rasped a hand over his jaw and decided to call it a day.

NADIA ENDED THE DAY feeling battered. Sick to her stomach, bruised head to toe. Remembering Ben Slater's chiding, she dragged herself to her kitchen and examined the contents of cupboards and refrigerator. She'd skipped lunch and had no appetite for dinner, but he was right—

she had to eat. Even a salad felt like too much work, so she settled for cottage cheese and a small bowl of strawberries. Finally, new lock or no, she carried a kitchen chair downstairs and braced it under the doorknob. In theory, there'd be an awful noise at the very least if someone tried to open the door.

Nadia watched TV shows that didn't really interest her until it was late enough to go to bed. If she'd had a sedative, she would have taken it. After very little sleep last night, she was mind-numbingly tired. But once she climbed into bed, lights out, she lay stiffly. The nausea soothed by her bland meal returned with a vengeance. As if she'd recorded today's phone conversations, they replayed in her head, some voices heavy with disappointment, others sharp. A few vicious.

Have you no shame?

I suppose you think we're country hicks, too dumb to see through your little story.

I won't be buying so much as a spool of thread at your shop again, and I hope every other woman in this county feels the same.

Plenty of people had been neutral, promising to let her know if the credit card had been run or check cashed. Perhaps half had promised to replace the money. A very small minority had been, like Louise Alsobrook, really nice.

Of course, it was what the nasty people said that was stuck in her head.

Nadia tried with the "sticks and stones may break my bones" thing, but still felt like an old woman when she opened the store come morning. Thank heavens she didn't have to teach a class today! She hoped makeup, applied more heavily than usual, disguised some of the signs of her exhaustion, especially the purple bruising beneath her eyes. The fact that her eyes appeared sunken…well, there wasn't anything she could do about that. Plus, her head ached, blinking almost took more effort than she could summon and she wasn't sure the muscles that would allow her to smile were functioning.

But this was the one day of the week she had no help, and the sign out front listed open hours that included Mondays, ten to five. If anything of her new life was to be saved, she couldn't hide in her apartment.

Mondays were the slowest days, business-wise, so she wasn't surprised, and was almost relieved, that no one at all came in to browse until after eleven. Then it was a husband and wife she pegged immediately as tourists. They exclaimed over the displayed quilts, gasped at the prices and bought a set of machine-quilted place mats.

Her next visitor was Colleen Hoefling, who wanted to hear what, if anything, the police had learned, and who purchased fabric for her next quilt, or so she said. Nadia suspected Colleen, like most serious quilters, already owned enough fabric for her next ten or twenty quilts. She was simply being nice.

Colleen also shooed Nadia upstairs to get some lunch, insisting she knew how to use a cash register.

After eating, Nadia came down to the sound of voices.

The first was scathing. "And who do you think stole the money if it *wasn't* her?"

"I don't know," Colleen said, hers distinctly cool, "but I'm appalled at the rush to judgment I'm seeing. Nadia has been nothing but friendly. She's warm and likable. Do you have any idea how much time she gave to make the auction a success? I'm not sure it would have happened at all without her." She talked right over the other woman, whose voice Nadia had recognized. Peggy Montgomery, whose consigned quilt was currently starring in the front window display. "What's more, Nadia is a fine businesswoman with a good eye for color. With the way she's selling our quilts online, she's giving all of us opportunities we haven't had."

"*And* making a sizable commission."

"This *is* her business. I, for one, am a terrible saleswoman."

Continuing to lurk out here made her a coward. Nadia girded herself and entered the store.

"Peggy," she said with a smile that probably

looked ghastly, but was the best she could do, "how nice to see you. Is there anything I can help you with?"

"Thank you, but no," she said stiffly. "I just wanted a word with Colleen." She turned and strode out the door.

Nadia waited until it closed behind her before she turned to Colleen. "I expected more people like her today." She wrinkled her nose. "What am I saying? I'm nowhere near halfway through the day. There's plenty of time."

"You heard her?"

This smile felt genuine. "And you. Thank you for the defense."

Colleen shook her head. "I don't know what's wrong with everyone. Peggy is a good example. She's a nice woman. This wasn't like her."

"I'm the newcomer. The outsider." Nadia had figured out that much Saturday. "Painting me evil is better than imagining someone you've known all your life stealing money that would have helped struggling people hold onto their land or rebuild."

The other woman sniffed. "I've lived around here all my life, and *I* have no trouble imagining a few of my neighbors feeling justified in doing whatever they pleased."

Nadia was laughing when the bell on the front door clanged. She turned to meet a pair of very dark eyes. Ben Slater wore his uniform today, a badge on his chest and his holstered gun at his hip. The visible weapon had the usual effect.

Her laugh had already died before she saw his stone face. "Chief Slater."

He bent his head. "Ms. Markovic. Mrs. Hoefling."

"I'm happy to stay a little longer, if you need to speak to Nadia," Colleen offered.

"That would be helpful," he said. "Perhaps we could go upstairs, Ms. Markovic?"

As chilled as she was by the expressionless way he was looking at her, Nadia didn't see that she had any choice. She thanked Colleen and led the police chief through the side door. She sidled by the chair she'd left at the foot of the stairs, since she had every intention of bracing it in place again tonight—and every night, for the foreseeable future. She didn't look back to see what Ben Slater thought about her primitive defense.

In the small living room, she faced him, chin high. She couldn't make herself ask how she could help him. Hating her awareness of him, she just waited.

"I'm here to ask if you would permit a full search of this building without my getting a warrant first."

"I feel sure you wouldn't have any trouble getting one," she said bitterly. "Given the local consensus on my guilt."

Something flickered in his eyes, but he said only, "You must realize this is something I need to do."

Nadia crossed her arms. "Shouldn't you have done it Saturday? Over the weekend, I could have taken the money box anyplace."

He didn't say a word. His expression stayed impassive. She stared at him, understanding embarrassingly slow to come.

"You've had me watched. Did somebody *follow* me Saturday?"

"I'm doing my job."

Air rushed out in what felt too much like a sob, but she clung to her dignity—and her anger and despair. "Do you know what it will do to my business once word gets out that the police suspect me to the point of searching my premises?"

"The sooner we can clear you," he said woodenly, "the sooner your reputation will be restored."

Her laugh was caustic. "What a nice, positive spin! I suppose practice makes perfect. I guess all that experience is why they made you chief."

The only satisfaction he gave her was the tightening of his jaw muscles and some tension at the corners of his eyes.

"When do you plan to do this search?"

"If you agree, immediately."

Nadia was so law-abiding she'd never so much as gotten a traffic ticket. The police officers who spoke to her after the shooting in Colorado had admired what they called her bravery. Now, seared by humiliation, she wanted to tell Ben Slater to get a warrant. *I should have hired an attorney*, she realized. She would, first thing tomorrow morning. But not anyone local.

Knowing her cheeks were burning red, she said, "Fine. Do it."

He took a step closer. Lines deepened on his forehead and his voice came out rough. "This is not meant to suggest we believe you stole the money."

"No? What other homes and businesses are you also searching?"

"You know there aren't any yet."

"I didn't think so. If you'll escort me downstairs, I'll let Colleen go home. I'd just as soon no friends were here to watch."

Nadia walked past him, pride all that held her together. She heard his tread on the stairs right behind her. Naturally. He couldn't let her out of sight, in case she tried to move her stash.

Alone in the store, Colleen had been studying a quilt hung on the back wall. Her eyes widened. "Nadia?"

"I'm fine. Thank you for staying, but I think I'll close up now."

"I'm sure people will understand." Colleen obviously didn't, but she knew not to ask questions. "Call me anytime, okay?"

"I will." Nadia gave her a swift hug and re-treated before she could burst into tears. "Thank you."

The other woman gathered her purse and bag full of fabric and thread, leaving after a last, worried look over her shoulder. Nadia hastened after her, flipping the sign to Closed and locking the door.

"Make your calls," she said with frozen dignity, and went to the back room to sit in front of the quilting frame. With her hands shaking, she couldn't so much as thread a needle, far less work on the half-finished Bear's Paw quilt in the frame.

She heard Slater's voice, coming from just outside the doorway. Which probably meant he hadn't taken his eyes off her for a moment. "It's a go," he told someone. "I'll wait here for you."

CHAPTER FIVE

"IF YOU'LL ALLOW US to search your car, I see no reason you have to be present while we're doing this," Ben said.

The woman sitting in the back room didn't even look at him. She'd gone deep inside; if he weren't watching carefully, he wouldn't have been able to tell she was even breathing. Horrified, he wondered if this was how she'd escaped a second bullet during the hours when she'd pretended to be dead.

"You wish," she said coldly.

"What?"

"I'm staying."

Ben almost stepped back, in case icicles had actually formed in the air. "Why?" he asked.

At last Nadia's head turned, and her gaze was the furthest thing from icy. Her magnificent eyes burned. "I intend to document every bit of damage you and your men do."

He might have taken offense, except he couldn't deny damage did sometimes occur. He knew of instances where a search left a house trashed. He'd never allow that, but in an old building like this, boards might have to be pried up. In the shop, the bolts of fabric sat on some kind of wood base. They had to be hollow, which meant his team would need to look inside however they could. Display quilts would be lifted or removed from walls in case Nadia had added a safe or cubbyhole beneath one. Damn near every possession she had, upstairs and down, would be handled. He couldn't help feeling some dismay when he looked at the hundreds of bolts of fabric. This space would be a nightmare to search. He'd remind people to wear gloves to avoid dirtying fabric that would then have to be cut off the bolt and discarded. And there were the quilts he now knew were each worth hundreds to thousands of dollars.

"My team will be here any minute."

Nadia turned her head away and stared straight ahead, although he knew she wasn't focused on anything. She couldn't see out to the alley through the large window, because a filmy blind covered it.

For just a minute, he looked at her straight back, squared shoulders and the pale skin and delicate vertebrae on her nape, visible beneath a heavy mass of gleaming dark hair confined in some mysterious fashion. Her complete stillness disturbed him anew. He couldn't see her forgiving him for this.

He had to do his job.

Teeth clenched, he left her, reaching the front of the store to see his sole crime scene investigator about to rap on the glass door. The couple officers Terry Uhrich had trained to assist him were only a few steps behind. Ben let them in.

"Ms. Markovic has chosen to stay," he said in a low voice. He nodded toward the back. "She's in there."

Uhrich didn't look happy. "You told her to keep out of the way?"

"I think she understands." Her sense of dignity wouldn't allow her to do anything so crude as to physically obstruct the searchers. But they would, one and all, end up ashamed of themselves for intruding so unforgivably. Ben remembered her horror at the idea of a man studying her sleeping, nearly nude body, and knew what he was doing to her was worse. Did he really believe he was doing what he had to? Or was that simplistic crap, justifying the fact that his investigation had gone absolutely nowhere? Right this minute, he was at war with himself.

They started with her car, parked in the alley, in case she changed her mind and decided to flee. Ben, of course, remained inside with her. Terry decided then to do the apartment, undoubtedly hoping Nadia would take refuge in it once they were done.

She followed the three men upstairs, Ben trail-

ing behind, and stood in the middle of the living
room with her arms crossed, glaring at each man
in turn as they searched her kitchen cupboards,
refrigerator and freezer and antique buffet holding dishes. The two officers pulled out the refrigerator; one crawled beneath her table while the
other lifted each chair to peer beneath the seat.
Cushions were removed from the sofa and arm-
chair, and both were turned over in case wads of
money were stuffed between the springs.

Ben was tempted to help, just to speed up the
process, but his role as lead detective was to
make sure the search was thorough, clean and
fell within legal parameters. Anyway, what was
he going to do? Sift through her lingerie? Study
the contents of her medicine cabinet and bathroom vanity? All he'd do was make any future
conversations with her even more difficult. Instead, he had to watch as she lost every shred of
privacy and yet clung to both dignity and fury.

Mercifully, his men managed to finish up here
without doing any damage. They even, more or
less, put everything back in place. The relative
care they took didn't make Ben feel any better.
His gut roiled as they continued with the necessary task.

The downstairs took hours. Just the peculiar
closet beneath the stairs consumed an inordinate
amount of time. It was jammed with plastic totes,
all labeled, but each had to be opened, the con-

tents examined. Nadia had installed cupboards and open shelves in the back room for some storage, but she needed most of the space for the quilt frame and to hold classes, so she had to live with the inconvenience of the oddly shaped closet. It must be a pain in the butt when she needed to find something that wasn't right in front.

Once they moved on to the store proper, Ben stepped into the hall where he could see the proceedings and Nadia while also making phone calls and checking email. He learned exactly how much money she had in checking and savings accounts, as well as an investment account. Given her mortgage, he doubted she had enough put away to allow her to hold out six months if sales in her store tanked. Not at all to his surprise, there had been no suspect deposits.

Suddenly, she exclaimed in anger and anguish, "You can't put those on the *floor*! Do you know the work that went into them?"

Ben hustled into the store to see Officer Ackley straightening with an armful of quilts, expression chagrined. "But…we have to take them down, ma'am."

"Lay them carefully over a row of fabric, or hand them to me and I'll find a place to put them temporarily. This one was made by Ruth Graber. Do you know her?"

Ben knew *of* her. The elderly Amish woman had lost her husband last fall. As it happened, the county sheriff, Daniel Byler, had married Ruth's granddaughter Rebecca in November. Who knew how many more quilts she'd make? Ben had also seen the tiny price tag pinned to the one Officer Ackley had been about to drop onto the floor. $2,800. He cringed to imagine a dirty footprint in the middle of an intricately hand-quilted white block.

He stepped forward to take the quilt from Ackley, making a point of twitching the tiny price tag into view. The officer's eyes widened.

Watching, Terry Uhrich shook his head and went back to inspecting walls.

Ben turned to find Nadia had resumed her rigid stance. Unfortunately, she'd crossed her arms, plumping her breasts above them. He had trouble dragging his gaze from the sight.

"You have to be beat," he said in exasperation. "For God's sake, why don't you go lie down? I'll keep an eye on them, I promise."

Not even looking at him, she said in a low, fierce voice, "You are the last person—" She shook her head, not finishing. She didn't have to.

He was the last person she would trust to look out for her interests. God help him, he couldn't blame her for feeling that way. She'd called the police for help, and, from her perspective, instead of looking for the real thief, they were subjecting her to this. They might as well have cuffed her, hauled her to the station and focused bright lights on her as they shouted questions.

He made a sound no one else would hear. *They?* Who was he kidding? In her head, the villain was *him*. And she wasn't even wrong—he had ordered this. He'd known they wouldn't find anything, any more than the warrant had turned up a grain of suspicious activity, and yet he still didn't know what else he could have done.

From what he was hearing, community opinion was solidifying against her. He wanted to be able to say, "Ms. Markovic is not a suspect." But would anyone believe him, after word got out about the search?

And it would—nobody had thought to lower the blinds in the front windows, and people had been peering in watching. A couple of times, the doorknob had rattled despite the closed sign. Nadia had kept her back to the windows, refusing to look at the curious.

Finally, Terry left his two men putting bolts of fabric back on the hollow bases and came to Ben and Nadia. "We're done, Ms. Markovic. I've lost track of which quilts hung where, but if you'll tell me, I'll be glad to put them back."

"I'd prefer you leave." Her voice was a husk of itself, dry and empty.

"But the ladders are out…"

She didn't say a word. Her gaze seemed fixed on a now bare wall.

Terry's eyes slid Ben's way. Ben gave his head a slight shake, and the other man sighed.

"Yeah, okay."

A minute later, the three left, the bell dangling on the front door tinkling in their wake. Nadia didn't move, didn't speak.

"They didn't put the fabric back in the right order," he heard himself say. He didn't love the idea of her spending an hour or more perched precariously on a step stool while she rehung the quilts for sale, either.

At last she faced him, the devastation in her beautiful eyes acting like a kick to his belly.

"I assume you're satisfied?"

"I didn't expect to find the damn money. I told you."

"And yet you decided to ruin me. Because you haven't been able to come up with another suspect, I assume." When he held his silence, her lip curled. "Unless you have any other indignities to offer, you need to leave. I don't want you here."

He couldn't tell her what else he'd done, because he'd continue watching her financial dealings for the immediate future, just in case she now thought herself safe and deposited some of the money. When she found out, as she inevitably would... Yeah, she'd see that as another indignity.

"I regret having to put you through this," he said stiffly. "I can only tell you I was doing my job."

"I've lost everything." She looked around in despair.

"You haven't." He wanted to grip her upper arms and make her meet his eyes, but knew better. "You have supporters. People will realize you would never have stolen that money. Just… give them time."

"I can't afford to give them time," Nadia said in the dry voice that held no vitality. "And…do I want people who condemned me without a second thought to become good customers? They would have to pretend, and I'd have to pretend…" She shook her head. "I can't stay in Byrum, not after this. Whatever happened, I'll never dare call the police again, I know that."

"Nadia—"

She took a step back. "You've worn out your welcome."

Despite the renewed ice in her voice, he hesitated, but recognized he couldn't make this better. Not now, maybe never.

He dipped his head. "Things will look better tomorrow."

She didn't dignify that with any response whatsoever.

When he walked out, she immediately locked the door behind him. Ben got in his car, started the engine then tipped his head back and closed his eyes. *Things will look better tomorrow?* Had he really said that? Why would she feel one iota better come morning?

Muttering a foul word, he drove away without allowing himself a last glance at the storefront.

NADIA MADE IT UPSTAIRS to her own bathroom before she dropped to her knees in front of the toilet, her stomach heaving.

When her phone rang and she saw her parents' number, she let the call go to voice mail. They'd spent the past year worrying about her. She wouldn't give them a new reason. If they knew what was going on, they'd want to rush to Missouri to support her. As much as she loved both her parents, she couldn't bear their surreptitious monitoring of her every word and move, the false cheer, the constant little suggestions.

And look how well her escape had gone, she thought bleakly.

Her skin crawled as she thought about the day. She should have left. They'd done nothing but their jobs, even Ben Slater. She knew that. And yet her entire goal had been making them all feel guilty for what they were doing to her, as miserable as she possibly could.

Except she knew perfectly well they'd put her out of their minds by now. Any of them who were unmarried had probably stopped at a bar for

a couple of beers and a game or two of pool once
they clocked out. The married ones would have
gone home to family chaos. And their chief?
He'd done what he felt he had to, staying calm
all day, and if he was a little ruffled by her con-
tempt and pain, he would shrug it off.

She was the only one who couldn't. This was
her life, or, at least, the one she'd been trying to
patch together.

Some of this bitterness that edged toward hate
had roots in Colorado, not present circumstances.
But that was the only other time she'd *needed* the
police, and they had failed her as completely as it
was possible to do. So, no, she wasn't being fair,
she knew she should hate the thief, not Chief Ben
Slater, but she didn't care. It almost seemed as if
he'd gone out of his way to make the search as
conspicuous as possible. If he'd cared, he could
have arranged it to be done after hours and not
had multiple marked police vehicles sitting in
front of her business. He could have pulled all
the blinds.

But, no. He had likely intended for the search
to be as visible as he could make it. *See? I listen
to the citizens of my town. Watch me do my job,
to hell with the woman I'm destroying.*

Feeling cold despite the sweltering temperature here upstairs, she tried to shake off the de-
bilitating effects of rage and humiliation so she
could think clearly.

What was she going to do? Pack up and return to Colorado?

She revolted instinctively at that idea.

Okay, try to make yet another start somewhere else? She'd be able to do that only if she could fund the start by a quick sale of the building. Otherwise…even if she took a job after moving and found a new outlet for selling her quilts, she wouldn't be able to earn enough to make payments on her mortgage here while covering the rent wherever she found to live. Go bankrupt? Couldn't do that until she really did run out of money. What's more, bankruptcy would mean no possibility of getting a loan to start over.

Anyway, if she put a for-sale sign out front, she would only increase Ben Slater's certainty that she had the money. If she was compelled to stay, for however many weeks, she had to keep opening the store every morning and hope she still had a few customers. At least she might bring in *some* income. It was safe to say nobody would hire her right now, making job hunting a non-option.

Panic joined the crowd of emotions elbowing for room inside her rib cage.

Nadia wanted desperately to run away. To pack a couple of bags and go. She could make long-distance arrangements for the quilts to be returned to their makers, for someone to clean out the apartment, to hire a real estate agent.

Her spine stiffened. She wouldn't run away again. Fail, have to move, maybe, but not quit when there was any possibility of salvaging what she'd built here in Missouri.

Making herself get practical, she decided she could get by for a while without replacing stock. No one would notice that the bolts of fabric were looser because no new fabric replaced what had sold. There might be stock in her store that could be returned to manufacturers, too, it occurred to her. Not much, she was afraid, but every little bit would help. The rest…she could donate it to Amish quilters. *My little bit of recompense*, she thought bitterly, remembering Julie Baird's suggestion.

Running the air conditioner after she went to bed so she could hide under the covers, Nadia made herself face reality.

Self-respect aside, taking off *would* make her look guilty. The smartest thing she could do, the bravest, was get up in the morning, do her best to restore her displays and open just as she did every other morning. If business was as slow as she anticipated, she'd have to let Hannah go. Maybe keep her or hire someone else just for the hours she was teaching classes—assuming anybody showed up for those classes. Unfortunately for her, given that the Amish were being supportive, they didn't need to take classes; they all had mothers and grandmothers and aunts to teach them the art.

One more thing she could do was refuse to talk to Chief Slater again without having an attorney present. Which put finding one next on her to-do list, after straightening up downstairs.

A little sleep would be really helpful right now, but every time she closed her eyes, she saw herself watching three strange men handle her most intimate possessions while she knew all the while that *he* was watching her.

If he expected his pressure would break her so she confessed all, he was going to be sadly mistaken.

LUCY'S CALL CAME the next day as Ben was leaving Aaron Hershberger's farm.

The poor guy was still scratching his head over Ben's interest in the gristmill on his property as he watched Ben get back in his car. *Ja*, Aaron knew Lyle Warren wanted to buy that land, but then he would not only restore the mill, he'd put in a parking lot and trails and signs, and Aaron did not want to live next to such a thing. He did say that Lyle had only repeated his initial offer, and not since spring. Warren apparently didn't have the money to increase it.

"I wouldn't sell it even if he offered double," the farmer had said with a shrug. "That building, it's falling down anyway. Already it's a nuisance. I chase teenagers away all the time."

Ben hadn't bothered telling him to call the sheriff's department. The Amish had as little to do with police as they could manage.

Braking at the foot of the lane, he answered the call.

"I'm ahead of schedule. I'll be there in about half an hour," his sister said with perkiness he knew was forced. She struggled with anxiety whenever her routine was altered. But he had to respect her decision to rent a car on her own after flying into Saint Louis so she wouldn't be totally dependent on him.

Had it taken the same grit for Nadia to make the move to Byrum?

"Can I stop by the police station and pick up a key?" his sister asked.

"I'll meet you at the house. You have the directions?"

"I printed them off," she assured him.

After promising to be there by the time she arrived, he turned onto the country road, noting where he'd parked Saturday but unable to see the mill from the road. Fortunately, it didn't take him over ten minutes to reach town.

When Lucy got out of her car in his driveway, he walked to meet her. "You've lost weight."

She made a face at him. "Most women would take that as a compliment."

"It wasn't meant as one." Yeah, Mr. Tactful he wasn't. But, damn it, his once slender sister had become painfully thin. Even since he last saw her at Christmas, she'd dropped weight.

His smart, pretty sister had always had an air of vulnerability. Sometimes Ben wondered if the rapist had picked her out from the herd because he'd seen her vulnerability. The thought never failed to enrage Ben.

Now he hugged her, disturbed by the sharpness of bones he shouldn't be feeling. He'd always been protective where she was concerned, but it grated that he hadn't even been able to help her heal. "You look like crap," he murmured against her baby-fine light brown hair, "but I'm really glad you came."

She stepped back with a tremulous smile. "I'm glad I did, too. I miss you, you know."

"Yeah." He had to clear his throat. "Ditto."

He carried her suitcase up to the somewhat bare bedroom across the hall from his. He had bought the bed right after moving into the old house in town. Only his parents had slept in it. Just a few months ago, he had seen the dresser in the window of an antiques store in town and bought it on impulse along with a rocking chair that was in the living room. Otherwise…he guessed he wasn't much for decorating.

"This is perfect," Lucy said, sounding as if she meant it. "What a wonderful house."

"A place the age of this one has some draw-backs, but there aren't a lot of new houses being built around here. I liked the porch." He had been sold the minute he saw the porch running the full width of the house. One of the few fur-nishings he'd purchased right away was a glider. He'd liked the rope swing in the backyard hang-ing from an old maple tree, too, even though he didn't have kids. He rarely had time to sit out on his front porch, either.

"It's a family house," his sister said softly, as if she saw right into his head. She'd always been able to do that.

"Yeah," he said gruffly. "Maybe someday."

"You haven't met anyone?"

Ben flashed on Nadia, lush curves, glorious eyes and fierce pride. Not happening. "No."

Lucy tilted her head to one side. "You're lying."

He gave a short laugh. "Maybe I didn't miss you."

She giggled, the unexpectedly merry ripple of sound somehow also sharp enough to pierce his chest, between the ribs and up into his heart.

"Are you going to tell me?" she teased.

"No." He sighed. "Maybe. But fair warning— there's no happy ending."

Her smile fading, Lucy searched his eyes. Ben didn't know what she saw, but she rose on tiptoe and kissed his cheek. The ache in his chest was so acute, he had to fight the need to press his hand to his breastbone to try to ease it.

"She's a suspect in a crime," he said harshly. "We…searched her apartment and business yesterday. Right now, she hates my guts."

Still studying him, still seeing deep, his fey sister asked softly, "Did you find anything?"

Ben shook his head.

Expression troubled, Lucy said, "She may understand better than you think."

"She told me I'd ruined her. That she'll have to leave Byrum. She said…she'd never dare call the police again."

His sister flinched.

"You feel that way, too?" he asked, reeling. She'd never told him anything like this.

"They made me feel so ashamed. I knew they had to ask questions, but…" She shifted, looking toward the window as if she no longer wanted to meet his eyes. "Do you know how it feels, to have that happen, and then have the police officers asking how often you date, whether you've been flirting with anyone, why your door was unlocked, why—" She choked to a stop, and he was shocked to realize she was blisteringly angry. "Because of course it was my fault," she finished, suddenly sad.

Damn. He'd felt more in the past few days than he had in years.

"You never said."

"No." She tried for a smile. "I knew what to expect. Rape victims all say the same. I suppose the police officers believed they were just doing their jobs."

This kick to his chest emptied him of air. His sister stared at him in astonishment. He couldn't explain. Wasn't sure, given her history, he ever would. Instead, he told her he had to desert her, but he'd be home as soon after five as he could manage.

After all, he had to go do his job, didn't he?

CHAPTER SIX

NADIA KEPT HERSELF BUSY restoring bolts of fabric to their proper places. Either the women signed up for today's class would show, or they wouldn't.

Business had been dismal. Yesterday, she'd held a session on enlivening quilt borders, for which only three of the seven participants showed, and that was the third of four sessions. She'd been sure they were all enjoying the class. Today's, focused on the Drunkard's Path pattern, was the opener, so no one was midproject, or committed beyond the check written when signing up.

A couple of her regulars had come shopping and left with fabric. Otherwise, tourists browsed and left.

Now, when the bell above the door rang, Nadia turned.

The petite redhead who entered wasn't signed up for any class. She didn't need to be. Somewhere in her fifties, although she didn't look it, Jodi Knowles was already a superb quilter. A large Sawtooth quilt of hers had sold for $1,600 at the auction. In the short time since Nadia had opened the store, she'd sold two of Jodi's quilts, one online.

"I'm afraid I need to take back the quilt you have," she said, with no preamble.

Nadia didn't bother asking why. She only said, "Of course," and went for her step stool so she could carefully take down the quilt that had been hanging from a thin rod that ran through the fabric sleeve on the back. A star variation, the quilt had only been in the store for a couple of weeks.

She gently bundled it in tissue paper and put it in a bag before handing it over. "This is truly lovely. I feel sure you'll find a home for it," she said.

Jodi lifted eyebrows plucked and penciled in. "I wouldn't want it to disappear," she said coolly, and marched out.

The moment the door closed behind her, Hannah, who had hovered in the background, burst out, "A week ago, I heard her telling someone how wonderful you are!"

"How quickly we forget," Nadia muttered, before sighing. "Hannah…I need you to know I may not be able to keep you on full-time if business stays this slow. I hope it doesn't come to that, but you deserve a warning."

Her plump assistant, wearing a lilac dress and apron today along with the traditional, gauzy white *kapp*, shook her head. "Earning money isn't so important for me. I have three sisters home to help my *mamm*, and I love the quilts. I can come when you need me, even if you can't pay me."

Tears stung Nadia's eyes. "You don't think I stole that money, do you?"

"No!" Hannah took her hand and squeezed. "Trust in God," she said kindly. "He will be your strength."

A lump in her throat, Nadia nodded even though the advice was more easily given than practiced. It had been a very long time since she'd been able to lean on anyone, and her faith wasn't sturdy enough to sustain her.

Two women did appear for the class, one quiet and not wanting to meet Nadia's eyes, the other cheerful and apparently oblivious to the weekend's events. Showing them how to use patterns to cut out the curved pieces and then how to hand sew them together without ending up with puckers, Nadia was able to put her troubles from her mind for the hour.

Once the class ended, she let Hannah go home. For the last hour, not a soul came through the door. She went back to restoring order, and chose another quilt to display in place of Jodi's.

What if several other women pulled their quilts, too? Ellen Shaw, for example; Nadia had three—or was it four?—of hers right now.

Worrying didn't do much good if she couldn't fix any part of her problems, and, right this minute, Nadia couldn't think of a single proactive thing she could do. Except remove Jodi's quilt from the website, she reminded herself wryly.

Somehow, the what-will-be-will-be acceptance didn't work for her. The knot in her stomach didn't loosen.

Closing and locking up was a relief. As was the fact that Ben Slater hadn't reappeared since she'd told him to get out on Monday.

Since then, Nadia had contacted an attorney who practiced in a neighboring county. They had an appointment scheduled tomorrow. The woman had agreed that she shouldn't talk to the police on her own again.

Of course, paying her might become a problem soon.

Nadia made a face. One more thing to worry about.

She settled for a salad for dinner, and picked at that. She did update the website, which had been designed to be user-friendly, thank goodness.

She fought exhaustion until nine o'clock, which seemed like an acceptable hour to go to bed. She might even turn her lights out before old Mr. Orton down the street did. Well, so what?

Tonight, sleep came before she could hop onto the carousel of worries.

Startled awake, she identified the sound of glass splintering. And…a *thud*?

Nadia's heart pounded. She scrambled out of bed, going to the window to separate blinds and peer out at the dark alley. Nothing looked out of the usual, or moved.

After pulling on yoga pants, she hurried through the apartment to look out over the street. Except for street lamps, she didn't see any lights. Only a few cars remained parked on this block at night. She waited, but nothing moved out there, either. Could the sounds have been part of a dream, or a nightmare?

Still, she went downstairs, moving as quietly as she could, unwedged the chair and nerved herself to unlock her apartment door. Before stepping out into the hall, she groped for the switch and flicked on the light. A scan reassured her that the back door was closed, as were the closet and restroom doors, just as she'd left them. Through the open arch, the shop was dark but for what light fell through the front window.

She didn't know why she was scared. The night was quiet. She couldn't even hear distant traffic, as she sometimes could. With her feet bare, she eased into the shop and flipped on those lights.

Immediately, she saw the big, splintered hole in the large front window. With a cry of dismay, she started forward. A jagged rock that had to be eight inches in diameter had scored the wood floor and come to a stop ten feet or so inside.

Movement just beyond the window made her jerk to a stop. A dark figure reared beyond the glass, the arm going back. Something shot through the hole, trailing sparks.

Nadia twisted and flung herself behind the case holding the display of thread. Her arms came up to protect her head as she hit the floor, seconds before a *boom* rattled the building and deafened her.

FISTS CLENCHED AT his sides, grinding his teeth, Ben stood on the sidewalk glaring through the shattered glass into A Stitch in Time Quilts & Fabrics. Damage was easy to see—blackened fabric, a splintered wood base—and the stench of smoke was acrid in his nostrils.

Behind him, lights flashed atop an ambulance and a police car. A raised voice inside said, "Ma'am? Can you hear me?"

Nadia had been close enough to the cherry bomb to be deafened. Furious that she'd been targeted, he stalked inside.

To his frustration, she was surrounded, and looked so shaken, so unguarded, he knew he had to leash his anger and the fear that roared behind it.

She sat on the floor, legs outstretched, back against the wall next to the arched opening into the hall beyond. Her hair was wild, her face bleached white. EMTs crouched to each side of her. One had fingers to her wrist and was presumably taking her pulse. The other used an otoscope to peer into her right ear. While Ben watched, the man and woman changed places so her other ear could be checked.

The minute he started forward, her gaze lifted to him. She didn't so much as blink, and he didn't think he did, either. He quit being aware of anyone else. When a place beside her opened, Ben dropped to his knees, able to see how shell-shocked she looked. Without even thinking about it, he took her hand, disturbed to discover that it once again felt icy.

"Nadia."

She kept staring at him, but didn't respond.

He wrenched his gaze from hers to look at the EMT holding the otoscope. Marty McClun. Ben knew him.

"How is she?"

"Her eardrums are intact, but her hearing is impacted. Shock may be disguising some injury, but she's refusing to be transported."

He made sure she was still focused on him. "Nadia, you need to go to the ER, get checked out."

She shook her head in mute stubbornness.

After a minute, Ben sank back on his heels. "All right. I'll drive her if she changes her mind."

The pair cleaned up and departed, leaving only the officer who'd been first responder, currently taking photos of the rock, window and damage.

"Let's get you upstairs," Ben said, rising to a crouch and grasping her elbow.

She hesitated, her gaze going to the shattered window.

"I've already called someone to cover it with plywood," he said, feeling like he was shouting but wanting to be sure she heard him.

After a minute, Nadia nodded and let him boost her to her feet. She went ahead of him, keeping a hand on the rail, him poised to catch her if she sagged or faltered. He had to curl his fingers into fists again to keep from reaching for her.

Partway up, she stopped, head hanging, and rested. If they had faced another flight of stairs, he would have scooped her up in his arms whether she liked it or not and carried her. She drew a deep breath, grabbed the railing and plodded on. She kept going through the small living room into the kitchen and sank down at the table.

As if he'd been here a hundred times, he put on water to boil and took the box of tea bags out of the cupboard. Caffeine wasn't ideal in the middle of the night—but she needed a stimulant. After spooning sugar into the mug, he turned to find her watching him.

"Why are you here?" she asked, her own voice pitched louder than usual.

"Your neighbors called 911. Please tell me you'd have done the same once you had the chance. Or called me."

Her chin tipped up. "I told you I wouldn't. In my experience, calling the police doesn't do any good. And you didn't answer my question."

What did she mean by that? Hadn't he responded every time she needed him? But he shoved aside her dig.

"The night-duty sergeant let me know what happened." He had a feeling his teeth were showing. "Damn it, Nadia, this was an attack on *you*."

"You don't know that. It was…it was vandalism."

"Yeah?" He took a couple of steps closer, the better to loom over her. "Why were you in the shop at three a.m.?"

"I heard the rock come through the window."

"And where were you when you heard it?"

Wariness in her eyes, she said, "In bed. The window breaking woke me up."

"So you got up, put on pants—or were you sleeping in them?"

Lips pressed together, Nadia shook her head. She wasn't a stupid woman. She knew what he was getting at.

"You turned on lights, made your way downstairs, stepped into the shop."

She continued to meet his stare, but her shoulders hunched just a little, making him think of a turtle.

"How long did that take, Nadia?"

Her lips tightened, but finally she answered. "I don't know."

"Five minutes? Ten?" Behind him the teakettle rumbled. It would be screeching any second. He ignored it.

"Maybe."

Bending forward, Ben flattened his hands on the table so he could get in her face. "He *waited* for you, Nadia. He waited to toss that bomb in through the window until he saw you. *You* were the target."

She seemed mesmerized. So much so, she jerked when the teakettle screamed.

He'd have kept ignoring the damn thing, but Nadia's ears had already suffered an insult. With a growl, he shoved off from the table and went to the stove, filling her mug and turning off the burner. He brought the mug to the table, setting it down in front of her.

Nadia looked at her tea, even stirring with the spoon he'd left in it. But then she lifted her gaze again. "It was meant to scare me. I couldn't have been hurt that badly."

"You could have two shattered eardrums if you'd been a few feet closer," Ben said flatly. "What if it had landed right at your feet and then

went off? Kids lose fingers or vision from fire-
crackers. This was a lot more powerful than a
firecracker." He knew his voice was rising.

"Don't yell at me!"

He planted his hands on his hips and glowered.

"And why would I call you?" Her voice was
almost soft now. "Give yourself a few hours, and
you'll decide I threw the thing through my own
front window. I could have, you know. I must
have wanted the attention. Or maybe I'm trying to make you see me as a victim instead of
the thief." She shook her head. "I didn't call you
because I don't want you here. You need to go.
My attorney told me not to talk to you again."

"Your attorney?" he repeated, incredulous.

Her look held pure dislike. "You should have
told me I was your principal suspect. I was foolish enough to trust you."

He was close to exploding himself. This burn
wasn't the fury that demanded violence; it was...
Shit. Hurt?

Not sure he trusted himself right now, he took
a step back and summoned an invisible shield
around himself. "If you're certain you don't need
to go to emergency, I'll leave you now," he said
impassively. "I'll make sure the window is covered before I go, and request drive-bys for the
rest of the night. From now on, pull the blinds
at closing."

Her lips parted. He didn't want to hear it, so he nodded and left.

A second officer had showed up and was hammering a large piece of plywood in place over the bottom two-thirds of the window. It looked like hell, but Ben presumed she'd get the glass replaced tomorrow. He spoke to the two, who promised to drive by at no more than fifteen-minute intervals for the remainder of their shifts, street and alley.

And then he went home, grateful when Lucy didn't emerge from her bedroom. Talking was the last thing he wanted to do.

HEARING THE BELL on the door, Nadia tucked her needle through the fabric and dropped her thimble onto the quilt as she rose to her feet. Hannah had come in for a few hours this morning, but with the absence of business, Nadia had sent her home. Now Nadia walked out of the back room to see a woman hovering just inside the door.

"Hi, can I help you?" Nadia asked.

The woman offered a shy smile. "Yes. I'm… well, visiting. I'd like to try quilting."

No more than midthirties, she was tall and model thin with ash-brown hair and eyes. Unlike with most beautiful women, nothing about her posture or clothes suggested she wanted to advertise. To the contrary.

Visiting. With sudden suspicion Nadia realized there was something a little familiar about this woman.

"You have family in town?" she asked, trying for casually friendly.

The newcomer wrinkled her nose. "I hoped you wouldn't notice."

"You're Chief Slater's sister."

"That would be me."

Nadia crossed her arms. "Are you here undercover?"

A smile lit her face. "Spying for him? No, he has no idea what I'm up to. What I said about quilting is true, but also... I guess I was curious. You have him tangled in knots, you know."

"*I* have him?" Nadia snorted. "Did he tell you I'm new in Byrum? He's pretty well destroyed any chance I had of making a life here. All he wants is to slap cuffs on me."

Which even she knew wasn't true; there was a definite spark between them, but he was doing his damnedest to stamp it out. Nadia *hated* that he'd come rushing to her rescue again last night. She hated even more knowing that she had lied when she told him she didn't want him here. Because she'd ached to feel his arms around her, to let herself lean against him and draw strength from him.

The man who'd humiliated her and, by shredding any reputation she had left, was driving her to leave town. She gave her head an unconscious shake.

"That's...not really true," Slater's sister said. "He told me—" She grimaced. "In confidence. Shut up, Lucy. Besides, that's not why I'm here."

Nadia forced another smile. "As you obviously know, I'm Nadia Markovic. You're Lucy...?"

"Slater. Unmarried. So." She looked around, her expression yearning.

Nadia remembered feeling that way the first time she'd seen an antique quilt at a friend's house. A Grandmother's Flower Garden. She could still picture it, feel the texture when she had tentatively touched it. She and her mother had taken a class together, Nadia not admitting her enthusiasm to her friends. She remembered rolling her eyes and saying, "It'll make Mom happy." Her mother enjoyed the new hobby, but Nadia had fallen in love.

"Is there any chance you have a beginning class?" Lucy asked. "And, if not, can you steer me to any books that would get me started?"

Nadia hesitated. "As it happens, I have an ongoing class for people in the beginning to intermediate stages. I keep it small enough to allow me to help everyone with whatever problem arises. When students start new projects, I steer them to ones that will be satisfying, just a little challenging, but not so frustrating they quit."

"When is the class?" Lucy asked eagerly.

"Actually, this afternoon. It's Tuesdays and Thursdays at two, and I hold additional sessions on Saturday afternoons for anyone who wants to come, but mostly to accommodate people who work weekdays."

"Sign me up. In the meantime, will you help me choose a project and buy the fabric?"

"My favorite part." Leading her to the library of well-thumbed books in the back room, Nadia said, "You may get my undivided attention this afternoon. Class attendance has dropped way off. I've become a pariah."

"I'm sorry. I don't know what's wrong with people."

That sounded like the voice of experience. Nadia looked at her sharply, but Lucy was focused on the books.

Nadia let her browse for a while, then sat with her to discuss patterns.

"I encourage beginners to start with a relatively simple pattern, which doesn't mean the result won't be gorgeous. A Nine Patch, for example, or even a Double Nine Patch." She found pictures, then showed Lucy examples of T-Block and Pinwheel quilts.

Lucy agreed bed-size sounded overwhelming. She wanted to do a wall-hanging, crib-size or smaller. Although admitting she loved the Ocean Waves, Bear's Paw and various star patterns, she decided on the Pinwheel for simplicity. Nadia left her alone to spend a happy hour among the fabrics before she finally asked for help with her final choices.

Nadia always found those choices to be revealing. Timidity or boldness came out, as did an artist's eye—or the complete lack of one. She had half expected Lucy Slater to choose soft colors, like Julie Baird did. Gentle or even bland colors went with Lucy's self-effacing manner and wrinkled tan linen pants and muddy-brown T-shirt.

She would have been wrong, though. Instead, Lucy seemed to instinctively understand she needed strong contrast and went with vivid colors on the dark end of the spectrum: a rich rose red, deep teal blue and navy against a pinkish-cream background fabric. Lucy bought several books, a hoop suitable for hand quilting smaller projects, and everything else she needed.

"And I have just enough time to hustle back to Ben's house and wash and dry the fabric before the class starts." Beaming, Lucy departed with her bags, leaving Nadia in a whole lot better mood than she'd been.

She couldn't help wondering what Lucy's brother would think of her new hobby, though.

CHAPTER SEVEN

BEN HAD ANOTHER crap day in what seemed to be a stretch of them. For June, the weather was damn hot, for starters. Sweating the way he was, he couldn't figure out how Amish men endured working out in the fields in the heat of the sun wearing long pants and hats. Straw hats, sure, in contrast to the black felt ones worn in colder months, but still. Their only concession to the heat was to roll up their shirtsleeves.

Driving out to talk to another couple who had attended the auction, Ben passed two men plowing under what must have been a spring crop of some kind, draft horses throwing all their weight into the harnesses, the men controlling the plows to dig deep into the rich soil. Neither even looked up at the passing vehicle.

Ben's morning had been spent canvassing Nadia's neighbors yet again in hopes someone had seen something last night. No surprise, they'd all been in bed, asleep. A couple had awakened when they heard breaking glass, just as

Nadia had, others the explosion. Three people had called 911.

He gritted his teeth. She'd rather be assaulted than call him. Hurt. Scared for her life. He hated knowing she felt that way, hated remembering her face as the search went on.

There had to be a way to get past her animosity, but he didn't know what it was. And, while he understood, he also remembered their first meeting and that flash of fear. She hadn't *expected* to be able to trust him. Why? In Colorado, the police had been the rescuers, not the accusers.

He shook his head. As long as she was a suspect, he had no business thinking about her the way he was.

He learned zilch from talking to the Wagners. The missus didn't see very well—used a white cane, in fact—and the mister had been bored, present only to please his wife who insisted on buying a quilt to help. They were distressed by the theft and had unhesitatingly replaced the check written that night. Neither had an opinion on who might have done such a thing.

Returning, he once again passed the gristmill, his eye caught by grass matted over time where cars had parked. A quick glint of metal in longer grass had his foot going to the brake, and, after checking the rearview mirror, he backed up.

A bicycle, laid on its side.

For no good reason, he decided to see who was here. A teenager? Could be meeting another one who lived within walking distance. The Amish didn't often use bicycles, but their teenagers sometimes did. Handy for when *Daad* was stingy with the horse-and-buggy privileges. Besides, not all farms in the immediate area were Amish owned.

Ben moved quietly, following a path that was more visible than the last time he'd been here. He kept just as wary an eye on the grass and vegetation to each side—he didn't like snakes *or* poison ivy.

As he approached the crumbling brick structure, he heard a rustling sound. He laid a hand on the butt of his gun as he took the last couple of steps to be able to see inside.

"Lyle?" he said in surprise.

The head of the historical society jumped and swung around. "Chief Slater? What are you doing here?"

"What are *you* doing here?" Ben countered. "Is that your bike by the road?"

"I ride for exercise." He lifted a plastic kitchen trash bag that appeared half-full. "I come now and again to clean up. I just can't stand to think of this place contaminated with beer cans and fast-food wrappers and what all."

Condoms presumably fell into the what-all category. Ben saw that Lyle had the common sense to be wearing heavy leather gardening gloves.

He hadn't had a bag to pick up trash the day Ben had run him down out here. So what *had* he been doing? Coveting?

"You do realize you're trespassing?"

Lyle snorted. "If Hershberger won't take care of a historic site on his land, I will. Would you really arrest me?"

No, not unless Aaron called with a complaint, which he wouldn't. And, heck, if all Lyle did when he came out here was clean up, he was doing the property owner a favor.

"I wonder if posting no trespassing signs would keep the teenagers away," Ben speculated.

"More like a few shotgun blasts over their heads," Lyle snapped. "I thought about setting some mousetraps disguised by leaves. At least it might give a scare to anybody who *defiles* a site like this."

"It's not a church."

Hate burned in Lyle's brown eyes. "It's part of our history. It deserves respect, not—" he hoisted the garbage bag "—*this*."

After a few calming remarks, Ben left the guy to his self-appointed task. Walking to his car, he pondered the disturbing conversation. For a second there, Lyle Warren's eyes had burned with the light of a fanatic. Was it really all about the gristmill? Or was something else going on?

FRIDAY, NADIA TOOK ADVANTAGE of Hannah's presence to go grocery shopping. Maybe if she hustled through the store during the late morning on a weekday, she could get her groceries without encountering anyone she knew.

She had forgotten the realities of living in a community the size of Byrum. She had no sooner pulled into the parking lot at the Hy-Vee than she spotted a regular customer of hers coming out with a laden grocery cart. Instead of continuing straight ahead, she turned quickly down the next row and parked. Then, head down, she hurried into the store, grabbed a cart and started with fresh produce.

Making her selections fast, Nadia had just added a container of strawberries to her cart when she saw trouble approaching. Allison Edgerton must have started on the other side of the store, because her cart was nearly full. Nadia tried to slink behind a display of bananas, but was too late.

Allison's expression froze. "I hear your little shop is still open."

Head up. "Yes, I have every hope that once the police arrest the culprit and recover the money, life will go back to normal."

"What a shame Chief Slater didn't find the money Monday," the older woman said disdainfully. "I trust he's checked your bank accounts, too."

"Why would you think for a minute that I kept

that money?" Nadia asked in genuine puzzlement. "Was I rude to you when you came into A Stitch in Time? Did you see me cheat a customer?"

Allison looked back at her without a grain of embarrassment. "Who are *you* accusing? Julie? Karen? How many people knew where to find the money, Ms. Markovic? It can't be many. And I know *them*." Turning her head away, she pushed her cart forward, to all appearances having dismissed Nadia from her mind.

Nadia stayed where she was, glad she had the cart handle to hang on to. She felt shaky. She'd never enjoyed confrontation, but being berated in public was a whole new experience. And to think she'd fled Colorado Springs because people were being too nice to her!

"What a bitch," a woman said behind her. "You should have slammed your cart into hers. Or…no, tipped hers over. Oh, oops."

Laughing despite herself, Nadia turned to see who was approaching. The voice wasn't familiar, but…the face was, even though she had to search her memory to know why.

The young woman—late twenties or early thirties—gaped at her. "I know you. Why do I know you?"

"I'm…not sure. Colorado?"

"No, I've never been."

The platinum blond hair didn't seem right

with the face. Well, it obviously wasn't natural; her eyebrows were too dark, and she had brown eyes besides. Had her hair been a different color whenever they'd met? Almost immediately, Nadia's mind formed a different picture. Brown hair, shorter then. Not as much makeup, either. And she didn't *know* know her, it had just been one of those casual encounters.

"Trenton," she blurted. South of Byrum, Trenton attracted tourists drawn to Amish goods and culture. "I remember now. We shared a table at a café because it was so crowded, and got talking."

The other woman—oh, what was her name? Or had they not introduced themselves?—looked astonished. "You're right. But…what are you doing *here*?"

"I live here," Nadia said, "although, as you may have gathered, I'm not very popular. I don't know if you heard about the quilt auction—"

"Oh, no! That's *you*?"

"Yes. I own the quilt shop here in town. I bought it about six months ago. My name is Nadia Markovic."

The woman blinked. "I had no idea. You bought the building from me. It was my aunt who died."

"You're…" What was the name? "Corinne Bissett?"

"That's me." She grimaced. "Obviously, I'm

not a sewer or quilter, much to Aunt Edith's disappointment. I work at the Harley-Davidson dealership."

"I'm surprised we haven't run into each other before this," Nadia said.

"*I'm* surprised we even recognized each other." For a second, she looked as if she wished they hadn't. Probably because of the rumors she'd heard. "That had to be six or eight months ago."

"More than that, actually. I'd been looking for the right location for a long time before I spotted the ad for your aunt's business. It was about a year ago when I flew out to look at Trenton and Jamestown and that general area."

Corinne didn't look as if she believed Nadia, but she gave a quick, dismissive shrug. "Well. I doubt we have the same friends, and we must not usually grocery shop at the same times. Still— I'm sorry about the mess you're in."

"I… Thank you."

She was talking to Corinne Bissett's back. She headed for the dairy aisle and was quickly out of sight.

How odd, Nadia thought. She had vaguely wondered if the old lady's niece lived here in Byrum. She remembered thinking that, if she did, Ms. Bissett would likely stop by to say hi. Well, if she'd had no interest in the fabric store and wasn't especially close to her aunt, she'd probably just wanted to sell quickly and take advantage of her inheritance, such as it was. With really short shorts, wedge sandals that made Nadia's feet hurt to look at and a skintight T-shirt, she was a contrast to Nadia in her flowing, gauzy skirt and far more modest knit shirt.

Starting slowly after Corinne, however, it struck Nadia that they did have something more in common than having shared a table for lunch in a crowded restaurant a year ago. Corinne would surely have been interviewed about her aunt's death, given that she was the heir. And Nadia would put money on it having been Ben Slater who'd interviewed her and probably done his best to scare her, too, in hopes she'd break down and confess all.

They really should have exchanged notes. Maybe Corinne could have given her some tips, Nadia thought wryly.

Hearing two women talking behind her, she remembered her mission: grab enough food to last at least a week and get out of here as quick as possible, preferably without encountering anyone else she knew.

"Do you know many of the Amish?" Lucy asked over the dinner table that evening.

Ben knew she'd been out most of yesterday; he'd seen bulging shopping bags heaped on the floor in her bedroom. He had no idea what she'd done today. Given her question, he had to wonder if she'd been hitting every Amish-owned shop in town.

And wasn't that what all visitors to Byrum did? If not for the Amish, travelers wouldn't stop here longer than it took to fill a tank with gasoline or buy burgers and fries to eat on the road.

"I know some, but not well." He reached for a third biscuit. They tasted good, even if they were out of one of those little tubes that popped open. Lucy had wished aloud that she had some sourdough starter here. Ben wasn't feeling picky; he was just happy to walk in the door to a home-cooked meal. "The Amish are friendly but reserved," he continued. "Like I said before, their mandate is to remain apart from the world. That's not to say real friendships don't form between Amish and *Englischers*, but how deep those go, I'm not sure. There are quite a few Amish businesses within the city limits, but not many of them live here. So I deal with an occasional buggy/car collision and complaints about horse patties on the streets and the grooves the steel buggy wheels wear in asphalt, while the Amish refrain from calling on the police whenever possible." That still frustrated him. Six or eight months ago, a rash of burglaries in the downtown could have been stopped sooner if the Amish business owners had reported their losses instead of admitting to them long after the fact.

Having an idea, he said, "I'll invite the county

sheriff and his wife over for dinner one of these evenings. I think you'd like his wife, Rebecca. Daniel is a lot more involved on the job with the Amish than I am, and both he and Rebecca have family among them."

"What a good idea." Lucy smiled at him while nudging the casserole dish in his direction.

Ben didn't really need seconds, but he helped himself anyway. When he and Lucy were teenagers, she hadn't been all that interested in cooking, but she'd learned somewhere along the way. He'd have assumed she'd developed the skill because she didn't want to leave her apartment more than she had to, but she hadn't hesitated about exploring since she had arrived to stay with him. At least, not during the daytime. She hadn't asked about nightlife. Maybe she'd guessed it was close to nonexistent. Byrum did have a two-screen movie theater, the only one in the county, and of course there were restaurants. Otherwise, unless a special event was being held—say, square dancing or bingo at the Grange hall—the town shut down early except for the taverns and bars.

He had a sudden memory of the day he and his parents had left her at the dorm at the University of Pennsylvania for her freshman year. Tears in her beautiful eyes as they were saying goodbye, but her cheeks pink with excitement and he could tell how conscious she was of some guys walking by in athletic shorts and sweat-soaked T-shirts. That Lucy was gone forever.

"You haven't told me what happened," he said, maybe too abruptly.

"What happ— Oh." Her expression dimmed.

Sorry he had raised the subject, Ben said, "We don't have to talk about it."

"No, it's okay. It really wasn't any big deal, just embarrassing." With her fork, she squished what was left of the casserole on her plate. "I went out with a guy a friend introduced me to."

He stared at her. "You went on a date."

Her eyes flashed to meet his, then lowered again. "You don't have to make it sound so unlikely. Like…like a robin hatching a chicken."

Ben smiled crookedly at the picture of a chick tumbling out of a robin's nest. Except then he realized how apt her analogy might be. Clearly, she hadn't been able to fly, either.

"I've been stagnating," Lucy said after a minute. "I was able to function at a certain level and hardly noticed when I quit trying for more. This guy was good-looking and he seemed nice, so I thought—" She hunched her shoulders, much as Nadia had done when uncomfortable. "Dinner was fine. He brought me home and walked me to my door. He, um, tried to kiss me—I freaked out—he fled."

Lucy had vowed not to have sex until she was in

college. What Ben had never known was whether she'd still been a virgin when she was raped.

"Okay," he said, since that was about what he had expected, "but I don't get how that precipitated a visit to me."

She'd quit playing with her food. He had a feeling she was wringing her hands beneath the table.

"I needed to push myself out of my comfort zone, but in a different way."

Lucy had gone on vacation a few times with their parents, but, from what Mom said, had clung to them.

"Is this the first time you've flown alone? Rented a car yourself?"

She nodded, looking hopeful. "That's something, isn't it?"

Ben smiled at her, this sister who'd secretly been his best friend as they were growing up. "It's something big." He hesitated. "Did it scare you when I went out in the middle of the night?"

"Not scared, exactly. I didn't sleep again until you got home."

"Would you rather I not wake you when I have to go out?"

Lucy shook her head vehemently. "No! If I woke up and found you gone—" She shuddered. "It's much better to know you're just doing your job."

There she went again, touching a raw nerve.

"It doesn't happen all that often," he told her. "Wednesday night, the sergeant wouldn't have called me if the vandalism didn't appear to be part of an ongoing investigation of mine. Normally, for anything short of a murder or kidnapping—" or rape "—I'd get the rundown the next morning. My two detectives aren't very experienced, so I'm taking lead on some crimes and using them as teaching opportunities."

Except, he hadn't been on this one. He'd been sucked in from the minute he met Nadia's eyes at the auction.

Why was it that every train of thought circled back to her?

HANNAH TOOK HER LUNCH at one o'clock to be sure she'd be back before Nadia started the afternoon class. This was the Saturday session technically for beginning to intermediate students, but really open to any student who needed some extra help.

Sitting on a stool behind the cash register in her empty store, she had the painful thought that eight days ago, at this exact time, she had been strolling from table to table during the quilt sale, watching for problems, laughing and talking with participants and buyers even as she felt a flicker of panic at knowing how little time they had to clear the ballroom before the night's auction began.

How much could change in one week.

She shivered, or maybe it was a shudder. She, of all people, knew how fast lives could change—and end. In bad moments, she still wondered whether either of Paige's boys might have lived if the police had acted sooner instead of letting hours pass while their father taunted the negotiator. She would never know about Colin, but Keenan...well, maybe doctors couldn't have saved him no matter what. Probably it was just as well she couldn't know exactly when they had died. Paige...*she* had been dead before she hit the floor.

The bell on the door tinkled, and Nadia returned to the present. Seeing who had walked in the door, she wasn't sure that was an improvement.

No matter how angry she was, Nadia couldn't help responding to everything about Ben Slater—his unruly dark hair, broad shoulders and lean hips, the long-legged stride that was always purposeful, his strong, shadowed jaw and sharp cheekbones. He looked good in the uniform that reminded her of who and what he was—a man very capable of violence, and one who likely closed his mind to the terrible consequences his decisions could have.

Too quickly, his intense, dark eyes captured her. She would swear those eyes hadn't left her face since he entered the store.

Instinct had her sliding off the stool. He still

towered over her standing, but the disadvantage was less.

She raised her eyebrows. "I hope you're not here to arrest me. I have a class beginning in fifteen minutes."

Creases deepened on his forehead. "You know I'm not."

"How would I know that?" She held on to a disdainful expression even if her heart was racing.

He came to a stop, only the counter separating them. "I don't enjoy what I've had to do, Nadia."

"Then you should have gone into another line of work, shouldn't you?" she shot back.

"There are days I think so, too." Rueful, deep, velvety, his voice seemed designed to undercut her resistance.

"I don't understand you." Alarmed, she didn't understand why she'd said that. This was the man who was helping ruin her life. Did it matter what drove him?

Was that a flinch, or only a nerve or muscle twitching beneath his eye? "I don't know if you'd like me if you did," he said, his eyes darkening, if that was possible.

I am in such trouble, she thought. Because… she hadn't been able to say, or even think, *I already don't like you*. She almost sank back onto the stool, but somehow fortified herself. *No, no, no.* She could not let herself trust him. Not given his profession or his capability for violence. *Oh, and remember the latest reason?*

"You've gotten access to my bank accounts."

He just looked at her for a minute. "How do you know?"

"Yesterday, one of my admirers was being nasty and said something, so I called the bank. The manager admitted the police did have a warrant."

He looked pissed. "Who told you?"

"You mean, at the bank?"

"No. The *admirer.* Nobody outside the department and the DA's office should have known about a warrant."

"Oh." He was right, except… "I think she actually said she hoped you were looking at my bank accounts."

"She?" He was implacable, and Nadia had no reason not to tell him.

"Allison Edgerton."

He grunted. "I hoped you'd never know."

"I'm sure you did hope I'd be stupid enough to wait a few weeks and then deposit the money," she agreed, sharp as the blade on her rotary cutter.

"Nadia, I don't believe you stole the money. I don't believe you have it cached away somewhere. But you were the last person who had it. You could have made up your story. I had to eliminate you. If you were in my shoes, wouldn't you have made the same decisions I have?"

She shook her head, and kept shaking it. "You could have handled all of this differently. What about this country's founding principle that says citizens are innocent until proved guilty?" Her voice caught. "You, and everyone else in this town, started with the belief that I'm guilty. Am I supposed to say I understand? I don't."

They stared at each other, and she had the startled awareness that she'd hurt him. No, she had to be imagining that. Why would he care what she thought of him?

Except…he did. He wouldn't keep coming back like this if he didn't. Unless he was trying to trick her into trusting him, of course. Only, she didn't quite believe that.

She lifted her chin. "You never did say why you're here."

Wait—she wasn't supposed to talk to him without her attorney at her side.

His laugh wasn't really a laugh. "I wanted to find out how you're doing. Whether your business is hanging in there, whether you're sleeping, eating." His mouth twisted. "I don't know about the business, but you're not sleeping well, are you? Or eating?"

Stiffening, Nadia said, "What a lovely compliment. And I thought I already knew how charming you can be."

He lifted a hand as if he was going to touch her, but aborted the gesture. "I don't like seeing bruises under your eyes."

She swallowed, her throat dry. "When I go to bed, I remember that locked doors weren't enough. Someone got all the way into my bedroom without my ever knowing it, could have been as close to me as you are right now. Call me sensitive, but that makes it a little hard now to settle down for a cozy night's sleep." And no, she wouldn't tell him she still had nightmares about those hours surrounded by the dead and dying.

Compassion and unexpected understanding altered the lines of his face. He opened his mouth to say something, but the bell on the door rang. Ben turned, even as Nadia forced herself to look past him.

His sister walked in, carrying her project stuffed in a tote. Only a few feet inside the door, she stopped dead when she saw Ben.

Nadia made the mistake of glancing at him just in time to see a flare of something intense—anger?—before he said with an unpleasant tinge of sarcasm, "Is there a little something you forgot to tell me about your activities this week?"

CHAPTER EIGHT

CLUTCHING THAT TOTE BAG to her chest as if it was her baby, Lucy opened and closed her mouth a couple times.

Ben shook his head, all his protective instincts bristling. As if side by side, he saw Nadia, dazed and shocked, being worked over by the medics— and Lucy, naked, battered, bloody, sprawled on that bed. Never again.

"You need to stay away from here," he said in a hard voice. "I'll see you outside." Taking for granted that she'd obey, he turned to Nadia in time to catch her expression of shock. No, worse than that: she looked as if he'd just cut her to the bone. Horrified by his sudden understanding of how she must have taken his reaction to seeing his sister here, he said urgently, "Damn it, Nadia…"

She backed away, her hands up as if to ward him off. "No. I don't want to hear it. By all means, be sure Lucy doesn't get contaminated by associating with me."

"That's not what—" She'd been so strong despite a trauma as horrific as the one Lucy had suffered. Would she understand that his sister was different, that she could be destroyed if she was even a bystander during an ugly incident?

But that bell was tinkling again, and Ben swung back to see another two women walking in, both carrying bags of their own. One of them greeted Lucy as if she knew her, and he realized Lucy had come here for the class—and that it wouldn't be her first. He also realized his sister hadn't gone outside when he asked.

She was forcing a smile for the benefit of the other women, giving him a second to glance over his shoulder. Nadia had retreated to the opening into the back room. She looked as if she wanted not to be here. As if she was trying to shrink into nothingness.

Ben took an involuntary step her way, but there was the bell again, and more voices, and Nadia wouldn't even meet his eyes.

Swearing silently, he went toward the door. "Lucy…"

Chattering, the others had streamed ahead toward Nadia and the back room.

"Don't even think about it," his sister snapped. "I want to learn to quilt, and Nadia is a good teacher. I *like* her."

"I like her, too. You know that. But a lot of people hate her right now, and if you're too close to her, you could get hurt."

"*My* decision."

He hadn't seen her angry and determined in a lot of years. Ben ought to be rejoicing. And it was true that an attack was unlikely in the middle of a business day. Which meant…he'd overreacted.

"You have no right to tell me what to do," she added, voice low but resolute. "Goodbye." And she walked right past him to join the other women.

He saw no alternative but to leave, knowing he'd screwed up again. Now the snapshot of Nadia's face replaced everything else, and he felt sick. If only he could explain why he'd been afraid for Lucy. Nadia would understand. She had to.

"Excuse me," a woman said.

Ben blinked, discovering that he'd come to a dead stop on the sidewalk, blocking the door. It was Hannah Yoder who waited politely to go by, the lenses of her glasses magnifying her blue eyes. She was as tidy as always. He glanced at the clunky black athletic shoes that didn't seem to go with a calf-length dress and stockings.

"Sorry, Hannah." He managed what he hoped was an apologetic smile. "I think I was *ferhoodled*. If that's the right word." So far as he understood it, *bewildered* fit within the meaning.

Hannah giggled. "*Ja*, it could be. You have a good day now, Chief Slater." She opened the shop door and, with a swish of her skirt, went inside.

He headed straight to his car parked a few storefronts down the block. Once behind the wheel, he sat frowning straight ahead, unable to shake the memory of how he'd hurt Nadia. A good start to redeeming himself would be finding out who'd stolen the money. Too bad he was flat out of ideas.

He had no witnesses, no strings to pull. If a local had taken the money, he or she might eventually brag to the wrong person about it, or spend it in a way that had neighbors wondering where the sudden wealth had come from. Otherwise... He didn't want to think about the *otherwise*, because it would mean another investigation going cold, another unsolved crime like Edith Jefferson's murder.

The usual uneasiness stirred when he reflected on the parallels. Same building in both; intruders had seemingly had a key. But Ben couldn't fit the two crimes together. The intent was different, and the victims had nothing in common except an interest in sewing and quilting. They'd never met; Mrs. Jefferson had been dead for over six months when Nadia moved here.

His attention snapped to his radio when voices crackled from it. A kid on a bike had been hit near the corner of Fourth and Oak. The officer pleading for an ambulance sounded frantic. Dread supplanting everything else, Ben pulled away from the curb and switched on his lights and siren to clear his way.

LUCY WHISPERED ANOTHER apology as she passed close to Nadia on her way around the table to an empty chair. Nadia managed a smile and a slight nod. Roiling with rage and hurt, she hadn't even been able to enjoy watching Ben's sister defy him. The very fact that he'd believed he could snap his fingers and his sister would jump to obey said a whole lot about him.

What it really did was reaffirm what she already knew about the man. To give him credit, he'd admitted there was reason she wouldn't like him. That he was the sexiest man she'd ever met, that her body felt tuned to his, that she had felt the gentleness in his touch, that sometimes she would swear she saw tenderness in his eyes... none of that could matter. Rats sometimes looked really good. Even monsters could. Paige's husband had been a handsome, athletic man who succeeded for a long time in hiding his sick, pathological anger and need to control from most people.

Nadia refused to let Ben ruin what was shaping up to be a great class. Six women had showed, the highest number this week. They were all enthusiastic, already oohing and aahing over each other's projects. Lucy was the newest, and those who hadn't attended the Thursday session gave rave reviews to her fabric choices.

"Are you planning to hand quilt?" Donna Adamski asked. "So far, that's my favorite part."

"Yes." Lucy beamed. "I bought a hoop. That seems the most practical for now."

Nadia let them talk for a few minutes, then encouraged them to get to work and asked if anyone had questions or problems. A couple of the women did. She helped them one at a time through the latest snag, and then focused a lot of her time on Lucy, the only real beginner. She'd made paper patterns and started cutting out triangles during Thursday's class. Today, she continued cutting out pieces and long strips for borders, after which Nadia talked her through sewing half-square triangles on one of the machines available for student use, then snipping off the corners of the triangles before pressing the squares flat.

My mother tried to teach me to sew, Lucy had confessed the day she first came into the store, *but I wasn't all that interested. I hope I remember at least some of it.*

It appeared she did, or else she caught on fast. Her excitement as she saw how the fabrics contrasted was contagious. Stories about initial disasters flew around the table, and the ready laughter felt like a balm to Nadia's wounds. This was what she'd imagined when she opened the store. Women helping other women. Supporting each other, learning. Friendships being stitched together as surely as were pieces of fabric.

Quilting had been her salvation after she got out of the hospital. She could concentrate on it in a way she couldn't on anything else. She could imagine the quilt she was hand stitching keeping a descendant warm a hundred years in the future. She dreamed about helping others, like Lucy, find the same passion.

So enjoy it, she told herself. *Don't think about all the crap or the people you* thought *were becoming friends. Especially don't think about Lucy Slater's brother.*

A couple of times, she heard Hannah speaking to customers, and in between Hannah popped into the room to admire the progress students were making and offer small tips of her own.

When the session officially ended, Nadia told them to feel free to stay if they'd like to keep working. Three women did, including Lucy, who didn't have a sewing machine at Ben's house.

As glad as Nadia was now to hear murmurs of conversation and the whir of sewing machines in the back room, she kept a nervous eye on the door in case Ben decided to find out why his sister hadn't left when she was supposed to.

Lucy was still in back when a middle-aged couple wandered in, looking for quilts. The husband appeared indulgent but disinterested as his wife looked at every quilt for sale, asking eager questions and exclaiming with pleasure. He became absorbed in his smartphone. Every so often, she'd say, "What do you think, honey?" and he'd shake his head. "You're the decorator, not me."

"He's actually color-blind," the woman whispered. "I do avoid red and certain shades of pink, because they look gray to him."

Which meant a goodly number of flowers must look gray. How odd that would be.

Nadia had hoped the woman was serious, and she proved to be when she chose two quilts, one full-size for a guest bedroom and a queen-size for their own room. The smaller of the two was a marvelous Texas Star quilt in soft shades, the queen-size an Irish Chain done in navy blue against a white background. When his wife showed him that one, the man blinked a few times.

"I thought quilts were all fussy."

"Using only two fabrics is actually quite common," Nadia said. Beaming, Hannah wrapped both while Nadia happily rang up the purchase. Having learned the couple was, appropriately enough, from Texas, she dropped a card in the bag, mentioning that most quilts in the shop were pictured on her website and available for purchase online.

Carrying her tote bag, Lucy appeared from

the back room shortly after the couple left. She looked in surprise at Hannah and Nadia. "What happened?"

Nadia knew she was still grinning. "A *huge* sale." Her percent would stave off bankruptcy for a month. Or let her keep Hannah on longer.

Lucy's gaze went to the blank place on the wall. "The Star quilt!"

"Yes, and a second one from the bed." A lacy, white-painted iron bedstead held twenty quilts or more, rotated so that each had turns being on top. And now another could go on the wall instead.

Lucy waited until Hannah went to collect a couple of bolts of fabric from the cutting table to return them to their place to repeat her apology.

"Ben was a butthead," she concluded.

Suspecting she ought to demur, Nadia said, "Yes, he was. But he's convinced I stole money raised for charity, so I guess it's no surprise he'd rather you didn't hang around with me."

"He didn't sound to me like he does think that," Lucy protested.

"He brought a CSI team in to search my building top to bottom on Monday." Her chest still tightened at the memory. "They went through my underwear drawer, turned over my sofa and chairs, poked through my medicine cabinet and lifted the toilet lid in case I'd taped the bag of money under there. Forgive me for thinking that denotes suspicion."

Lucy made a face. "He says he had to do it, if only for appearances."

"Appearances." Nadia had never laughed with so little humor. "He could have lowered the window blinds so passersby couldn't see what was going on. He didn't. If you'd been a customer here, how would that search *appear* to you?"

Lucy hesitated, then admitted, "Not good."

"Except for your purchase, I've hardly sold a thing all week. The store is empty for hours on end. Most people who signed up for classes aren't attending. Today's was the best I've had, and that's probably because the women are mostly beginners who weren't involved in the auction. The couple who just bought two quilts were tourists. They didn't know they'd stepped into a den of iniquity."

"Aren't most of the quilts sold to tourists?"

"Yes, but I need the fabric store to make a profit, too. Quilt sales are occasional, not steady. And—" She shook her head, aware of Hannah now listening. "No, that's enough whining."

"Tell me." Lucy's expression was fierce.

Oh, what difference did it make? "I've had three quilt makers stop by to pick up ones they'd consigned for sale. They're all locals. If more follow their example and quit trusting me with their quilts, I'm done."

Hannah had been quietly listening. Now she

said, "The *Leit* will keep bringing their quilts here. I haven't heard any bad talk about you."

Nadia smiled shakily at her, aware the Amish called themselves the *Leit*—the people. "That's good to hear. Speaking of… I won't be able to get the cash until Monday, but will you be able to drop it off at Emma Troyer's? And…maybe she has another quilt ready for sale?"

"*Ja*, for certain sure! So glad, she'll be."

Nadia smiled, hating the poison of bitterness she'd let leak out. "And I'll call Jennifer Bronske right now."

She told Lucy she was welcome to come in and use a sewing machine anytime the room wasn't otherwise occupied, after which Ben's sister left. Nadia thought they could become friends if Lucy wasn't in town only temporarily…and if Ben wasn't so opposed to it.

Hannah turned the sign to Closed and locked the front door while Nadia dialed Jennifer's number. When Jennifer answered, Nadia said, "I hope I didn't call when you're in the middle of dinner preparations, but I wanted to let you know that your beautiful Texas Star quilt sold. I can mail a check to you or—"

"I prefer cash," the other woman said with noticeable coolness.

Because her checks were certain to bounce? Nadia choked back what she really wanted to say. She couldn't afford to burn bridges.

"That's fine." She managed what sounded to her like a pleasant voice. "Obviously, I won't be able to get to the bank until Monday morning. If you want to come by and pick the money up, anytime after I open would be fine."

"I'll be there." Then she was gone.

Would she bring another quilt to be sold? Doubtful. Nadia wanted to think it would be a cold day in hell before she'd accept it if Jennifer did offer another one, but as long as she was trying to stay in business here in Byrum she'd have to keep swallowing her pride. But, oh, she hated doing it.

Hannah suddenly said, "Jacob is here, I must go," and let herself out the front. Indeed, a horse and buggy had stopped at the curb. Jacob and their father, Roy Yoder, owned the cabinetmaking business down the block. Hannah had sometimes helped them in the showroom, which was why she'd immediately noticed when Nadia opened the fabric store again. She waved out the window and thought Jacob lifted a hand in return. He seemed like a good man, as did his father who always had a twinkle in his eyes. Jacob had his own place, but his wife had died from a separated placenta during a third pregnancy, leaving him a widower with two young children now cared for by his mother and younger sisters during the day.

Nadia had turned out the lights when she saw

Ben passing the front window. A moment later, he knocked on the door. Nadia froze where she was, at the end of a row of fabric. He scanned the dim interior but apparently didn't see her. When he pulled out his phone and bent his head, she ducked, even though she felt foolish. Hide-and-seek.

Her phone, left beside the cash register, rang. If he could hear it, he'd know she was still downstairs somewhere. Did it matter? She couldn't take one more apology from him. Really, she should walk over, grab her phone and keep going without even turning her head to look at him.

Since that wasn't in her nature, Nadia stayed where she was until a peek told her he had given up.

Trudging upstairs, she tried to recapture her delight at how well the class had gone followed by the sale of two—count 'em, *two*—quilts, but couldn't quite pull off the trick. *Thank you, Ben and Jennifer.*

NADIA WASN'T ANSWERING her phone.

Thanks to his sister, Ben was currently leaning on a shovel in his front yard, filthy and wiping sweat off his brow. Lucy had decided to take on clearing a couple of flower beds, one in his front yard, one in back. Both were choked with weeds, but some stubborn roses and perennials were still hanging on and blooming, if sparsely.

Instead of being able to take advantage of his day off to sit around reading in the air-conditioned house, he'd had to pretend enthusiasm to join her laboring out in the hot sun.

He'd insisted on doing the heavy digging on the bed in the front yard. All the while, he kept an eye on his phone, sitting on the railing so he didn't miss a call. He would have kept it close no matter what, of course, since he needed to be available to his officers 24/7. Them, he'd rather not hear from on a day off. What he had hoped for was a return call from Nadia once she calmed down and listened to his message.

Using the hem of his ratty T-shirt, he wiped sweat out of his eyes and spared a scowl in the general direction of the phone.

"Are you waiting to hear from someone?" his sister asked. Still on her knees holding a trowel in one of her gloved hands, she had paused to look at him.

"Your nose is pink," he said. "You know the sweat is washing off the suntan lotion."

She snorted. "You don't really think Nadia will call, do you? After you were such an ass?"

He turned the scowl on her. "I didn't mean what I said the way she took it."

"Really?" She tipped her head to scrutinize him over the top of her sunglasses. "You ordered me out of the store. Because your delicate, innocent sister needed to stay away." She pretended to ponder. "I think that was it."

"I didn't imply—"

"Sure you did." She looked distinctly unfriendly, considering he was her beloved brother. "You hit two targets with one shot. She's inappropriate company for me, and I'm too fragile to… I'm not sure. Resist the temptation if she tries to recruit me to join her in a criminal spree?"

He growled a word he didn't use around her— okay, he *did* think of her as somewhat fragile— and snapped, "I told you about the cherry bomb tossed through her window. You saying that wouldn't scare the shit out of you?"

"No more than it would anyone else," Lucy said hotly. "I have…particular issues. That doesn't mean I'll faint if I happen to be around when someone is nasty to her." She paused. "Which is fortunate, given that *you* were downright vicious."

"I wasn't." The protest came automatically even though he still winced at the memory of Nadia's face when he said what he had.

His sister only stared unrevealingly at him through the lenses of those dark glasses, then bent her head and went back to work ripping out weeds and dropping them in the rusting bucket he had found in the shed that also held the temperamental lawn mower the former owner had left for his use. He might have been better employed mowing today than clearing a flower bed he would now feel compelled to keep weeded.

When his phone rang, Ben took his time stretching before he reached for it even though he doubted he was fooling Lucy. Nadia's name did not show on the screen. Instead, the caller was Danny Carroll, the officer he intended to promote as soon as he could make other shifts in the department.

"Danny?"

"Chief? I know you're off today—actually, I am, too—but I heard something I thought would interest you. If you're busy…"

"Doing yard work. Nothing I mind being interrupted."

The other officer chuckled. "I know what you mean. Well, this probably isn't anything big, but the Neeleys live about a block from me. I know Carol was involved with the auction committee, and Ron helped with setup. I guess some carpentry know-how was needed."

"I talked to her," Ben agreed.

"Well, my next-door neighbor mentioned that the Neeleys are going on a ten-day Alaskan cruise in July. And that Ron is talking about buying a boat. Something he can use for fishing and maybe even water-skiing. Last time I talked to him, he was complaining about how slow construction has been, and how he didn't like having his wife work but Carol was looking for a job to help out."

"Could she have found a good one?"

"She was talking about cashiering at a convenience store or at the Hy-Vee if she was real lucky. That's not the kind of work that pays for luxuries."

"No, it isn't," Ben agreed. He couldn't quite picture the woman he'd met conspiring to steal money raised for charity…but someone had. "I'll talk to Ron. I won't mention you."

"Thanks. We have a friendly neighborhood. You know how it is."

"I do." Ben thanked him and put his phone on the railing.

Naturally, Lucy had been eavesdropping and he had to explain to her. She encouraged him to shower and go talk to the man *now*. "You don't know how awful this has been for Nadia."

She was wrong; he had a good idea. Which motivated him to take one of the quickest showers on record and head out the door.

The Neeleys lived in a modest rambler. It was Carol who came to the door, obviously surprised to see him on her doorstep.

"Just thought I could catch your husband at home on a Sunday," Ben said easily. "Is he here?"

"You bet." A pleasantly rounded, middle-aged

woman wearing a lot of pink, she led him into the living room, where two recliners faced the TV. When she called, "Ron, Chief Slater is here to see you," a man appeared from the kitchen. A good foot taller than his wife and rail thin, Ron Neeley was losing his hair.

Ben didn't see even a hint of wariness on either face. He took a seat at one end of the sofa and waited until both had perched on their respective recliners.

"I imagine Carol told you the kinds of questions I was asking," he began.

Shaking his head with apparent regret, Ron said, "I don't think I can help you at all. I put together some racks first thing that Friday morning, then came back to help dismantle the sales tables and set up for the auction. I didn't even stay for it. Carol drove herself so I didn't have to go back for her."

"I suppose you've heard all the talk."

It was Carol who answered. "Yes, but we've been distracted. In fact, we were away for the two weeks before the auction. I don't remember if I told you that. I felt guilty not being here to help, but it's been a crazy past few months. My mother passed away in May, so Ron and I have been going back and forth to Springfield ever since, clearing out her house. Ron kept it in good shape for her." She smiled at her husband. "It sold right away, thank goodness."

Ben said the conventional, "I'm sorry for your loss," and knew this visit was another dead end.

"Oh, I'll miss her, but we were starting to talk about nursing homes, and Mom would have hated that, so…"

They mentioned the Alaskan cruise and how excited they were. As soon as he reasonably could, Ben stood and said, "I don't see any need to bother you any more on a Sunday. I'm getting a little desperate here, so I just wanted to make sure I didn't miss talking to anyone involved with the auction."

They both accompanied him to the door, Carol shaking her head over such wickedness but also telling him she worried about Nadia. "Such a hard worker, and with a kind word for everyone. I've been meaning to stop by the store to tell her I don't believe any of those people bad-mouthing her, but with so little time to quilt, I haven't needed to shop for fabric."

Her husband gave her a sidelong look. "As if you ever need to, with a closet stuffed full of fabric you haven't used."

Ben left them still amiably arguing about the issue. They were such nice people, he was ashamed to be disappointed that they hadn't turned out to be crooks.

Although it wouldn't hurt to do a little research, make sure he hadn't just been conned, he decided.

CHAPTER NINE

SUNDAY WAS COMPLETELY UNEVENTFUL. Nadia wished she could think of it as peaceful, but truthfully she felt more as if she was waiting for the other shoe to drop. She didn't once go downstairs. A couple times, she looked to be sure the chair was still wedged in place. If somebody broke in to her shop or vandalized the exterior, they did it quietly.

Monday morning, dread crawled through her even before she opened her eyes. The days of being excited about her new business and the auction were gone.

Don't want to get up.

Maybe from now on she should keep the shop closed on Sundays *and* Mondays.

Something to think about, but right now the sign promised she'd be open, so she needed to get moving if she didn't want to alienate any of her remaining customers. Plus, she needed to dash to the bank for the money she owed Jennifer and still be back before ten.

Thinking about the bank during the five-block

walk, Nadia became aggrieved anew that her financial information had been handed to the police. Okay, the bank manager might have been legally required to cooperate, but he could have called to let her know about the warrant. Wasn't she owed something as a customer? Byrum did have branches from two different banks, so she could move her money. Although, why bother, when the chance was so good that she wouldn't be staying?

As many buggies passed as cars. At least half the downtown businesses were either Amish owned or employed Amish workers. Small paddocks and sheds off the alleys were shared to shelter the horses during the day.

Barely over a week ago, Nadia would have enjoyed the walk. Today, she was grateful to see so few pedestrians this early in the morning.

Her business at the bank didn't take long. The teller divided the cash she needed between two envelopes, one for each of the quilters. Seeing increased foot traffic as soon as she stepped out of the bank, Nadia walked fast, purposefully, on the return trip.

When she came abreast of the Amish Custom Cabinet Shop, though, Jacob Yoder stepped out. *"Gute mariye."*

Smiling politely, she said, "Good morning to you, too." Had he been watching so he could waylay her? They'd never had a real conversation before. It was possible, she decided, that he was concerned she'd have to let his sister go.

Solidly built and around her own age, Jacob wore a blue shirt with the customary black pants and suspenders. The straw hat shaded his face. His chestnut-colored beard signaled that he was—or, in his case, had been—married. Only unmarried Amish men shaved their jaws. It had taken Nadia a little while to get used to seeing bearded men with clean-shaven upper lips.

Jacob met her eyes, his sympathetic. "Hannah says business has been slow for you."

So she'd been right that his worry was for his sister. "Did she tell you what a good day Saturday was? Maybe I've turned the corner."

"*Ja*, I hope that is so." He glanced over his shoulder. "*Ach*, I think that is *Daad* yelling for me. I must go, but call for us anytime if you need help."

His kindness gave her a lump in her throat. Maybe he was thinking about her as well as Hannah. "Thank you. *Denke*," she ventured.

Jacob laughed. "So you speak *Deitsch*, do you?"

Nadia couldn't help laughing, too. "So far, some polite phrases. Oh—because of the name of my shop, Hannah did teach me to say, *En schtich in zeit is neine wart schpaeder naus.*"

A stitch in time saves nine.

Eyes twinkling, Jacob agreed she had needed to learn that much.

Her uplifted mood lasted about one minute. First, she saw Jennifer Bronske getting out of a car parked at the curb, and realized a second woman sat in the passenger seat. Then she saw an approaching police car, slowing to pull in behind Jennifer's black Mustang.

What's more, a man was walking fast toward her on the sidewalk. A stranger. She wanted to be relieved, but he didn't avert his gaze the way most passersby did. *Should* she know him?

Her thoughts jumped. Jennifer had to be well aware that the store didn't open until ten. Was she really so afraid she wouldn't get paid?

But Nadia forgot Jennifer now that she was close enough to see the burning intensity of the stranger's stare, trained on *her*. She stepped sideways toward the vacant storefront next to A Stitch in Time, giving the man plenty of room to go by.

But he didn't. Her heart thudded as he came straight to her. The cords in his neck stood out and his face was flushed an angry color. He stopped barely a foot from her, his hands balling into fists at his sides. And then he spit on her face.

BEN ERUPTED FROM his car in time to hear Nadia's assailant snarl, "*That's* what I think of you, bitch."

He covered the distance in seconds. The two

formed a frozen tableau when he reached them. Grabbing the creep's shoulder, Ben yanked him around. "You are under arrest for—" The words died in his mouth. Oh, hell, he knew this guy. Not to meet, but he'd seen his face. One of the spring tornadoes had ripped a swath through his dairy farm, destroying his barn and taking the roof off his house. One of his kids had been killed. There'd been a lot of devastation this year, but only the one death.

The man just glared at him. Behind him, Nadia hadn't even lifted a hand to wipe off the spittle dripping down her cheek. She looked stricken. Meantime, Ben had heard brakes applied as a passing motorist stopped to watch the scene, and he was well aware Jennifer Bronske and some other woman had home-plate seats to the action.

Ben said evenly, "I'm aware of your troubles, Mr…?"

The man's Adam's apple bobbed. "Hixson. Leonard Hixson."

Ben nodded. "Mr. Hixson. I'm the chief of the Byrum police department. Whether you know it or not, you just committed the crime of battery on a woman who worked very hard to raise funds to help you among many others." He raised his voice slightly, wanting to be heard. "There is *no* evidence to support any belief that Ms. Markovic took the money. To the contrary. How are you going to feel when we arrest someone else?"

Hixson blinked a couple of times. The crazed fury in his eyes became confusion. "I didn't…"

"You did." Now Ben let his voice harden. "Spitting is considered battery as much as striking another person would be."

His mouth fell open. "But…"

Ben propelled him around to face Nadia, who had finally taken a tissue from her purse and was wiping her cheek.

"Ms. Markovic," Ben said formally, "this is Leonard Hixson. His farm suffered severe damage this spring from a twister. Worse, his son was killed."

Shock and pain transformed her face.

Ben continued, "He has good reason to be feeling a lot of anger, but there is no excuse for directing it at you this way. I'm very willing to arrest him if you want to press charges—"

As he'd expected, she was already shaking her head. "No. No, of course not." Tears stood out in her eyes. "I'm so sorry for what you went through, Mr. Hixson. I can only promise you that I didn't take that money."

Hixson's face crumpled. "Thank you. Thank you. I don't know what I was thinking. I have to go." He staggered as he turned away from her, his shock showing when he saw the growing audience. Then he bent his head and began walking. By the time he reached the corner, he had broken into a run.

Ben exhaled when he lost sight of Hixson. He took Nadia's arm and said quietly, "Let's get you inside."

"Yes, I—"

Cheeks crimson, she still held her chin high when she looked at Jennifer Bronske, who hadn't moved an inch since Ben arrived on the scene. If the woman had looked pleased, he'd have been tempted to arrest *her*, but he thought shock was what held her in place.

Nadia delved in her big handbag and pulled out what was obviously a bank envelope. She held it out to Jennifer. "As promised."

A flush spread on the other woman's face, too. She lifted a hand, hesitated and then took the envelope. "What happened… I'm sorry, I didn't mean…"

Nadia simply nodded and said, "Please excuse me." Her hand shook when she took her ring of keys from her bag.

Ben deftly removed them from her hand and unlocked the front door of the shop. While ushering Nadia inside, he didn't so much as look at Ms. Bronske or any of the several other people who had clustered on the street out of sheer nosiness. After relocking the door, he steered Nadia toward the archway that led into the hall. That she didn't once protest told him how raw she felt.

Once they were out of sight in the hall, he gave her a nudge. "Go wash your face."

"Oh." Her hand lifted toward her face but stopped short, as if she didn't want to touch it. "Yes."

With her in the bathroom and the door shut, Ben stalked from one end of the hall to the other. Had he done the right thing, not arresting Hixson? Would the guy have also hit Nadia, if Ben hadn't been there to intervene? And what was the deal with the bank envelope Nadia had handed over to Jennifer Bronske?

The rush of fear-fueled adrenaline still had him on edge. That moment, when he'd realized a man was closing in on Nadia… If he hadn't been here, if he'd gotten a call she'd been seriously injured and was being transported to the hospital…

He couldn't think like this. He didn't know how his feelings for her had gotten so out of hand, but—

He spun around when he heard the bathroom door opening. Nadia emerged with her composure almost reassembled. Only her eyes betrayed the aftereffects of the ugly scene.

Without even thinking, he took the couple steps to reach her and pulled her into his arms. For a moment her body stayed rigid, but then her purse clunked to the floor and she wrapped her arms around him, too. She shuddered as she laid her head on his shoulder, and in back she grabbed handfuls of his shirt.

"It's okay," he murmured into her hair. "I was proud of you. You kept your dignity. He ended up ashamed the way he should be. This will pass. It will."

Yeah? Who was he trying to convince? But he knew. *Both of us, that's who.* Because if this didn't pass, she'd move away. No question. And he didn't want her going anywhere.

As boneless as she felt right now, only the knuckles digging into his back told him she wasn't truly relaxed. He fell silent as he became disturbingly aware of her body, pressed up to his. All those curves. Breasts flattening against his chest. If he let one of his hands stray, he could follow the dip of her spine down to another equally luscious and curvy part of one of the most feminine bodies he'd ever seen—or touched.

And, damn, if he didn't inch away from her, she couldn't help but notice his growing arousal. The timing was lousy. She needed comfort, not him coming on to her. Especially not him. Except, she did trust him enough to let him hold her. That meant something, didn't it?

Finally she sighed and began to straighten away from him. One hand released his shirt, then the other. The color in her cheeks hadn't subsided— or maybe it was new heat in her cheeks. Yeah, she couldn't have missed the erection straining against his zipper.

JANICE KAY JOHNSON   171

When her eyes met his fully, he saw that they were dilated. He wondered if she was aware that, after releasing him, she had placed one hand on his chest, her fingers spread. When those fingers flexed slightly, he almost groaned with pleasure.

"Thank you." Nadia nibbled on her lower lip. "I'm still mad at you, but…I don't know what I'd have done without you." Her huff was almost a laugh. "Well, I suppose you were just doing your job."

"No." Not smart. He made himself elaborate anyway, be completely honest. "Yeah, I'd have intervened for anybody, but…I wouldn't have been so scared."

"Scared?" she whispered, searching his eyes.

He'd startled her. Maybe more. "He could have had a weapon. No matter what, he was a lot bigger than you are. I didn't know if I could get to you in time."

Her hand moved in a circle, comforting—still unconsciously, he thought.

"But you did. And…I doubt he meant to hurt me."

"I hope not."

"This is why you didn't want Lucy near me."

"It is." What else could he say? "But I don't think she's as fragile as I believed her to be." He shook his head. "How could I have just let Hixson walk away? I should have asked if he just happened to see you, or came looking for you. Either way, he's an angry, depressed man."

Pain infusing her voice, she said, "Who might have been helped with some of the money I lost." Her hand falling to her side, Nadia started to step back.

Ben caught her before she was out of reach, his fingers sliding beneath the bundle of hair at her nape to hold her. "The money was stolen. You didn't lose it."

She stared back, not lowering her chin. "Unless I took it."

"You didn't." When he saw no softening on her face, Ben lost what grip he'd had on his self-control. The distance he'd had to keep, her anger, had been eating at the lining of his stomach and causing a chronic ache beneath his breastbone. He couldn't prevent himself from bending his head and kissing her.

NADIA HAD FELT too much in such a short period of time. Mad and frightened, grateful and yearning. Somehow, Ben's mouth covering hers was exactly what she needed.

With a whimper, she rose on tiptoe and flung her arms around his neck, meeting his hunger with her own. He bit her lower lip, the sting part of this urgent tide that made her blood feel as if it was hot and thick in her veins. She nipped him back, and he took advantage of her parted lips to drive his tongue inside her mouth. The delicious stroke had her squirming to get closer.

His hands roved, one kneading, then gripping her butt to lift her higher against him. She stroked the back of his neck and tangled her fingers in the heavy silk of his dark hair. His jaw rasped her skin, part of the startling intimacy with this man.

She'd wanted to hate him.

I can't.

He was turning her in a slow circle, as if this was a dance. She wanted to climb him to assuage a cramping need, low in her belly. She could wrap her legs around his waist, rub herself against the hard ridge. Except…during one of those slow twirls, something *else* that was hard bumped her side. His gun.

She froze.

Nadia put both hands on his chest and pushed.

Ben lifted his head, his eyes almost black, the dark color of arousal running over his sharp cheekbones. "Nadia?" he said hoarsely.

"I have to open my shop. You're parked right out in front. People will think…"

An indescribable sound tore from his throat, and his hands fell from her waist and hip. He backed up until he hit the wall.

"I didn't mean…"

"To kiss me?"

His gaze lowered to her mouth, then lifted to

meet hers again. "I've been wanting to kiss you since I set eyes on you."

At the auction. The reminder was painful, but needed.

"I'm still…" Nadia hesitated.

"A suspect?" He shook his head. "Not in my eyes."

She retreated a couple steps, needing distance to regain her common sense. "How can you say that?"

"Easily…" He ran a hand over his face. "No. I won't push. You have a lot to deal with."

Yes, she did. But the kiss, him telling her he believed in her, changed something fundamental.

After this, it would hurt even more to have him turn on her.

What if a customer was peering in the front window wondering why the door was locked and the lights weren't on? "I need…" She gestured toward the archway, even as she couldn't seem to quite look away from his dark eyes.

"I know. I have to get to work, too." He didn't sound any more motivated than she felt. But after a minute, Ben grimaced. "I'll call later. I should talk to Bill Jarvis and find out if there isn't something that can be done to help the Hixson family."

Nadia nodded. "A lot of the people who paid with credit cards or by check have reimbursed us. That's nowhere near enough money, but…"

"Most people's losses were at least partially covered by insurance. I wonder if his weren't."

"It might not be that," she said. "Grief changes a person. But also, when I started working on the auction, I was told that some companies specifically exclude windstorm damage. It can come as a shock to people who didn't read the policies carefully."

Ben grunted his agreement. "Some of the folks who got hit had coverage on their houses but not the barns, tools, livestock. For a dairy farmer, that would put him out of business."

"Does he have other children?" She had to ask, even though she doubted it lessened the agony of losing a child. Ben's expression suggested he knew she was remembering Molly...and Molly's brothers.

"Two younger, if I remember right. The boy he lost was the oldest, out exploring with his dog, too far away to make it to the house. I know Hixson kept the door to their storm shelter open as long as he could."

Praying, she thought. He would have had to let himself believe the path of the tornado would miss his son, that he would come running after it had passed, calling for his mom and dad. They would have climbed out of the shelter, looking frantically in every direction, uncaring of barn or house. She imagined the desperate search—

"Nadia." Ben squeezed her shoulder. He

waited until she focused on him. "It was a tragedy. You can't save every child."

"I already know that." How well she'd learned that lesson. She backed away. "I'm okay. I am," she repeated, when she saw that he remained unconvinced.

"All right." He gave her a quick, hard kiss. "I'll call later."

It surprised her that she could smile. "I might even answer."

His husky chuckle made it easier to see him leave, and to greet a woman who appeared minutes later.

She only bought two rolls of thread—but she hadn't had to go somewhere else because A Stitch in Time was inexplicably closed.

BEN NEEDED A decent cup of coffee, which he wouldn't get at the station. Only after he had accepted the job and moved to Byrum had he discovered he couldn't get anything but an old-fashioned cup of coffee anywhere in Henness County. He'd bought an espresso machine and resigned himself, but six months later a drive-through coffee stand with a serious drink menu opened on what had formerly been a vacant lot two blocks off the main drag.

Today he bought a double espresso on ice that should hold him for a couple of hours. After one long, cold drink, he drove the short distance to the police station and parked in his reserved spot, taking the cup in with him.

After letting dispatch know where he was, Ben settled down to work in his office on scheduling for August.

Boyd had put in for vacation—two weeks, which Ben had approved back in March. And, crap, Jose Garcia was getting married the first Saturday of August and then taking a honeymoon. Their absences overlapped by only a few days, but if anyone got sick—

His desk phone rang, the internal line. "Slater."

Sherry, the fount of gossip, said, "Chief, Jim Wilcox is here to see you."

The locksmith? If he'd suffered a loss of some kind, why wouldn't he have called 911?

"I'll be right out."

What few dealings Ben had had with Jim Wilcox, he'd liked him. Somewhere in his forties, the man had a way of sliding into the background. Just one of those unmemorable faces.

When Ben opened the door into the waiting room, Wilcox stood. He picked up a brown paper bag from the seat beside him and brought it along. They shook hands, and Ben ushered him into a small conference room.

Once they were seated, Ben said, "So what's this about?"

"Someone managed to shove this through the

mail slot in the door of my shop." He pushed the bag across the table, looking glad to get rid of it.

Ben had never been in his store, but had seen ads. Wilcox made copies of keys and sold a variety of padlocks and dead bolts as well as safes for homes and businesses.

The brown paper sack in front of Ben was the kind just about every grocery store used when customers didn't want the plastic ones. This one was plain, lacking a store name or logo. It had been folded several times and the whole thing flattened. Ben opened it and looked inside. From long practice, he suppressed his jolt of surprise. He didn't reach in. In fact, he regretted handling the bag at all without having put on latex gloves first.

He met the locksmith's troubled brown eyes. "I assume you took a look to see what was in here."

"Sure, I thought it was for me. The first check I picked up was written for forty-seven hundred dollars. I know the woman who wrote it. I'm thinking this is some of what was stolen after that auction."

Ben tapped his fingers on the table as he thought. "Why you?" he finally asked.

"I don't know." Wilcox appeared less than happy. "A lot of folks in town know me."

"I wonder if your mail slot is deeper or wider than some."

The locksmith shook his head. "I don't know.

I never paid any attention. My building is an old one. The mail slot is brass, an old-timer."

"Do you mind if I fingerprint it?"

"No, of course not."

"All right." Ben pushed back his chair. "Thanks, Jim. We'll see if we can get lucky and find someone who saw this being delivered."

Visibly relieved to have off-loaded a problem, Wilcox left, and Terry Uhrich came in response to Ben's summons.

He studied the bag without noticeable enthusiasm. "Well, paper absorbs oils so it's ideal for picking up fingerprints. But this one isn't crisp out of the store. Fact is, I'll probably find lots of them. I'll have to get yours and Jim Wilcox's for elimination. And that's just the beginning. Presumably a grocery clerk or bagger and at least one customer handled it. And people keep these around and reuse them. There could be an innocent reason for just about anybody leaving a print on it."

"And the guy who decided out of the goodness of his heart to give back the credit card slips and checks probably wore gloves."

"Unless he's never watched television or read a book or newspaper," Terry agreed.

"Or just got careless."

Terry shrugged. "It happens. Anything I lift from here would mostly be useful to match up once you have a suspect." Peering inside, he said,

"I'll see what I can do with a couple of the top and bottom slips and checks, too."

"Go for it," Ben said, and went straight to his office to call Nadia. She deserved to hear the news first.

CHAPTER TEN

NADIA HUNG UP the phone, her hand not quite steady. She didn't know what to make of Ben's news. Had somebody suffered from a guilty conscience? If so, not enough to return the cash—the irreplaceable part of what was stolen.

She'd be happier if the return of the credit card slips and checks cleared her of suspicion, but anyone who had already condemned her wouldn't have any trouble believing she had been the one to jam the sack through the locksmith's mail slot. It was logical to suppose that, under suspicion, she would have decided to get rid of the physical evidence.

The bell on the door let her know she had a customer, so she arranged a smile on her face and stepped around the counter. The smile immediately became natural.

"Katie-Ann!" Besides Hannah, Katie-Ann Chupp was the only Amish woman she considered a real friend. "And Ruth!"

Elderly and tiny, Ruth Graber was widely considered the finest quilter in the area. Nadia had been captivated from their first meeting by Ruth's bright eyes and mischievous smile.

Today, both women carried bundles in their arms. Quilts, Nadia saw, and gave silent thanks. This was their way of expressing support.

"Do you have room to display more?" Katie-Ann asked, as if there was any doubt. "Mine is only crib-size, but Ruth's is for a bed."

"For you two, I always have room." Nadia hurried forward to take the larger bundle from Ruth. The top of her head barely reached shoulder height on Nadia. "I'm excited to see what you've brought."

Their voices must have carried, because Hannah and Lucy emerged from the back room. Lucy had arrived shortly after the shop opened to use a sewing machine. Nadia introduced her.

"Learning to quilt?" Ruth surveyed Ben's sister and nodded with apparent satisfaction. "Smart, you are, coming to Nadia. A fine teacher she is."

Lucy beamed. "I think so, too. Do you mind if I peek at your work, since I'm here?"

Of course they didn't; quilters almost always welcomed newcomers. And although the Amish abhorred pride—they said someone was taken over by *hochmut*—the finest of craftsmen and women surely wouldn't strive for such perfection and grace without feeling gratification anyone else would call pride, or so Nadia suspected.

First, she spread Katie-Ann's crib quilt atop the pile on the bed. The Tumbling Blocks pattern used fabrics shading from the palest lemon in one corner through richer yellows and vibrant greens before flowing into blue at the opposite corner.

"Oh," Lucy breathed, reaching out to touch it reverently with her fingertips. "If I had a little boy…" Sadness crossed her face as she withdrew her hand.

Nadia filed away what she'd seen, wondering if Ben's sister was unable to have children or had lost a baby. Not the kind of thing she could ask.

And then they all sighed with pleasure as Nadia unrolled Ruth's Sunshine and Shadows quilt that truly seemed to capture sunlight contrasting with secret corners that were never quite illuminated. Yellow, gold and bronze, it glowed. The tiny, perfectly spaced stitches made it a masterpiece.

"I'll take pictures of this today for the website," Nadia said. "I predict it will sell by the end of the week. I think it might be the most beautiful quilt I've ever seen."

Ruth demurred, of course. *Ach*, she knew so many fine quilters! She did her best, she said, but her eyesight wasn't what it had been, which Nadia didn't believe for a minute. Not after seeing her stitches in this newest quilt.

She took Ruth's hand, small, calloused and arthritic, and Katie-Ann's, no softer but stronger, and said, "Thank you for bringing these. For… trusting me."

The wrinkles giving Ruth's face a crepe-paper-like texture deepened into crevasses. *"Was der schinner is letz?* Not trust you? Who would not?"

What in the world is wrong? she had asked. Hadn't any of the women told Ruth what was happening? In Nadia's experience, the Amish grapevine was lightning fast despite the fact they didn't use telephones.

"You know about the stolen money?" she said.

"Ja, sure."

"Quite a few people think I took the money myself. They are no longer shopping in my store, and…" She made a face. "Several women have taken their quilts back. I guess they're convinced I won't pay them."

Ruth's grip tightened until it almost hurt. "Moderns. A good shake, is what they all need! You are honest as the day is long. Any fool can see that."

"Denke," Nadia said shakily.

Ruth turned her fierceness on poor Katie-Ann. "Why did you not tell me?"

"You've had enough troubles—"

She snorted. "If I don't know, I can't talk sense into people. This must be set right."

"Chief Slater called a few minutes ago," Nadia said. "Um, he's Lucy's brother."

Hannah already knew, of course. The other two women stared at Lucy for a moment.

Nadia told them about the credit card slips and checks being returned via the mail slot on the locksmith's door. "I told him to take them to Julie Baird. There's enough distrust of me—I can't handle them. A lot of the people have already stopped payment at their banks or credit card companies. There are a few from people we were unable to contact, and those we can cash."

"So more of the money can go to help people," Hannah said with satisfaction.

"Yes. But, no matter what, it isn't even half what we brought in. A third of the total, maybe? So many people paid with cash, and whoever took it didn't give that back."

Ruth gave a firm nod. "What I earn from this one—" she nodded at the Sunshine and Shadows quilt "—you will give that money in place of what was stolen."

Katie-Ann beamed. "*Ja*, you must do the same for mine. I will talk to other quilters."

Nadia's eyes stung. "You can tell them that I won't keep a commission if they're willing to donate their part, too."

"No, no." Ruth squeezed Nadia's hand and let it go. "You must keep your part. What will we do if you go out of business? What I offer is for you, too."

Katie-Ann nodded vigorously.

Nadia swiped at damp eyes. "You're making me cry."

"In a good way, I hope." Katie-Ann hugged her.

Laughing through her sniffles, she said, "Of course, in a good way! Thank you both. *Denke.*"

Eventually Ruth and Katie-Ann went to the back room to see what Lucy was working on, and approved both her fabric choices and the care she was taking in cutting, sewing and ironing. So many beginners thought they could be slapdash, not realizing how the tiniest imperfection would cause problems down the line.

Nadia caught sight of a buggy stopping in front, the glossy brown horse calm even as a motorcycle roared past. "Is that your ride?" she asked.

Following her gaze, Katie-Ann exclaimed, "*Ach*, Elijah is here already."

"So soon?" Ruth chuckled. "Well, *blabbermauls*, we've been, ain't so?"

Hannah walked them out, and Nadia saw the three out on the sidewalk, their heads close together, and guessed they had switched to Pennsylvania Dutch. The better for Hannah to tell them hastily about this morning's events. Nadia touched her cheek, remembering how filthy she had felt, when a baby's spit wouldn't have bothered her at all.

Knowing she did have friends warmed her inside. The effect lingered even though by lunch-time her sole sale of the day was the two spools of thread.

BEN HAD KNOWN before he and his officers began canvassing people who worked up and down the street from Wilcox Lock and Key that the odds of finding a witness to the bag being poked through the mail slot were about one in a million. Few buildings here had upstairs apartments. With no restaurants or taverns, the street shut down at five o'clock. Yeah, there were street lamps, but it wouldn't have taken a minute for somebody to pull up to the curb, hustle over to shove the sack through the slot, then drive away.

Still, they'd had to try.

When he returned to the station after the fruit-less quest, Terry reported finding fingerprints from eight different people on the bag, but none of those were also on the checks and credit card slips that had been on the bottom and top of the pile. Except for Wilcox's and Ben's, Terry ran the prints from the bags, but Ben's gut feeling was that this thief wasn't anyone who'd already be in the system. Not to say the individual hadn't stolen before, but nothing about this had been impulsive. Somehow, he or she had had a key. He—if it was a man—hadn't taken the oppor-tunity to rape Nadia.

Not for the first time, Ben wished he'd followed her home and made sure she got inside safely. If so, he might have seen someone else watching.

Had the thief savored the irony of returning that envelope via Wilcox Lock and Key? Or was it an outright taunt? *I have a key, didn't need a locksmith?* He gave passing thought to Lyle Warren but, odd as the man was, Ben couldn't fit him into any believable scenario.

He forced himself to set aside the brooding in favor of a few hours dedicated to the frustrating administrative stuff. He and the principal had a lengthy discussion about what presence the police would have at the high school come fall semester. An officer who'd done a lot of the safety talks at the elementary school had taken a job elsewhere, so Ben now had to decide who could replace him. He took a call from an irate father who didn't want to believe his daughter had actually shoplifted.

Midafternoon, Ben checked in with Lucy. She mentioned having spent several hours at A Stitch in Time. He asked her to hold dinner to give him time to stop by and talk to Nadia before coming home. What he'd have liked was to invite her to join them for dinner, but he didn't dare, not yet. He had been told that the city council had erupted in some hot debates before he had been offered the job of police chief. He felt sure he knew which councilmen—and every damn one of them was male—hadn't wanted to hire a brash, know-it-all Northerner. Ben had worked hard so far to do his job effectively while not giving anyone ammunition to get rid of him. However he felt about it, Nadia was still a suspect in the eyes of too many influential members of this community.

He slipped away early enough to park in front of her building just as she was turning the sign to read Closed. She waited, opening the door as he crossed the sidewalk to her. He wanted to sweep her into his arms and resume this morning's kiss, but restrained himself. Nadia had had reservations about him from the first, even before the theft, and he needed to know why before he presumed too much.

She locked and said, "You do know everyone who sees your Explorer out front will wonder why you're here."

"It's not a police car. Why would anyone notice it?"

Nadia's look said, *Get real.*

"How do you know so much about small towns when you didn't grow up in one?" he grumbled.

"Being the subject of vitriolic gossip is a speed-learning experience," she said tersely. "Are you staying long enough to come upstairs?"

"Yes."

Without comment, she led the way, her reserve solidly in place. Maybe he *should* have kissed her the minute he walked in the door, to hell with the chance of being seen.

"I made lemonade earlier," she said without looking at him as they entered the apartment. "Would you like a glass?"

"That sounds good. Thanks."

Another nod, and she disappeared into the kitchen. Not liking this uncertainty, Ben hovered in the small living room, listening to the sounds of her moving around. The cupboard door, the refrigerator, the clink of glasses. Soft but unmistakable. Would she really have slept through those kinds of sounds while an intruder searched her place?

Yeah, but if she'd turned lights on and off quickly on the way upstairs, an interested observer might rightly have assumed she hadn't stopped long enough along the way to hide the money. And what if the only light she turned on in the apartment was in her bedroom? The intruder could have started the search there. With a penlight, he could have seen the money box immediately.

When she returned with the lemonade, he sat on the sofa, her on the easy chair facing him.

"Walk me through what you did when you got home that night."

"What?" Shock showed on her face.

"You parked out in front and let yourself into

the store. Did you turn on any lights down-stairs?"

"The hall, just long enough for me to check that the back door was still locked. And then the ones above the stairs, of course."

The light in the hall would show as a glow through the store's front windows, for sure, and more faintly through the back window. The stair-case lights probably couldn't be seen from out-side at all, front or back.

Needing to pin her down, he said, "But not in the store."

She shook her head.

"Upstairs?"

Her eyes briefly became unfocused. "As I was going up, I thought about having a glass of wine. But I was so tired, I think I was weaving a little, so I went straight to the bedroom."

"No lights on the way."

She frowned at him. "What's this obsession with lights?"

He explained, and she said, "How will that help you figure out who he was?"

"It probably won't, but you've satisfied my cu-riosity. It kept bugging me. How could somebody search out here without waking you?"

"I was awfully tired—"

"I know, but I also think we all have a strong sense of self-preservation and an internal filter. We ignore a lot of noises when we sleep. But there are noises that *shouldn't* be there. A cupboard door closing, a footstep outside your bedroom door—"

Shivering, she carefully set her glass on the coffee table. "But…he or she must have come with the intention of searching thoroughly."

This was the part that still chilled him. "Yeah."

"If I *had* woken up…"

"Thank God you didn't," he said roughly.

Nadia blinked a couple of times. "Yes." She was quiet for a minute. "You won't give up, will you?"

"No. I'm not good at quitting." He heard more heat in his voice than he'd intended to give away.

She searched his eyes and finally nodded. "Thank you." She cleared her voice. "I've said that a lot today."

When he asked, she told him about Katie-Ann Chupp and Ruth Graber's visit, and their kindness. There was awe in her voice when she mentioned Ruth's offer to donate the entire amount earned from her quilt sale—and Katie-Ann's immediate willingness to do the same.

"It's their way," Ben said simply, and Nadia nodded.

"So I'm discovering." She smiled at him. "Ruth's quilt is spectacular." Some less welcome thought had her smile dying. He'd swear she was challenging him when she added, "I'll bet Lucy will tell you about it."

Ah. He'd hinted, but they never had put that incident to rest. Unfortunately, he couldn't explain why he'd reacted the way he had without violating his sister's privacy. And the last thing he wanted to tell her was that he still wished Lucy would keep her distance until he made an arrest or the community uproar died down.

So all he said was, "She mentioned that she planned to use a sewing machine at your place."

"I can assure you that she left in good health."

"I am worried about her," he admitted, knowing he couldn't lie to her. "And no, it's not because I think you'd be a bad influence on her. It's her. And I can't tell you any more."

Nadia's chin lowered. "Today, she said something…" She rubbed her hands over the arms of the chair. "Katie-Ann's crib quilt made her sad. I wondered if she'd lost a child, or—"

Ben shook his head. "Not that." He knew how much Lucy wanted children, but in the normal course of events you needed a man for that. He'd be sorry if she decided the only way she'd ever have a baby was to go to a sperm bank, but he and—he felt sure—his parents would accept that. "I'll talk to her about it tonight. I stepped in it big-time, and she might take pity on me and let me tell you why I'm nervous about her being here if anything else like the cherry bomb happens."

Worry shadowed her eyes. "Don't push her

too hard. I don't want her to be uncomfortable with me."

Not surprised that her first concern was Lucy, Ben nodded and decided to change the subject. Before he could, she said tentatively, "Do you have other siblings? Lucy hasn't said."

So she wanted to know more about him. Did that mean forgiveness was possible?

Ben shook his head. "Just the two of us. We're only a year and a half apart in age. Two pregnancies so close together probably convinced Mom that enough was enough."

Nadia's chuckle lifted his mood another notch.

"Having two kids in diapers at the same time might have had something to do with that."

Ben laughed, too. "Yeah, that could be. I'm pretty sure I was an oops baby. At least an 'oops, not yet' baby." Intensely curious, he asked, "What about you?"

"Like you, I have only one sister, several years older than me. We were pretty good friends, even though Sonya always was bossy. After... you know, she wanted me to get over it. It was like she couldn't stand not being able to fix me." Her forehead crimped. "Her and Mom, both. They're..."

When she seemed to be searching for words, he suggested, "Overbearing?"

She hesitated. "I know they love me and want the best for me."

In other words, yes.

Unhappily aware that he should shove off and leave her to her dinner plans, he asked if she'd heard from Julie.

"No." She appeared unsurprised.

From his interviews with the volunteers, Ben knew that Nadia had been the driving force behind the fund-raiser and had committed a daunting amount of time and energy. In contrast, Julie Baird mostly liked committees and having a reputation for charitable work without having to seriously apply herself. He had a few things he'd like to say to her but, given his position, never would.

"Did you talk to Bill Jarvis about Mr. Hixson?" she asked.

"I did. And you were right. Their coverage on the house excluded wind damage. He didn't have insurance at all on the barn, farm equipment or animals. Raising three kids, and having a relatively small operation like his, they had to be tight with their money. Bill says right now the Hixsons are living with the wife's sister and her family. He has the impression they're getting desperate. Leonard hasn't had any luck finding a job, but doesn't want to sell the land."

"Would anyone buy it, given the obvious tornado damage?"

"Maybe. Farmland usually does go, but without buildings? Anyway, what he'd get wouldn't support a family for long." He sighed. "The Hixsons are near the top of Bill's list, but there just isn't enough money to go around." Seeing Nadia's expression, he said, "Don't go there. The rest of the money you raised would have been welcome, but spread it around between two or three families, and it wouldn't get any of them back on their feet."

"No, but… It's too bad the farmers that were impacted didn't have Amish-style barn raisings."

"They'd have had to be able to afford the lumber. And what good is an empty barn?"

"Not all the cows were killed, were they?"

"Probably not, but he may have had to sell the herd. Anyway, dairy farming is mostly automated these days, even among the Amish. You need tanks to keep the milk cool and sterile, and I'm guessing that's just the beginning."

"It's not right!" she exclaimed in frustration. She'd obviously forgiven Hixson and ached to help him, giving her a lot in common with the Amish women who had rallied around her.

Despite everything going so wrong with the auction into which she had poured so much energy, her generosity and compassion remained alive and well. Aware of a sharp twinge in the region of his heart, Ben smiled at her.

"No, it isn't right. But you did something extraordinary to try to help, and that's more than most people do." He needed to get out of here before he pushed for something she couldn't possibly be ready to give.

When he expressed his need to go and stood, Nadia rose, too. "You didn't find out anything about the checks and credit card slips being returned."

He shook his head. "I didn't expect to. Whoever he is, he used his head."

And why did he keep thinking of the thief as "he"? If someone involved with the auction took the money, "he" was more likely a *she*.

Convenience, he decided. And reality was that he arrested way more men than he did women.

"Why do you suppose the person bothered?" Nadia asked.

"I don't know," he admitted. "Burning the pile would have been easy and less risky."

"Maybe he does feel guilty."

There she went again, holding on to faith that everyone had a heart. Given that she'd seen the darkest side of human nature, that was a miracle.

How would she classify the rage that kept a coal burning white-hot inside him? Would she believe it was justified? Protective? Or would she see a man like her friend's husband, ready to explode at the right provocation?

And are you so sure that doesn't describe you?

Yes. He was sure. But whether Nadia would agree was another story. He still hadn't forgotten the fear darkening her eyes when they met.

That's long past.
Ben wanted to think so, but he was careful to keep his kiss light and not demand more before he left.

CHAPTER ELEVEN

LUCY ARRIVED NOT ten minutes after Nadia opened A Stitch in Time the next morning. Her tote bag bulged, and this time she'd brought the large wooden hoop.

After greeting her, Nadia nodded at the tote. "Are you ready to start quilting?"

"Not quite, but all I have to do is add the borders and cut out the backing and batting. Well, and pin it. And…I don't need to mark it if I'm just planning to quilt straight lines, right?"

Nadia laughed. "No, you don't. Don't sound so nervous! Remember, if your first stitches are huge or crooked, you can pull them out. Besides, this is your first quilt. You can't improve if you don't start."

"I know." She scrunched up her nose. "I'm a perfectionist, which means I drive myself crazy."

"I understand that," Nadia admitted. "It bodes well for you as a quilter, though. The best are, you know."

Lucy looked thoughtful. "That makes sense.

I've been studying the quilt in the frame in back. Hannah told me it's yours."

"It is." She hadn't touched it while she was so shaken after the auction, but in the past few days she'd had plenty of time to work on it. No annoying distractions like customers.

"The stitches are incredibly tiny and so even. Which says *you're* a perfectionist, too."

"I am, but part of it is just practice. I've done it so long, now I can quilt with my mind a million miles away, or while I'm carrying on a conversation, and my hand just knows what to do. I use a really small needle, and almost always pack twelve stitches on it."

"But you don't count."

She shook her head. "I don't need to anymore."

Lucy sighed. "I'm hoping you'll give me a quick lesson before I start that part."

Nadia smiled. "Of course I will. And no, we don't have to wait until the class this afternoon. If things stay quiet, I'll be glad to have something to do."

Lucy looked around. "Where's Hannah?"

"Not coming in until noon. Yesterday was so dead…" *Quiet.* That's what she meant.

In a different voice, low and almost timid, Lucy asked, "Do you have time to talk for a minute?"

Ben must have kept his promise, but now

Nadia felt guilty. Did she really need to know the details of what his sister had suffered, instead of being willing to accept that he had reason to be extra protective of her?

"Of course I do," she said, "but…if this is because of Ben, you don't have to tell me anything, you know. I don't want you feeling coerced."

"No, I don't mind telling you. Really. I'd like to think we can be friends."

Nadia hugged her. "Me, too. Okay, let's sit in back."

She brought them both bottles of water from the dorm-size fridge she had under the checkout counter, and sat at the worktable where she could see into the store.

"I was raped," Lucy said.

"Oh, no." From their first meeting, Nadia had seen the same darkness in Lucy's eyes she saw in her own sometimes when she looked in the mirror. But by body language and her choice of clothing, Lucy carried it further. Whether consciously or not, she was trying to pass unnoticed, certainly by men.

"It happened the summer after my sophomore year. I didn't go home because I had a job showing prospective students around the campus and doing some filing and data entry for the admissions department. I was living in an off-campus apartment. Then…one night I woke up and he was ripping my clothes off. I tried to scream and he clamped a hand over my face." She stopped, swallowed, distress coming off her in waves. "He—"

Nadia took her hand and squeezed it. "You don't need to tell me. If…it helps to get it all out, I'll listen, but please don't relive it for my sake or your brother's."

Lucy held on to Nadia's hand as if desperate for the connection. Despite dry eyes, her devastation was easy to see. "Thank you. I'm sure you can imagine what happened. What woman hasn't known it could happen to her?"

A lump in her throat, Nadia nodded.

"The rape was…really brutal. When he was done, he hit me, over and over. He must have thought I was dead when he left. The irony was, he'd used a condom and worn those thin plastic gloves, but when he battered me, they must have ripped, because he left blood on me."

"So police had his DNA."

"Yes. I'm told that usually the state lab wouldn't have run it until the police had a suspect, but I was lucky enough to have a detective who kept up the pressure until he got the results even though he and the other investigators never identified the man. So the DNA is out there in case he commits another crime, but it's been sixteen years, and there's never been a hit." She smiled wryly. "Ben calls the detective at least once a year."

Of course he did. Nadia admired him for it.

"The rapist. How is it possible he hasn't done it again?" she said.

Lucy shook her head. "Maybe there was something about me—"

Nadia wouldn't even let her finish the sentence. "You know better than that."

Lucy tried to smile again, the result pathetic. "I do. What I really believe is that he's raped a lot of other women since. The gloves might not have ripped again. Or the condom. And the vast majority of rapes are never reported to police, you know."

Nadia had read that up to 90 percent of rape victims didn't go to the police. "If he injured any other women the way he did you, how could it *not* have been reported?"

"Maybe he didn't. Maybe he got home and freaked when he saw that the gloves had ripped and his knuckles bled. He'd been careful otherwise. He could have learned his lesson. And… I've read that a lot of identified rapists don't come across as frightening. They can be nice guys, really successful, well liked, even married and with children."

"And now you look at every man you meet and wonder," Nadia said slowly.

That same, twisty smile. "I do."

"Who found you? Did a neighbor hear, or…?"

"No, the next morning was Saturday and my parents and Ben decided to take me to breakfast. When I didn't answer my phone or the door, they let themselves in. Ben had a key because he slept on my couch sometimes."

"Oh, no," Nadia whispered again. Ben would have just finished his freshman year in college, which meant he was only nineteen. To see his sister like that… Of course he'd become a cop. Of course he was still intensely protective of her.

"I was lucky. If not for their surprise visit, I'd have lain there all weekend. Even if I hadn't showed up for work Monday morning, who knows if anyone would have come to my apartment to find out why?"

"You were still unconscious."

"Yes. Doctors called it a coma. It was Sunday before I regained consciousness. I had lots of broken bones, including my cheekbones." She touched her face lightly, seemingly without being aware she had. "I was in the hospital for two weeks. I didn't go back to school there, because I was afraid the rapist was someone I knew. How else would he have targeted me? I did eventually finish my degree, but I've lived with a lot of anxiety. I don't go out at night if I can help it, I check the locks about twenty times before I go to bed and I still wake up with a start, thinking I've heard something, at least every half an hour all night long." Her fingers bit into Nadia's. "Don't tell Ben that, please. He worries enough. Anyway, here with him, I've slept better than I have in forever."

"I won't. I promise. He's good at making a woman feel safe." Except, of course, when he suspected her of a crime, when he had the opposite effect. Nadia hesitated. "Did he tell you about what happened to me?"

"You mean, someone getting into your bedroom to take the money?"

"No. Before I moved here." When Lucy shook her head, Nadia described her own ordeal in more detail than when she'd told Ben. "I can't completely understand what you went through, but maybe better than most people. I still have nightmares. And I don't trust as readily."

"Yes." Tears welled in Lucy's brown eyes. "But I'm letting life pass me by, and I want to change that. Coming here was a first step." She tugged a corner of her pieced quilt top from the bag. "Maybe this is one, too."

"I hope so."

The bell over the door was followed by women's voices.

"Friend or foe?" Lucy murmured, even as she wiped away the tears.

Nadia was able to laugh. "Keep your fingers crossed for me."

SOMEHOW, SHE WASN'T SURPRISED when her doorbell rang soon after she closed the store. A second later, her phone rang, too.

Ben.

"Hi," she said, answering. "Is that you downstairs?"

"Yeah. I should have called sooner. I just realized you might be nervous having to come down
without knowing who's at the door."

She would have been, if she hadn't guessed
Ben would stop by. All she said was, "I'll be
right down." But, setting aside her phone, she
almost wished she'd made an excuse. Or ignored
call and doorbell alike. The intensity of her attraction to a man who reminded her of the worst
moments of her life made her wary.

Although, she reflected on her way down, apparently not wary enough.

He still wore his uniform, which reminded
her every time of all the good reasons she had
to keep her distance from him.

Nadia opened the door anyway, but he didn't
move.

"Don't look at me that way," he said roughly.

Not liking the way *he* was looking at *her*, she
took a cautious step back. "What way?"

"As though…" He shook his head and walked
in. "I remind you of someone, don't I?"

She blinked. "No."

"I scare you."

It was disconcerting to discover how easily those dark eyes read her.

"I just get...flashes."

His knotted jaw told her he wasn't happy about her admission.

"Do you have time to come upstairs?" she asked.

"Maybe that's not a good idea."

"I don't expect you to attack me."

After a moment, he nodded, following when she started up. Feeling strangely awkward once they reached her apartment, Nadia took refuge in politeness. "Can I get you something to drink? I haven't started on dinner yet, but..."

He accepted again, allowing her to flee to the kitchen. There, she took a few deep breaths and tried to figure out why she felt so vulnerable. The answer wasn't hard to find. Lucy's story, and then retelling her own, had opened doors she tried to keep shut.

Returning with two glasses and a pitcher of iced tea, she found Ben studying the framed photos atop a mahogany bookcase.

"Your family?"

"Yes." She set down the pitcher and glasses and joined him. "You must have seen these when you did the search."

"No. I was keeping an eye on the men, and on you. I didn't let myself get distracted."

"God forbid you let yourself be moved by anything like family photos."

Ben slanted a glance at her. "I don't blame you for being ticked, but would you really have wanted me getting that personal? Maybe asking about your family?"

Nadia looked away. "No." After a moment, she focused on the photo he held in his hand. "That's my sister with her husband and kids. She's a paralegal, he's an attorney. She stayed home for a few years, until the kids had both started school. He went out on his own recently, and now Sonya works with him."

"You don't look much alike."

"I took after Dad—really my grandmother on his side—while she took after Mom."

He studied her parents. "Yeah, I can see that. Does anyone else in your family quilt?"

"Mom. She talked me into taking a class with her. I was the one who got hooked. She pieces and machine quilts things like Christmas table runners. Me, I found a passion."

As if her choice of word had triggered something, he carefully set the photo down in the same place it had been, then turned to face her. "Why aren't you married, too?"

She remembered him asking about previous relationships as part of his investigation. "I just… haven't met the right man." Or should she have said, *I* hadn't *met the right man*? On a wave of shock, she thought, *No, no.* She was attracted to him, sure; sometimes she even liked him. But that wasn't…whatever she'd been thinking.

His eyes narrowed, telling her he'd seen her perturbation. No more than that, she hoped.

Retreating to her favorite chair, she poured iced tea and waited until he'd taken a seat, too, before saying, "What about you? I assume you're not married."

His dark eyebrows rose. "Are you trying to insult me?"

"Maybe?"

He shook his head, but one corner of his mouth lifted enough to tell her he'd suppressed a smile.

"Never been married. I've had relationships, but I think I was too driven by the job to give enough to satisfy any woman."

Nadia noted his verb tense, just as she had hers earlier. "Something changed."

His "What makes you say that?" didn't come across as relaxed as he'd probably meant it.

"You left your big-city job and moved here." She held his gaze in a kind of challenge. "I told you why I did."

Ben took a long swallow of tea and then grimaced, looking at it. "Like a little sugar, do you?"

"Yep."

He sighed and set down the glass. "Lucy told you what happened to her."

Nadia nodded. "And that you'd found her. I assume that's why you went into law enforcement."

"I will never forget what she looked like." Roughened by rage, his voice was even deeper. "Her face a bloody mess…" He swallowed. "That son of a bitch destroyed her, physically and emotionally. Lucy could be bossy when we were growing up, but she was also my best friend. Seeing the change in her just about killed me. She was alive, but the light had been snuffed out. She was always shy, but not timid, not afraid of experiencing everything she could. Her standing up to me that day in your store was the first time I'd seen her show any spirit since the rape."

"That's a good thing, isn't it?"

"Yeah. It worries me, too, though. If she were attacked again…" He shook his head, as if he was trying to block even the idea. "The possibility scares the shit out of me. Could she come back from that?"

"I don't know," Nadia said softly. "But what kind of life does she have if she never takes any kind of risk?"

A nerve twitched in his cheek. "You're right, but I don't have to like it when she does."

"I'd feel the same." She sat quiet for a minute. "Maybe it would be better if she *didn't*—"

Ben was already shaking his head. "As she reminds me, she's an adult. I'm seeing the Lucy I remember, Nadia." Astonishment and what might be joy made him look younger, probably more like the boy he'd been before he found his sister battered and barely alive. "This quilting thing has given her something she needs. You're responsible for that."

Nadia shook her head. "She came to me because she wanted to learn." Nadia prayed that quilting would give Lucy both satisfaction and the knowledge that she was creating something that would outlast her. What could be more healing than that?

"She wanted to learn, huh?" His crooked grin was ridiculously sexy. "I think she was just making an excuse to take a look at you. Me and my big mouth."

Nadia knew she was gaping. "What did you *say*?"

His grin widened. "Not going to tell you."

"What? Then you shouldn't have hinted." She shrugged. "I'll just ask Lucy. She'll tell me."

"Not a chance. She's always on my side."

"Like you're on hers."

His expression softened. "I guess so."

"You're trying to distract me, aren't you? This whole thing started with me asking why you threw over big-city law enforcement in favor of Byrum."

"You don't have to say it that way. You chose to move here, too."

"This wouldn't have happened if I'd picked

any other town." She could tell he didn't like that. Because they wouldn't have met if she'd bought that fabric store in Willow Springs in the Ozarks, or in any of the other states where she'd searched real estate?

"Your business was doing well. It will do well again."

That remained to be seen, but she only nodded.

"I didn't choose Byrum," he said abruptly. "I wanted to make a change to small-town policing. I interviewed for several jobs that were open. This one felt right." He moved his shoulders as if uncomfortable. "I've always had a special rage for rapists. No mystery why."

She nodded.

"Even though my last promotion had me spending a lot of time behind a desk, I'd taken lead in hunting down a man who we were pretty sure had raped at least half a dozen women. He was developing his style as he went, getting off on hurting them. The last one died."

Nadia listened in horror, Ben's near-monotone delivery raising the hair on her arms.

"He screwed up with her, though. A neighbor, an older man who doesn't sleep very well, had seen this guy parking and then walking away down the sidewalk shortly after midnight. It bothered him, because this was a residential neighborhood. Most people had garages, which left plenty of street parking. Why leave his car there if he wasn't going to one of the houses on the block? The guy shrugged it off, but he was woken up a couple hours later by a car engine starting. Same car. He didn't even know why, but he wrote down the license number. When he saw the flashing police lights, he called 911 and told us what he'd seen. Turned out, the car belonged to a woman who had reported it stolen the evening before. Middle of the night, we went to talk to her. Funny thing, I'd been to that same apartment complex several times. Investigating the rapes, a name kept coming up. This time, thanks to the witness, we were able to move fast, catching him arriving back at his apartment. Later, we found out he'd ditched the car a mile away and hoofed it. His hair was wet, like he'd just washed it or dunked his head. He didn't want to explain. He was carrying a duffel bag. I asked him to open it, and he ran."

Nadia rubbed her arms, unable to take her eyes off his face. It was expressionless, but he couldn't do anything about his eyes. They were turbulent, betraying everything he'd felt.

"We'd come straight from seeing that woman's body. It looked too much like—" For the first time in this speech, his voice broke, but he recovered quickly. "I wanted to kill him." He paused. "I think I would have if one of my men hadn't stopped me."

The unemotional tone and the words didn't go together. Nadia grappled with what he'd said. She'd always known his capacity for violence. Maybe...maybe *this* was what she'd sensed, the first time she set eyes on him.

Even while wearing a badge, he would have freed his rage and killed a man instead of taking him in.

Nadia had such mixed feelings about his confession, she couldn't figure out what to say. *Why weren't you arrested?* Well, that was easy— nobody, including him, had told his superiors that he had lost control. *I'm shocked?* She was, but...something else lurked beneath.

The silence must have stretched too long, because he stirred. "Now you know you were right to be afraid of me."

"No." Wait. *No?* "What you felt, what you almost did," she began slowly, "was because you're human. If you'd gone through with attacking him, you would have violated your own beliefs." She had to think this through even as she talked. "But he was vile. And he'd reenacted your worst nightmare."

Ben stared at her, not even blinking.

"And would you really have done it? Hit him, maybe, but to keep on until he was dead? When you hadn't even seen yet what he had in that duffel?" Nadia found herself shaking her head. "I don't believe it."

"I told you."

"How many times in your life have you really lost control?" A thought darted into her head: even making love with a woman, would he?

He still hadn't blinked. "Twice," he said hoarsely. "The first time was after we found Lucy and got her to the hospital. Once I was home, alone in my bedroom, I lost it. I threw things, punched holes in the walls, broke my hand. Sobbed."

"That doesn't really count, you know."

"Why?"

"Because you waited. Even as a teenager, you had the self-control to know you needed to be alone before you vented everything you felt. How many hours did you hold it in? Eight? Ten? More?"

Ben shuddered and closed his eyes. She wanted to think he was seeing the past in a new light, but he could as well be angry that she presumed to know him better than he knew himself.

She blurted, "I wished—"

When she didn't finish, he opened eyes now red rimmed. "What did you wish, Nadia?"

Despite the rasp in his voice, he sounded gentle, the way she remembered him being so many other times.

"The police in Colorado Springs. The cops who just stood around outside the house. For *hours*. The crisis negotiator." She'd hated him most of all, the burn worse than the pain from her wound. "He was calm and deliberate and sympathetic. And I know that's what he is supposed to do! But Damon refused to let any of us talk on the phone. Why did they give him a hundred chances? Why didn't they *understand*?" She was crying, yelling and didn't care.

Ben moved fast, kneeling in front of her and spreading his hands on her thighs. "That none of you were capable of coming to the phone? That you were suffering, waiting?"

"That our lives were in their hands," she whispered. "Trickling through their fingers, and they never got mad at what he'd done. Why didn't they care more about *us* than they did *him*?"

"You do know they thought they were protecting you by bringing him down slowly, don't you?"

Face wet, eyes blurry, Nadia nodded. In her head she did. But not in her heart.

"You and Molly held out."

"But Keenan didn't."

He rocked back. "Another of the kids was alive?"

"Yes. I don't know exactly when he died, but if they'd mounted an assault in the first hour, he might have survived. Their job wasn't to pacify a monster, it was to rescue *us*. I was so angry." She balled one hand into a fist and pressed it to her stomach. "I still am. That's why—"

"You reacted the way you did to me. Oh, honey." In a single motion, he got to his feet and scooped her up, then sat in the chair with her in his lap.

And she cried. Hot, angry tears, sad tears, tears that stung. She pounded his chest with a fist, hearing his murmur, "That's it. Hit me all you want." In the end, exhaustion brought emptiness that might even be peace.

Ben kept holding her.

CHAPTER TWELVE

DAYS LATER, NADIA still hadn't come to terms with her breakdown. How could she not have known how much she'd been keeping pent up inside? Struggling with grief, that was one thing, but anger corrosive enough to eat through the walls… That was different.

Too much like what Ben had gone through, after finding his sister?

And why did it disturb her so much to discover they had this in common?

She had managed mostly to avoid him since Tuesday evening. Lucy had been here almost every day, but Nadia hadn't seen any questions in her eyes. There'd been no searching looks, or pity. Which meant Ben hadn't told her about their talk. He must have come up with some excuse for being later than Lucy had likely expected him that evening, but whatever it was couldn't have borne any resemblance to the truth.

See, I told her I'd tried to kill a man, which led to Nadia confessing that she wished the police back home had killed the guy who shot her.

She told me a little boy died when he didn't have to, and that made her so furious, she sobbed and punched me.

No, Lucy would not be looking at her the same way if she'd heard that story.

Hannah and Lucy had left a few minutes ago to have lunch together. Even though Nadia had declined their offer to bring her a sandwich, she half expected them to return with one of the fabulous— and fattening—Amish goodies. A slice of shoofly pie, maybe, or perhaps a butter cookie.

Two browsers thanked her and departed without making any purchase. She had to hope they'd be back. A few real shoppers *had* come and gone. Not enough to justify paying Hannah for eight hours, but this was Saturday, usually the busiest day.

Now the bell tinkled and another woman walked in. Ellen Shaw, a quilter who lived right here in Byrum. She'd become a good customer and Nadia had sold half a dozen of her crib- or wall-hanging-size quilts. In fact, just yesterday she had called Ellen to let her know one of the small ones she had on consignment had sold.

Nadia smiled and took a few steps to meet the stocky woman who at a guess was in her early sixties. "Oh, I'm glad you came by. I can give you cash or a check, whichever you'd prefer. The young woman who bought your quilt was so excited. She didn't show yet, but said she's almost four months pregnant."

Any of the Amish women would have expressed pleasure that the work of their hands had found a *gut* home. The right home.

But Ellen only nodded, her expression cool. "Cash would be handy. And I'd like to take back my remaining quilts, Nadia."

Nadia went still. "I would regret losing you as a friend and customer."

"I kept waiting for you to do the right thing. Since apparently that isn't going to happen, I can't continue to support your business."

Stung, she still kept it together. Maybe she had developed an emotional callus, if such a thing was possible. "I loved the place I was making for myself here. I offered to work on the auction out of a desire to help other people. How can you believe I would steal the money we raised?"

"If somebody had really broken into your place, I have to believe the police would have made an arrest by now."

She knew arguing was hopeless, but had to try. If she could convince one person… "Whoever it is had a key."

Ellen raised her eyebrows. "And who might that be?"

"I don't know. Mrs. Jefferson might have handed out keys to any number of people. How would I know?"

"All thieves, of course."

"You might recall that one of those people killed her."

Ellen took a step back. "That was never proved. She might have fallen."

"Chief Slater seems certain."

"If someone did push her, he hasn't managed to arrest *that* person, either, has he?"

The spiteful tone told Nadia she was wasting time and hope. "Excuse me. I need to get the ladder to take down your quilt."

Neither spoke while she carefully lifted a queen-size Lady of the Lake quilt from the hooks, climbed down, and folded it and two smaller quilts before putting them into bags. At the end, she opened the cash register and carefully counted out bills. She also brought out the forms she had every quilter sign, setting the terms of their agreement, noted the sale and money she was giving Ellen, and asked her to sign all four forms.

She should have insisted Jennifer Bronske count the cash she'd been given and sign, too.

Ellen's signatures were closer to slashes than the more rounded handwriting she'd used when she'd brought these quilts in.

Nadia said, "You do beautiful work. I hope you have luck selling these."

"Thank you," Ellen said stiffly, dropping the

cash into her purse before she gathered up the bags and walked out.

Watching her go, Nadia felt all-too-familiar humiliation, anger and dread. Whatever Ben believed to the contrary, she couldn't see how bouncing back from this was possible.

SUNDAY MORNING, BEN and Lucy attended church services.

He had drifted away from organized religion after he left home. College life was new and exciting, and there were better things to do on Sundays. The faith he had taken for granted as a boy probably lingered—until the attack on Lucy. If God existed at all, Ben was too angry to worship Him. Later, nothing he encountered on the job led him back to that faith. He saw too much brutality and hate, too many senseless deaths.

But it had become clear to him shortly after moving to Byrum that he was expected to choose a church and show his face every Sunday morning unless he was desperately needed elsewhere. Amish, Baptist, Methodist or Seventh Day Adventist, the people in Henness County were believers, and they'd look askance at a police chief who wasn't.

He wouldn't have blamed Lucy if she hadn't wanted to join him, but the first Saturday of her visit, she'd asked him what time they needed to leave for church in the morning. This week, she seemed to take it for granted they would go.

After the service, he suggested they go out for brunch. Instead of eating in Byrum, he drove to Hadburg, the next-largest town in the county. He knew the food was good at the Amish-owned Hadburg Café, and he hoped to pass unrecognized.

The minute they walked in, he saw Henness County Sheriff Daniel Byler and his wife, Rebecca, alone in a booth. He'd learned the previous week that they were in San Francisco, where Rebecca was testifying in court at the trial of one of the men who had tried to kill her last year.

Now he paused beside their booth. "Bet it's a relief to be home."

Strain briefly showed on Rebecca's fine-boned face. "I pray they won't need me again."

Daniel and he clasped hands, and Ben made introductions.

"Please join us," Rebecca urged, so Daniel switched sides to sit beside his wife, and Lucy and Ben slid into the booth across from them.

In no time, Rebecca and Lucy were chatting like old friends, while Daniel and Ben caught each other up on their jobs—including the theft of the proceeds from the auction.

Rebecca, a beautiful blonde, jumped right in once that subject came up. "Just yesterday, *Grossmammi* told me all about it," she said.

"She's outraged that so many people are convinced the owner of the shop kept the money."

Ben glanced at his sister. "Rebecca's grandmother is Ruth Graber, who you met."

"Oh, she's sweet and fierce both!" When Rebecca laughed, Lucy said, "You're so lucky to have her. And the quilt she brought in for sale is exquisite. Even Nadia said it was the most beautiful one she'd ever seen."

"She is talented. And I think quilting has been a lifeline to her since my grandfather died last fall. She really believes he's with God and she'll join him when her time comes, but she seemed lost without him. Making a quilt for our wedding gave her a purpose." Rebecca frowned. "She won't admit any possibility Nadia would have done such a hateful thing."

Daniel raised his eyebrows at Ben.

"It's been ugly," he said. "I'm getting the feeling people rushed to blame her so they didn't have to look around and wonder who might have taken the money. Better to see horns and forked tail on the outsider than imagine them on your next-door neighbor or your cousin."

Lucy jumped in to tell the other couple about the quilters who no longer trusted Nadia to sell their work, or who insisted on a cash payment instead of a check. Lucy puffed out a breath of frustration. "Because, of course, she's not trustworthy."

"According to Ruth, the Amish all trust her," Daniel put in. "I asked my mother to be sure it isn't just Ruth, but *Mamm* said the same."

Lucy explained why Nadia's store was in trouble anyway. Amish women might offer enough quilts for her to sell, but most didn't purchase their fabric from her. And Nadia didn't want them to, not when it would take business away from the fabric store in Hadburg.

Rebecca looked as fired up as Lucy was. "*Grossmammi* said some man actually *spit* on her?"

Ben explained Hixson's story without naming him, and told them how quickly Nadia had come around to wanting to help the man and his family.

He'd been aware of a couple in the booth behind him, a good reason to have kept his voice low and avoid using names.

But he'd no sooner finished than he became aware that the woman behind him had slid off her seat to plant herself in front of their table.

This was why he'd wanted to get out of town.

"Chief Slater." She nodded at him, then frowned at Daniel. "You're Sheriff Byler, aren't you?"

Daniel agreed he was. Ben saw that he wasn't the only one whose instant reaction was wariness.

She switched her gaze to Ben. "I don't usually eavesdrop, but I couldn't help hearing. I was already mad enough about what Nadia has gone through, but now I realize how complacent I've been. I donated a quilt to the auction, convinced I'd done my part, but none of us have done enough."

A man behind her said, "Colleen, maybe you shouldn't bother these folks while they're eating."

Ben shook his head. "We don't mind." And he didn't, not once she'd said her piece. He hoped he spoke for the rest. "You look familiar..."

"Oh, I should have introduced myself, shouldn't I? I'm Colleen Hoefling, and this is my husband, Rob."

Lucy leaned forward. "Nadia pointed out one of your quilts in her shop. It's gorgeous."

"Thank you. That's kind of you. Are you a quilter?"

"Only a beginner. I'm taking a class—" His sister shook her head. "Never mind that. Do you have an idea about how we can raise more money?"

"No, but there must be a way."

"And if you manage to help one family, what about the others?" Ben felt obliged to insert.

"Even one family is a start." This Colleen sounded as stubborn as Nadia could be.

"Ruth Graber and Katie-Ann Chupp have offered to donate the money they would otherwise earn when quilts sell to the aid organization," Lucy put in.

"That's a lovely, generous idea," Colleen said decisively, "and I'll do the same. But it's not enough."

Rebecca leaned forward. "What about doing something online?"

Colleen's face lit. "Crowdfunding, right?"

"Yes," Lucy crowed. "Ooh, that's a great idea!"

Daniel grinned at Ben, who shook his head bemusedly. The women were off and running... and he knew darn well Nadia would be right with them.

Which was probably one reason he was falling in love with her, he thought ruefully, without feeling any surprise at using a word as new to him as the term *crowdfunding* probably would be to the Amish.

Of course, the Amish lived the concept, it occurred to him. Only the technology was new.

He tuned back in to find the women had already agreed on a meeting to make plans. They'd aim for Tuesday evening. Colleen had offered to host it and would ask friends to join them. Lucy promised to invite Nadia.

"I know Sondra Vance, the staff photographer at the *Henness Herald*, took hundreds of photos of the damage done by this spring's tornadoes," Ben contributed. "She was all but chasing the things. I'll bet she'd let you use any you want for an online appeal."

Rebecca said thoughtfully, "I remember the

ones in the paper. They were really powerful. People picking through the ruins of their homes, animals injured, this horrible swath of destruction."

Colleen nodded. "That one of dairy cows lining up to be milked in front of a flattened barn really got to me."

Fired up, the three exchanged phone numbers and email addresses. Colleen's husband grinned over his shoulder at the other two men as he and she left. Apparently, her instinctive urge to jump in with both feet had come as no surprise to him.

The rest of them finished eating, paid and walked out together. Daniel dropped back to join Ben. "I thought you said your sister is just here for a visit."

Gaze on the back of Lucy's head, Ben said, "Something tells me it's going to be an extended visit." Months instead of weeks. Or…forever? Watching as the two women hugged in parting, Ben wondered what Lucy really did have in mind.

NADIA JOINED IN the laughter as the Amish women teased each other. She had been flattered to be invited to this quilting bee—or would the Amish say it was a *frolic*? In fact, she was the only *Englischer* among them, but the eight women had gone out of their way to make her feel welcome.

Katie-Ann's youngest daughter was due to

have her first baby two weeks from now. Every time she had tried to stand up today to help in the kitchen, a chorus of voices ordered her to rest.

When Nadia arrived, two frames had been set up in the living room. The group had separated to hand quilt two crib-size bedcovers for the new *boppli*, as the Amish said.

As they worked, there had been much teasing about which group would finish first. Susan Byler, who had introduced herself as the county sheriff's mother, had only chuckled and said, "Fast is not always best."

Their hostess Katie-Ann had only quilted intermittently. She was occupied with feeding such a crowd, which included her husband, two sons and a teenage grandson who had also appeared midday for a meal, taking over the kitchen while the women ate outside, in the shade of a large, spreading maple tree.

As the chattering women prepared to depart, Nadia stopped to look closely at both quilts, needing only the binding to be finished. With so many hands wielding needles, she would have expected more variation in stitches, but these were astonishingly uniform.

When she remarked on it, Katie-Ann said comfortably, "*Ach*, we have done this so many times! The finest quilters make their stitches just a little longer, and those who are not so skilled do their very best."

Nadia had quilted the way she always did, and wondered now if she hadn't been steered to a group of women with similar expertise to hers.

"These both came out beautifully," Nadia said. Mary King, Katie-Ann's daughter, hadn't had an ultrasound and therefore didn't know whether she was having a boy or girl, so both quilts used fabrics and colors that would work for either gender.

"You will stay to eat, *ja*?" Katie-Ann asked. "Driving in the dark in a car is not so bad, ain't so?"

Of course the other women would prefer to be home before dark, given that they were driving buggies. Yes, the local Amish all had battery-operated lights on their buggies, but they weren't as bright as her car headlights. And at the speed a horse-drawn buggy was overtaken by a speeding car, the lights could be seen too late.

Katie-Ann's menfolk were currently harnessing the women's horses and bringing one buggy after another around front. A few of the quilters had come in pairs; one had walked, although Susan Byler insisted she would drive her home. Others must have miles to go.

"No, I don't mind driving in the dark," Nadia said, "but you don't need company for another meal."

"The more people at the table, the happier I am," Katie-Ann assured her. "I have talked about you before. I think Elijah is glad to get to know you."

In a quiet way, Katie-Ann's husband had seemed curious, so Nadia agreed with no more argument even though, after the bounteous offerings at midday, she wasn't hungry at all. Katie-Ann allowed her to set the table and pour drinks. Once they sat down, the crowd was nearly as large around the table as it had been for lunch. Mary was staying in her childhood bedroom for a few days since her husband, part of a carpentry crew, was away on a job. One of Katie-Ann's daughters-in-law joined them with her three children, the oldest of which, a girl, hurried to help her grandmother with the meal although she couldn't be more than eight or nine years old. The adults spoke English except when murmuring to the two younger children.

Elijah told Nadia he was sorry about all the foolishness over the money. "Ashamed, they will all be, when the truth comes out."

"If it does," she said wryly.

"You must have faith," he said, and she knew he meant it literally.

Her smile and nod seemed to satisfy him. *"Gut, gut,"* he declared, before applying himself again to his meal.

Despite her hostess's protests, Nadia insisted on helping clear the table after dinner and dried dishes while the others put away food. A cheerful woman who might have been a younger version of her mother, Mary was once again urged to "Rest."

"I can help—"

"No, no, sit," her sister-in-law told her sternly.

Nadia caught her rolling her eyes, and the two of them laughed.

Katie-Ann walked her out to her car. Bats darted against a deep purple sky. The wide doors on the barn stood open and the yellow light of lanterns showed inside, as the men had excused themselves from the table to feed animals. Without even a hint of a breeze to stir the leaves on the trees, the silence was uncanny.

There'd been no way she could turn down the leftovers Katie-Ann pressed on her. After setting the heavy basket on the passenger seat, Nadia closed the car door. She winced at the noise.

"It's so quiet." Instinctively, she kept her voice soft.

"*Ja*, we don't have so many cars down this road, and the closest *Englischers* are Don and Gale Amundson, on the corner by the stop sign. Nice people they are, but we're glad not to have their outside lights right next door, or the sound of their television and the music their fifteen-year-old son plays so loud."

"I've never lived in the country. Even in a town as small as Byrum."

"Small, is it?" Katie-Ann chuckled. "To me it

seems so busy. Cars and stoplights and people rushing in and out of stores."

"I can see that." Nadia gave her a quick hug. "This was a wonderful day. Thank you for inviting me. I'm excited to hear when Mary has her baby."

"You are *wilkom* anytime." This time, Katie-Ann initiated the hug. "Elijah is right. People are acting crazy. They will come to their senses."

Nadia's smile was more forced, but she said, "I hope you're right. Good night, Katie-Ann."

By the time she drove away, the murky light had deepened toward full night. As she turned onto the paved road, her headlights picked out a small animal racing across in front of her. A rabbit, she thought, but as fast as it moved, she couldn't be sure.

Just for now, she didn't let herself think about her problems. She had made up her mind last week to close the store on Mondays, and updated the sign and her website to reflect the change. Taking today off had been a relief. Plus, she loved quilting with other women who felt the same, and the sense of achievement was heartwarming. The friendliness and generosity with which she'd been met gave her a lift, too.

Full night had fallen by the time she turned into the alley behind her building. The only light was one above a door at the far end. Mr. Orton must have already gone to bed, since no glow shone from his apartment window. She'd have left her own back light on if she'd expected to stay as late as she had, but really it wasn't far to the door once she parked in her usual spot out of the way of the garbage truck that would lumber down the alley Wednesday morning to empty the Dumpsters. It wasn't as if she hadn't returned after dark before, especially in the late winter and early spring, when days were shorter. Besides, she wasn't carrying anything of value this time, she thought wryly.

Getting out of her car and locking, Nadia wondered whether the thief had waited out here that night, expecting to be able to knock her down, maybe, and grab the money box without entering the building at all.

She hurried to the back door, keys in her hand. With touch alone, she fumbled a little getting the key in the lock. She hadn't yet turned it when she heard an odd noise behind her. Metallic? Nadia turned to look even as her brain supplied the answer. A dog or raccoon or even a person had bumped the Dumpster. The metal had rebounded with a small clang.

Something moved between her car and the big bin. She had no chance to react before a shot rang out and almost simultaneously something pinged off her metal door.

A bullet.

With a gasp, she whirled, hunched low and

turned the key. *Bang. Bang.* Time slowed, and the air felt thick and hard to move through. Her shoulder burned and she couldn't seem to lift her left hand. Too far away, voices called out. She pulled the door open, only her grip on the knob holding her up.

And then she fell forward through the opening, into darkness.

CHAPTER THIRTEEN

"Ben?"

If Nadia's name hadn't come up when he answered the phone, he wouldn't have recognized her voice in the single, shaky word.

"Nadia?"

"I know I said I'd never call you again, but…I think I need you."

He lunged forward in his recliner, stabbing a button on the remote to turn off the television. Lucy was calling something from his home office where she had been researching crowdfunding on her laptop, but he was focused entirely on the phone.

"Tell me what's wrong."

"Somebody tried to shoot me."

His heart lurched.

"I guess somebody *did* shoot me." Nadia sounded vaguely surprised, which told him she was in shock. "Again."

"Where are you?" he asked urgently. "Are you safe?"

"I feel kind of strange. I think I'm going to be sick." A clunk told him she'd dropped the phone.

He moved fast, grabbing his gun from a side table and his keys from the small dish where he dropped them whenever he got home.

Lucy had come out into the hall, alarm on her face.

"I have to go," he said. "Lock behind me."

Using his lights and siren, Ben drove faster than he should have. On the way, he called dispatch, to be told units were already en route. Either she'd called 911, or neighbors had. With traffic scant, he made it downtown in less than four minutes and swerved into the alley.

A police car blocked the far end. He braked where he was, left headlights on to illuminate the stretch right behind her store and ran.

A uniformed officer standing in the door opening turned at the sound of running footsteps.

"Chief. I was just going to call you."

"Nadia did."

Officer Ackley held up a hand. "Wait. You better not come in this way. There's blood on the door and concrete pad. I unlocked the front for the paramedics."

Ben wanted to swear viciously, but managed to hold back. Dennis Ackley was right to stop him from contaminating the scene. And at least Nadia was already receiving care.

"Nadia?" he asked anyway.

"Awake and talking."

All Ben wanted was to get to Nadia, but he had to do his job. Story of his life.

"Have you searched out here?"

"Only to shine a flashlight behind the Dumpsters and the parked cars, but I didn't see anybody. They must have taken off."

"Okay. I'll find out what happened from Nadia. When backup gets here, I want the alley taped off."

"Yes, sir."

Ben ran the way he'd come, turned off the headlights but left on the flashing lights, and then on foot circled to the front door of her building.

A few people clustered on the sidewalk to stare, even though all they could see was the ambulance parked at the curb. From their nightclothes, he guessed them to be apartment dwellers on this block. Lights shone in several apartments above stores.

Ackley waited for him just inside. "The EMTs are with her."

Ben kept going.

Until he was well down the hall, he couldn't see much but the broad back of a man crouched, looking down at someone. A turn of the head allowed Ben to identify Marty McClun.

Marty glanced up at his approach. "Déjà vu."

From that moment, all Ben saw was Nadia,

lying on the floor, eyes closed, blood staining her shoulder and arm. The same woman paired with McClun last time, Rhonda Foster, was using scissors to cut away Nadia's shirt.

McClun got out of Ben's way.

He crouched beside her and took her good hand. "Hey."

Her lashes fluttered and her eyes opened. "You came."

"You called."

Her mouth curved just a little. "So much for vows."

"Yeah." His voice had been scraped over asphalt. "You hanging in there?"

"Uh-huh."

"We gave her something for pain," Marty said behind him.

No wonder she seemed to have trouble focusing on his face. Ben squeezed her hand. "Can you tell me what happened?"

"I got shot." She sounded both perplexed and indignant.

"Yeah, I can see that." A woman who didn't hold a high-risk job had been shot twice now. How could that be?

Foster was wiping away blood to give her a better look at the wound. She pressed a thick gauze pad to it. Marty sidled around to help her ease Nadia onto her side so they could clean up her back, too.

"Exit wound?" Ben asked.

Marty nodded. "Looks like. Saw a nick in the wallboard. Bet you find the bullet there."

It had punched through her and into the wall. Ben bet on a hunting rifle. Seemed everyone in these parts owned one or more. Kids around here learned to shoot and hunt before they were old enough to get behind the wheel of a car. Many of the families depended on the meat to supplement their incomes.

Nadia's eyes had started to drift closed again, but he went to his knees and bent forward to lock gazes with her. "Talk to me. Why were you going out back?"

She shook her head. "Not. Coming home. Parked. Wished I'd left an outside light on."

"Did you park in the same place as always?"

"Uh-huh."

He wormed the story out of her. There wasn't much to it. If she hadn't heard something—she thought the shooter bumped the Dumpster—there wouldn't have been any warning at all. As it was, she'd managed to make herself a smaller target, the first and maybe a second shot missing her. She was pretty sure there'd been at least three and possibly four shots fired. They ought to be able to find bullets that had ricocheted off the door or brick wall in the alley. If the shooter was cool enough, he might have picked up the shells before fleeing.

When he asked Nadia if she had heard footsteps, she mumbled, "Uh-uh. Hit my head."

McClun made an exclamation and began exploring her head. When Nadia winced, he said,
"Yep. You have a goose egg, all right."

"When you hit your head, was the door still
open?"

"I think so. I sort of fell inside. There wasn't
anybody here when I woke up. I called you." She
frowned. "You weren't here first."

Door open, Nadia unconscious, completely
vulnerable. The realization felt like a gut punch
to Ben. He couldn't forget she'd been shot before,
and lay waiting for medical assistance for hours,
unable to so much as twitch or whimper without
drawing the attention of the man who'd believed
she and the little girl she protected were dead.

Not relevant, he told himself. *Think about tonight.*

Something had scared away the shooter. A
passing car? The neighbors' voices? He could
get some of the sequence from Ackley as first
responder.

"You didn't call 911?"

"Uh-uh."

"Then someone else did. Gunshots have a way
of grabbing attention."

"Good thing," Rhonda said. "Brought us here
quick." Her eyes met Ben's. "We're ready to
transport."

"Okay." He gently placed Nadia's hand on her stomach, then let himself cup her cheek. "I need to get things started here, then I'll follow you to the hospital, okay?" He had an idea. "I'll call Lucy. Unless there's someone you'd rather have with you?"

"No, but if she's in bed—"

He skated his thumb over her lips. "No, she heard me talking to you."

"'Kay." Her eyes closed, her dark lashes forming fans above her too pale cheeks.

Ben made himself release her, stand and step back. She groaned as she was rolled again to allow a stretcher to be slid beneath her. McClun raced off to bring a gurney, and Ben retreated to the shop, where he called Lucy.

He told her Nadia had been shot and was on her way to the hospital. "I know you don't like to go out at night—"

"You have to stay to search for whoever shot her, don't you?"

The shooter was long gone, but he would have left traces of his presence. Those were what Ben would be looking for.

Not necessarily a *he*, he reminded himself. Plenty of women hunted, too, and had equal expertise with a rifle.

"We'll block off the alley until daylight so we can get a better look," he said, "but yes. I want to find the bullets and where the shooter set up."

"I'll go to the hospital. She should have someone with her," his sister said sturdily.

"Thanks." He had to clear his throat. "I'll see you when I get there."

Time to shut down the emotions and focus on the details that would tell him how and why this crime had been committed.

NADIA AWAKENED TO a sharp, throbbing pain in her shoulder and a headache that made her reluctant to open her eyes or move a single muscle.

But the antiseptic smell and the sounds of far-off beeps told her she wasn't home.

She slitted her eyes open enough to see gray light seeping between the slats of window blinds. And she saw something else: a man sprawled in a chair right beside the bed. Ben, slouched low, asleep.

The hospital—yes, she did remember that, but it was Lucy who had been with her, asking questions, smoothing hair back from her forehead, reminding her how to use the pump that supplied the painkiller through an IV.

Not that she'd needed the lesson, given her previous hospital stay. The first time she'd had a GSW. Never having been a fan of murder mysteries or thrillers, she'd had to ask a cop interviewing her what that meant after he used the acronym. He'd appeared a little embarrassed and said, "Gunshot wound."

How unlucky was she to have a second GSW in her life?

She really hurt, and she was procrastinating. Nadia opened her eyes the rest of the way and groped for the button. To find it, she had to turn her head, which made her gasp.

When she pressed the button, relief spread through her.

"You're awake." Ben, but his voice a rasp.

"I woke you." Very, very carefully, she rolled her head on the pillow. "I'm sorry."

"Don't be. I've dozed on and off."

Exhaustion or something else carved lines in his face she was sure hadn't been there before. Furrows in his forehead, others between his nose and mouth. Dark stubble covered his jaw and throat. His hair stuck out every which way. He wore a gray T-shirt and worn, faded jeans instead of his usual uniform. Even tired and disheveled, he was sexy.

Oh, heavens, what did *her* hair look like? The throbbing inside her skull didn't let her cling to the worry. "Wasn't Lucy here?" she asked, puzzled.

"Yeah. I sent her home when I arrived."

"Oh." Nadia thought about that. "It was dark. Wasn't she scared to go out?"

"Maybe, but she did it anyway. And no, don't even start feeling guilty. She offered, and she did it. I walked her to her car, and I'm betting she had left on every light inside and outside the house. She texted to let me know she'd made it, safe and sound."

"Okay."

He moved from the chair to sit beside her on the bed. His hand lifted to her face, his fingertips gentle and somehow knowing. He stroked her forehead and applied just the right amount of pressure to her temples. His touch felt so good, Nadia moaned.

"How do you feel?" he asked.

"I've been better." She searched his face. If anyone would have answers, it was Ben. "Somebody shot me."

He smiled crookedly. "Yep."

"I could have been killed."

The smile disappeared, leaving him grim. "I'm guessing that was the idea. This wasn't meant to scare you in hopes you'd sell out and move. Your death wouldn't bring the money back. It's hard to figure what anyone had to gain."

Reluctantly, she said, "Leonard Hixson?"

"A county sheriff's deputy drove out to where Hixson and his family are staying with the wife's relatives. He was there. He and the brother-in-law had watched the same Cardinal game I had on when you called me. Both their wives were home, half a dozen kids. They couldn't have all been lying when they said he'd been there all day and evening. The deputy told me he said, *After what I did, I can see why she'd think*— And then he got all choked up. His wife fired up and said Leonard would never do anything like that."

"Oh." She relaxed. "I'm glad."

"Someone else in the same boat he is could be holding a grudge, though. We'll need to take a look at other people who lost everything and are still waiting for help."

The fingers softly caressing her face went away. She would have protested, except that suddenly his large, warm hand had slid between her neck and the pillow, and now he was kneading aching muscles. Her mind hazed with pleasure, making it hard to think. But what he'd said…

"If it was a million dollars, I could sort of see it. But the seventy-eight thousand dollars that's still missing wouldn't go very far. Is it really enough to make someone kill?"

Ben shook his head, but she didn't see the same disbelief she felt on his face. Bleak knowledge infused his voice. "A punk will kill a convenience store clerk for twenty-five bucks. Abusive men have beaten their wives to death because dinner wasn't ready. Normal people, no. These farmers who lost everything could see you as a scapegoat, though. A symbol. From their point of view, they've been screwed over by everyone, from insurance companies to FEMA and every aid organization that hasn't done anything for them. But you, you're an individual, easy to find, a convenient focus for hate." His expression altered at whatever he saw on her face. "I'm sorry. I was thinking out loud, and I shouldn't have been. What I said—that's unlikely. You know that, don't you?"

It was as if some small insect had stung her all over. Her skin prickled, burned. She found the bed controls, and raised the head of it. Ben's hand dropped away from her.

The focus for hate. Me.

"Who else could it be?"

They looked at each other, his conflict showing. She could almost, but not quite, see all the things he didn't want to say there on his face. There were only the two of them, existing in a bubble.

"I don't know," Ben admitted finally. "I can't help wondering whether this really has anything to do with the auction or the money."

Breathing became a struggle. "You mean, someone *else* hates me?"

He frowned at her. "I want you to come home with me. You shouldn't be alone."

She ached to agree, but knew she shouldn't. "I have a dead bolt lock at the foot of the stairs," she argued. "There's no other access to my apartment."

"Someone could shoot through a window."

She tried to hide her flinch. "I'll keep the curtains and blinds drawn."

Frustration thinned his lips. "You *want* to be alone?"

"You can't be the investigator if I'm living with you. Right?"

"I could explain—"

"And what if me being there endangers your sister?"

"Crap!" he said explosively. Clearly, he hadn't thought of that, and Lucy came first. He ran a hand over his face. "I'll think of something else."

Right. He thought he could unload her on one of his officers? She could imagine it—awkward conversation, trying to sleep in a guest room while she listened for any sound outside the window, or even in the hall. With the new locks and the sturdy chair braced under the doorknob, getting to her in her aerie wouldn't be easy.

What about a fire? She'd be trapped.

With a sort of fatalism, she knew she wouldn't feel safe anywhere. She might as well toss and turn in her own bed as anyplace.

"The doctor might not even release you today," Ben said. And wouldn't, if he had anything to say about it, Nadia suspected.

"I'll be fine with pain meds." She hesitated. "Hannah will show up. She has a key. Can you make sure someone lets her know what happened?"

"Of course I will. No reason she can't tend shop until you're back, is there?"

"I suppose not." Of course there wasn't. Hannah could teach this afternoon's class as well as she could. With business so slow, Nadia knew she wasn't needed at all, a thought that left her feeling hollow. Or maybe that came from facing the harsh truth that some faceless, unknown person wanted her dead. "Did you find anything last night?"

"Bullets. They're thirty-five caliber, common as dirt. Both we found last night are in bad shape." His teeth could be heard grinding. "One bounced off the metal door. The other is the one that went through your shoulder. We were able to dig it out of the wall."

"Common?" she said uncertainly.

"It's a caliber used for hunting everything from coyotes to deer. Works in the most popular rifles, like the Remington 700. I'm hoping in daylight we can find a casing, because there could be a fingerprint. Looks like the shooter picked them up, but in better light I'm hoping we spot one he or she missed. Both you and your neighbors think there were four shots taken, so we'll be looking for a less damaged bullet, too, with rifling that could be matched to a particular weapon."

Nadia latched on to one word. "She?"

"Women hunt, too," Ben said simply. "Didn't it cross your mind that the attacker might be a woman?"

Well, yes, it had. But her, she'd never so much as picked up a gun of any kind. Neither her parents nor brother-in-law owned one. The men she'd been involved with in the past were hikers, skiers or mountain climbers, not hunters. Until she met Ben, the closest she'd ever come to a gun was looking down the barrel of the ugly black pistol Paige's husband had used in his rampage. No wonder she'd been startled when she felt the hard bulk of the grip of Ben's holstered gun when he kissed her. In fact, it should have been more of a mood-killer than it was, considering how literally gun-shy she was.

Without any advance warning, the overhead light came on and a woman in purple scrubs appeared at the foot of the bed. She pushed back the curtains and smiled approvingly. "Good morning! My name is Nancy Jones. I'll be your nurse today. Time for me to take your temp and check your blood pressure so you're ready for breakfast. The carts will be here in no time. If you need to get up…" She looked inquiring.

"Yes." And, oh, Nadia didn't look forward to the trek.

Of course, Ben took the nurse's arrival as his cue to leave. He made Nadia promise to let him know what the doctor had to say, and insisted he'd pick her up if she was released.

Once he disappeared around the curtain, she couldn't hear his departing footsteps any more than she'd heard the nurse's approach. He was just gone. She became more aware of her pain… and that he would be scouring the alley for the most minute of evidence that might identify the person who had come so close to killing her.

THE DAY WAS as maddening as Ben had expected it to be. Of all crime scenes, he thought he hated alleys the most. At best, they were filthy. At worst…well, he didn't have to worry about that in Byrum. There wasn't a lot of homelessness in a town this size, and garbage service was reliable. Since taking the job here, he'd yet to go Dumpster diving. Today, he'd have volunteered, if Terry Uhrich thought there was any chance the shooter had tossed something in.

He didn't. "Sounds like there would have been a window of only a few minutes when Ms. Markovic was unconscious and wouldn't have heard the clang of someone lifting that metal lid and letting it fall," he said, contemplating the bin. "We'll take a quick look, but I don't believe this assailant was stupid enough to dump shell casings or anything else right behind her building."

Another officer was currently fingerprinting the trunk, back fenders and bumper of Nadia's car. The shooter had almost had to be standing or crouching in the four feet or so between the rear of her car and the side of the Dumpster. Terry himself was presently flat on his belly, peering beneath the garbage bin.

Ben's phone rang, and he turned away. It was Nadia letting him know the doctor wanted to keep her one more night. She grumbled about missing the meeting to plan a fund-raising strategy for the Hixson family's benefit. Even so, Ben couldn't decide if she sounded genuinely unhappy about being stuck in the hospital, or relieved. He knew which he was. The hospital administrator had agreed to have a security guard patrol her hall today, until Ben was able to return. Damned if he'd have been able to drop her off at her apartment and head home to a good meal and his own bed. She might not like it, but no matter where she stayed tonight, he intended to be there, too. She'd find it harder to ban him from her hospital room than from her apartment.

He kept the call brief, and had just ended it when Terry murmured, "Will you look at this?" before he began wriggling backward, holding up tweezers he'd used to grip something. Sunlight lit the thing on fire.

Ben stepped forward. "What in hell?"

"Earring."

Terry dropped it in a small brown paper evidence bag, but held it open so they could both study it.

"Is it a real diamond, do you think?" Ben asked. If so, that had been a pricey set of earrings, because this was noticeably bigger than the one-carat diamond studs his dad had bought for his mom for Christmas a few years back. Two carats, at least?

It was a simple post earring, the stone set in silver or white gold, or even in platinum. No back, of course.

"Don't know," Terry said, "but it looks like it could be."

"There's no surface that would hold a fingerprint."

"No, but the post would have DNA, if we get that far. When I'm done here, I'll take this by Larson's." The town's one and only fine jeweler.

"If it's a diamond, somebody had to miss this," Ben said thoughtfully.

"Oh, yeah. If we're lucky, Larson will recognize it and still have a record of sales. I don't think it's been here long. No dirt even under the prongs. Let me see if I can find the back. You might look under the car."

It wasn't there, but Ben located it a few minutes later, in a weedy area of cracked pavement running along the windowless, cinder block back of an abandoned building that had once been a mattress manufacturer. The woman could have taken a couple steps before it fell. Or it could have been kicked away. Terry could be mistaken about how long the earring had lain there.

Ben had picked up some hairs with his tweezers, too, but this *was* an alley. The proprietors in buildings all down the block brought their garbage either here or to the Dumpster near the other end. People probably cut through here. The garbage collectors might get out of their trucks on occasion. Ben would have bet one long, dark hair was Nadia's.

They didn't find a single rifle shell. Of course, they lifted multiple fingerprints from the back of Nadia's car and the side of the Dumpster. In the case of the Dumpster, *years* worth of them.

And Terry did finally lift the lid and hoist himself in, but he didn't stay long. "Almost everything in here is bagged, neat as can be. Nothing dropped on top."

Canvassing didn't tell them anything, either. None of the people who'd heard the gunshots had been able to see the alley. Mr. Orton, who could have looked out a window, had slept through the whole thing. Apparently, even a siren didn't wake him.

Neither the neighbors nor anybody else within a radius of several blocks had seen anyone on foot in the dark, far less someone carrying a rifle. Nobody had particularly noticed a car engine starting, or driving away, but why would they have? They didn't remember hearing Nadia driving into the alley and parking, either.

The diamond—if it was a diamond—was the only significant find.

Having noticed Nadia's ears were pierced, he called to ask if she'd lost an earring.

"Not that I've noticed," she said immediately. "I pretty much wear plain yellow-gold balls. I can't remember the last time I took them out."

In the city, Ben wouldn't have leaped to assume a woman had lost it. Men wore post earrings, too. But not here. Anyway, aside from the fabric store and the barbershop, most of the businesses on the block were Amish owned and had Amish employees. "Prettying themselves" up with jewelry wasn't their way.

He went home, showered, shaved and changed into his uniform, ate lunch with Lucy, then went into the station to work on the myriad administrative tasks always waiting for him. Terry called to say that their diamond was indeed real, and the jeweler agreed with his estimation of two carats and said it had excellent clarity. A rough valuation lay in the five- to ten-thousand-dollar range. Unfortunately, it had not been purchased at Larson's.

Ben checked, but no one had reported it missing or stolen to the police. Shaking his head, he tried to imagine a woman wearing her best diamond earrings to an attempted assassination.

And if they belonged to the shooter, it seemed to rule out the farmers who might have been enraged thinking Nadia had kept money intended to help them rebuild. Wouldn't anyone have sold earrings that valuable, if they'd owned them in the first place?

What he found himself thinking uncomfortably about were some of those auction volunteers he'd interviewed in the first round. Julie Baird, Karen Llewellyn, Jennifer Bronske and a few others. Women likely to wear diamonds.

What he couldn't understand was why any of them would hate or fear Nadia enough to want her dead.

CHAPTER FOURTEEN

NADIA HAD MADE the front page of the *Henness Herald*.

When Ben appeared at the breakfast table, Lucy had said, "You need to read *that*." Loathing filled her voice.

A snippet about the late-evening shooting in the business district had appeared in yesterday's paper. Today's article expanded on it. By the time Ben reached the second paragraph, his blood pressure was soaring.

> Anonymous sources identified Nadia Markovic as the victim. Markovic was previously named as a suspect in the theft of over $100,000 raised during a community-wide charitable event to benefit victims needing help to rebuild after tornado damage.

Previously named? Presumably an anonymous source for that statement, too, since in fact the police department had not named *any* persons of interest.

The article continued with more details about the shooting, including a mention that Markovic remained in the hospital, recovering from her wound. There was a suggestion that the "widespread anger Markovic stirred in the wake of the charity event" left investigators flummoxed as to where to begin seeking this perpetrator. Police had declined to comment, as did the Amish co-chair of the quilt auction and sale, put on with such hopeful intentions.

Declined? Ben hadn't been asked for a comment, and no one in his department would have done anything but refer a call from the newspaper editor to him.

With a growl, Ben turned to the next-to-last page, where editorials, political cartoons and letters to the editor appeared. The editorial had to do with a noise ordinance the city council was considering. But the two letters to the editor concerned Nadia and her "alleged" theft of the money, and were both vicious and small-minded. He'd have liked to call them actionable, but all the right qualifiers had been inserted, and he'd be willing to bet the editor and principal reporter of the newspaper had taken care of that. Nice way to make his point without *his* name being appended.

Ben had clashed with Dave Rutledge before, but this time he'd gone too far. As pissed as Ben was that Rutledge had made clear how inept he thought "investigators"—read Ben—were, it was the slaps at Nadia that enraged him.

The front-page article wasn't news; it was a thinly disguised editorial. And by God, Ben was going to force a retraction. He'd be stopping by to chat with the two authors of the letters to the editor, too. Their nastiness made them prime suspects in Monday night's attack on Nadia, as far as he was concerned. He might even "name" them as such. Let Rutledge publish that.

"Does Nadia subscribe?" he asked.

"I think so." Lucy sounded as shaken as she was angry. "She's being released this morning, right? I'll go by and ask Hannah to get rid of this morning's paper before Nadia can see it."

The article and, even worse, the letters to the editor were another slap to cement her certainty that she couldn't stay in Byrum.

Didn't these fools realize that only the Amish were keeping this town alive at all? That the vacant space next door to her store where a florist had gone out of business, that the abandoned building behind hers where a small manufacturer had probably once employed twenty people or more, were only a few of the empty commercial buildings and storefronts in Byrum? Nadia was the first outsider in a long time to open a business in Byrum—replacing one that had been closed—and make it thrive. A business that offered products locals needed, and drew tourists as well.

Her success might have inspired someone else to try. But it would seem the good citizens of Byrum and Henness County in general would rather suffer a continued economic decline than welcome anyone they hadn't known their entire lives.

Right this minute, he despised the people he had sworn to serve and protect. Ben didn't much like the feeling.

"Much as I hate knowing how this crap will make her feel, I think we need to let Nadia see this," he said. "Sooner or later, someone will mention it. She wouldn't appreciate being unprepared."

"But…"

"Nadia is strong," he said quietly. "You'll see."

Not looking at him, Lucy nodded and pushed away from the table. "I wish I could say that about myself."

"I wasn't comparing you."

"I know you weren't. I was comparing myself."

A moment later, he heard her footsteps on the stairs.

"I CAN SIT behind the cash register and ring up sales," Nadia told Hannah in the late morning Wednesday, "if you'll take over the class this afternoon." Fortunately, this was their block of the month class. Not that canceling would be the end of the world, she thought. At best, two or three of the registrants might show up.

Hands planted on her hips, expression stern, Hannah looked like a mother taking on a recalcitrant teenager. "You should lie down."

"I've been lying down for two days. I'll go crazy if I have to stare at another ceiling." Accepting her determination to spend at least a little time in the shop, Ben had taken her medication and hospital paperwork up to her apartment.

She hadn't admitted to him that she felt a teeny bit light-headed every time she stood up. With her left arm in a sling at the doctor's insistence, she wouldn't be able to heft bolts of fabric onto the cutting table, either. But, by heavens, she could sit here. Probably she should use her time to look at mail, catch up on her newspapers, but she wasn't ready for a dose of reality on top of the pain pills. Bills could wait.

And, if any customers materialized, she could operate the cash register.

Hannah threw up her hands. "*Ja*, fine. *Ach*, you are as muleheaded as Jacob."

Nadia laughed. It hurt—but it felt good, too.

"Someone is here," Hannah said, looking past her.

The tension in her voice had Nadia swiveling on her stool. An extra-long van had pulled up right in front. It seemed to be crammed full of people. An attack squad? Protesters?

Well, attack squad was probably out, since the passengers seemed to all be women, some young enough to spring out of the van, the middle-aged and elderly passengers taking more care. They streamed toward her door.

Nadia braced herself.

The first through the door swept the store with an avid look. The second, middle-aged, wore a hot-pink T-shirt that said "Old quilters never die. They just go to pieces."

She grinned at Hannah and Nadia, both of whom were probably gaping. "We're a little over-whelming, aren't we? We're all quilters from Kansas City. Every six months or so, we hire a van and take two days to travel from one fabric store to another. You weren't here the last time we came to this part of the state."

In Colorado, Nadia had belonged to a group like this. They were all hungry to find that one special fabric or a color and pattern perfect for a quilt in the planning. No two stores carried the same stock. Nadia made a point of searching out new and unusual lines.

"We've only been open six months. Welcome!"

The women spread throughout the store with gasps and cries of delight. Several others, she saw in passing, also wore T-shirts with slogans. The most apropos was one that said "Ever hear about the quilter that had too much fabric? Me neither." She counted—it felt like more, but there were nine women in the group.

They exclaimed over quilts on display, but most plunged right in between rows of fabric. In no time, they were heaping bolts of fabric on the cutting table, where Hannah worked nonstop with the rotary cutter.

"Oh, I'm not sure there's five yards left on this bolt," she'd say. "Let's see." Then, "*Ja, ja!* Chust enough." Her accent seemed to be thickening with the excitement.

A minute later. "Three yards of each? I will chust pile them here, see?"

Nadia directed several of the women to her displays of fat quarters and fat eighths—small pieces perfect for accents. She bundled many that went together.

The crowd stayed for almost two hours, and spent an astronomical amount of money, sweeping out at last with bags bulging with fabric, thread and a few quilting books.

"This is a fabulous store," one woman assured her, while another said, "We'll be back!"

The women piled into the van. As it pulled away from the curb, waving hands could be seen.

Neither Hannah nor Nadia moved for a minute. Then they looked at each other and laughed.

"I think I need to lie down now!" Hannah declared.

"Oh, my. It was like two weeks' worth of customers all in two hours."

"The blade on the cutter was getting dull."

"It felt like a whirlwind."

Hannah giggled. "*Ja!* That one woman—did you see her? She bought thirty yards, and some fat quarters, too."

If gloating was prideful, Hannah didn't remark on it. Unfortunately, the anesthetic properties of all that excitement wore off with the speed of a birthday balloon losing its helium, and Nadia realized if she didn't take a pain pill and lie down, she'd be flat on her face any minute.

Hannah shooed her upstairs, where she ate a couple soda crackers in hopes they'd protect her stomach, swallowed a pill and lay down very carefully on her side in bed. She couldn't decide if her shoulder or her head hurt the worst. But thank goodness she'd been stubborn! Hannah couldn't have coped on her own, not with so many eager shoppers at the same time.

A smile curved Nadia's mouth as her eyelids grew heavy. But it wasn't the numbers she'd rung up on the cash register she was thinking about as sleep sucked her in. No, she pictured Ben in the chair beside her bed the past two nights. Every time she started awake, he seemed to know and would soothe her back to sleep with gentle touches and the deep velvet of his voice.

She hadn't overcome her fears where he was

concerned, and she winced away from the memory of the humiliating search and the scary and hurtful knowledge that he believed she had stolen the money. But…the Ben who hadn't left her side all night, who had held her hand and kept her safe, he was hard to resist.

When she woke up two hours later, heart pounding from a dream that slid away from her while leaving a weight of dread, she moved stiffly to the kitchen where she ate cottage cheese and a peach, then went downstairs.

Somebody tried to kill me.

And that was why Ben had stayed at her side. Not out of passionate devotion, but because he was determined to keep her alive.

She nodded at the women just arriving for the class session, puzzled when their gazes touched on her sling and slid away. Neither asked how she'd been hurt. Because they already knew?

Lips pressing together, she marched to the hallway where her mailbox was located. Mail and newspapers went in from the street side; she unlocked a small door to retrieve what had been delivered.

The handful of envelopes probably did contain bills; she didn't really look at them. It was the two newspapers she hadn't yet seen she set on the counter beside the cash register. The Downtown Shooting headline caught her eye immediately.

Within seconds, nausea hit.

Markovic was previously named as a suspect in the theft of over $100,000 raised during a community-wide charitable event to benefit victims needing help to rebuild after tornado damage.

Still absorbing the other veiled allegations, she read the rest of the newspaper mechanically, not really taking any of it in.

But she did take in the vitriolic content of the letters to the editor. Oh, yes. She did.

AFTER CONTEMPLATING THE surprisingly full parking lot, Ben walked into the Harley-Davidson store on the outskirts of Byrum. The place was busier than Hy-Vee, the only large grocery store in town. He scanned the store as he did any space when he entered it, his eye catching on a cluster of guys in their late teens or early twenties ogling a bike, chrome and black leather and a powerful engine, not to mention a price way out of their means. Dreaming was a lot of fun, though, and it appeared the salesman was being indulgent.

He recognized the woman he'd come to see, working behind the counter. Her hair wasn't the same color it had been, but he knew her, all right. She was tied up right now, apparently helping a pair of women make a decision on…he couldn't tell from this distance. Coffee mugs? Maybe.

Another customer was hanging back waiting for her attention.

It was logical that the store offered replacement parts and accessories for the motorcycles, as he'd have expected, and, okay, riding pants and chaps, helmets, boots and bandannas. But regular clothes? Men's and women's departments both carried shirts, jeans, caps, distinguished by the Harley name or logo. There was even luggage. When he finally approached the glass counter, he saw the coffee mugs, along with barware, clocks, sunglasses and heated gloves. No, not just gloves—heated vests, jacket liners and pants, too. Seemed like cheating to him.

"Chief Slater." The platinum blonde behind the counter said. "Did you find something that interests you?"

"Afraid not," he said easily. "I was passing by, thought I'd stop by to check in with you."

"With me?" Alarm flickered in her eyes, but he didn't get excited; most people got worried when he came looking for them. "Have you found out something about Aunt Edith?"

"Afraid not. Although I've been in and out of her place a lot these past few weeks, as you probably know."

"There does seem to have been some excitement there." She gave a quirky smile. "I kind of pay attention, since I owned the building for a little while."

Thirty years old in March, Corinne Bissett must have been a lot prettier before she started looking hard. He guessed she smoked, which had an aging effect. Or maybe it was just the heavy makeup, the too obvious cleavage and the white-blond hair contrasting with darker roots. Ben's gaze flicked to her hand—no wedding or engagement ring. She did have pierced ears, along with probably 90 percent of the other women her age, today wearing something dangly.

"Seems odd, doesn't it? Your aunt getting killed, and then the woman who bought the building having so much trouble."

Just as she always had, she argued, "I still can't believe anyone pushed Aunt Edith. Why would they? She was a nice old lady. She'd lived there forever and ever. Everybody *liked* my aunt."

That was true enough, although a few times Ms. Bissett had slipped a little, revealing the sharpness and irritation she had felt for Mrs. Jefferson. That in itself wouldn't have been enough to make him suspect her of her aunt's murder. The young often had reason to find the elderly exasperating. Corinne probably hadn't expected to be stuck with the responsibility of an aging aunt. But she was the only remaining family— and she was Edith Jefferson's heir.

She'd had an alibi. He'd verified her airline tickets and the hotel room in New York City, where she and a couple of girlfriends had met up to sample big-city life. He'd had to rule her out, even though she was the only person who seemed to benefit from Mrs. Jefferson's death. That, and he'd seen right through her pretense at grief.

"You know why we're certain she didn't just fall." He kept his response mild, although she'd *seen* the spot dented in the wall by her aunt's head. Common sense said Edith Jefferson couldn't fly. Still, denial was a normal human failing.

Ben didn't like coincidences, though, and the idea of two intruders in the same building, albeit a year apart, both seemingly having keys to let themselves in, nagged at him. She was one of only two people who'd admitted to having a key, and the other one was a dear friend of Mrs. Jefferson's, also in her seventies. Ms. Bissett could have kept a key. There'd been nothing to stop her from making as many copies as she wanted before she signed the papers selling the building.

All of that would bother him even more if Ms. Bissett had any interest in the value of quilts or had showed her face that day at the auction.

He had solved other crimes this way, though. He didn't let people drop from his radar. A cop stopping by to see them now and again tended to make people edgy. Especially people with guilty consciences. Edgy enough, sometimes, to do something stupid.

Corinne was tough, though. He could tell she didn't like having him here, but she stayed calm.

Ben settled himself comfortably against the counter. "So, were you able to buy a house once the inheritance came through?" He didn't add, "What about a really nice pair of diamond earrings?" He couldn't imagine she'd admit that, not if she'd happened to lose one in the alley behind Nadia's building.

Her chin rose as if he'd made an accusation. "Yes, I did. I was really tired of always having to share to cut costs." Only then she wrinkled her nose. "Sometimes I'm sorry, though. I didn't think about having to mow my own lawn."

Ben laughed despite himself. "I have to admit, I don't love mowing."

She grinned. "Can't call the landlord to whine if the shower starts dripping or the furnace craps out, either."

"But you can call a repairman without waiting days to hear from your landlord first."

With them both laughing now, he left it at that. His only goal had been to remind her that he had his eye on her, and he'd accomplished that.

"I WANT TO sue them all," Nadia snapped. "Starting with that creep—" her gaze strayed to the newspaper on the table "—Rutledge. He was sweet as shoofly pie when he came to interview me about the store opening. I've never talked to the man again!" She slapped the paper. "He doesn't know me *at all*, but he despises me?"

"No." Ben almost told her to sit down, but knew better. Wounded or not, she needed to vent some of her anger and pain. "He wants to make people talk. Sell papers and advertising. I doubt he gives a damn about you one way or another."

She stopped to look at him. "You don't sound as if you like him, either."

"I don't. And the feeling is mutual. Whatever the crime, if we haven't made an arrest by the time the paper goes to print, he gets in a few jabs. He's all but accused me of police brutality, or condoning it in one of my men, but he always stops just short of setting himself up for a lawsuit. If we bring someone in for questioning and determine they had nothing to do with the crime, we've sullied the reputation of a fine citizen of this community." He didn't even try to hide his bitterness. "Not *we*—it's the police chief 'some members of the community now believe was mistakenly imported from New Jersey by the city council, who may be questioning their own decision with this latest outrage.'"

Nadia pulled out a chair and sat across her kitchen table from him. "That sounds like a quote."

"It burned itself into my memory."

"So I'm not the first person he's insulted."

"No, and you won't be the last. Hey, didn't you notice a jab or two aimed at me in that article?"

"You mean the part about you being flummoxed?"

"Yeah." He rubbed a hand over his jaw. "I shouldn't let the jackass get to me."

Her distress appeared to have eased. Because misery loves company?

"Police brutality?"

Figures she'd home in on that.

"On top of all his other sins, he's a bigot. If someone with a smartphone catches one of my officers wrestling with a black or Latino suspect who has resisted arrest, you won't see a mention in the *Herald*. Make it a seemingly upstanding white citizen—even if, really, he's brewing meth in his spare bedroom or has raped a woman who didn't think one date meant she'd agreed to have sex with him—and Rutledge jumps right on it." He was getting pissed all over again, and probably grinding his molars to dust.

"Figures." Nadia sniffed.

"We'll make him grovel once we arrest the person who really stole the money."

"That would be nice." She went quiet for a moment. "But what are the odds after all this time?"

Not good, but Ben wasn't going to admit as much.

"The whole thing's a puzzler," he did say.

"Right now, I'm more worried about who ambushed you."

"You don't believe it's the same person?"

"It's not logical." He probably sounded as frustrated as he felt. "He got away with the money. How can you be a threat to him?"

"Because I know something I don't know I know." She made an awful face. "That didn't come out so well. But you know—"

Laughing despite the topic, he said, "I do know what you mean. And, yeah, I guess that's possible."

"What if he's afraid I saw him?"

"If you had, why wouldn't we long since have arrested him?" Ben countered.

Nadia lifted a shoulder to concede his point. "Well, what if someone wants to take over my store? Or just buy my building?"

Why *would* somebody be desperate to take over the building? And if they did…it had been for sale not that long ago. So maybe owning it wasn't what mattered—it was having free access. A chance to retrieve something left here? Or to search for something that had been hidden?

Terry Uhrich's crew had done a pretty thorough search already, he reminded himself, albeit they hadn't pried up floorboards or blasted holes in the walls.

Frowning, Ben said, "Far as I know, there's

never been so much as a rumor that Mrs. Jefferson might have stashed anything valuable here."

"Who owned the building before her?"

"No idea. I do know she ran that fabric store for something like forty years."

Troubled eyes met Ben's. "But somebody murdered her. And now, somebody tried to kill me, too. What could we have in common?"

The fabric store. A love of quilts. And the building, which wasn't anything special. The very similar one next door was vacant, available for sale or lease.

But he also could not believe Mrs. Jefferson's death and the shooting weren't connected somehow.

Right now, he just shook his head.

CHAPTER FIFTEEN

SHE SHOULDN'T HAVE let Ben win the argument, Nadia thought, unsettled to have a man lounging on her sofa as comfortably as if he lived here. The worst part was that his insistence on staying sharpened her fear. She couldn't push it back, even for a few minutes at a time.

She worried about Lucy, too. How would she sleep tonight, with her brother not home? She had been so determined not to let Ben know that she was sleeping better than she had in years because he made her feel safe.

All of the above was true, but Nadia wasn't into self-deceit. The real reason his presence disturbed her was because of the attraction between them. She had to make an effort not to stare. Okay, not to stare too *obviously*. It was really, really hard *not* to look.

He'd taken off his shoes earlier, removed his belt and slung it over a chair back and stripped off his uniform shirt to reveal a plain white T-shirt beneath. His holstered handgun he'd set on the end table within reach of the sofa he had taken over.

After asking whether she minded, he stacked his feet on the coffee table and took possession of the remote control. To all appearances, he was absorbed in a baseball game while Nadia pretended to read. With the volume low, the commentators' voices and occasional crack of a bat connecting with a ball were background noises she could ignore.

As she stole another look at him, he stretched, flexing all those muscles, and then clasped his hands behind his head. His intensity and restlessness, the way his dark eyes bored into hers, usually kept her from being able to absorb details, like the dusting of dark hair on his tanned forearms or the shape of his ears or the tendons in his strong neck. He had broad palms and long fingers, she had noticed, with a few hairs curling on the backs of those fingers. But given how heavy his beard growth was, she'd have expected his arms to be hairier. And she could make out the definition of powerful chest muscles, so surely if he'd had a lot of chest hair, she would have been able to see that, too. He had distinct stubble by evening; once, he'd run his hand over his jaw, and Nadia had heard the rasping sound. It would be scratchy, wouldn't it, if he kissed her…

That was the moment when she realized he was watching her, too, his eyes even darker than usual.

"I don't suppose you'd like to join me," Ben

said, voice husky. He lowered a hand to pat the cushion beside him. "We could cuddle."

Nadia gave her head a panicky shake. She was too vulnerable right now. If he held her, if he kissed her, he'd end up in her bed. She was too uncertain about him to let that happen.

"Nadia. I won't ask for more than you're ready for."

He'd read her mind. She cleared her throat to be sure she sounded at least seminormal. "I know."

"Do I still scare you?"

Her "No-o" didn't sound as decisive as she meant it to. His eyes narrowed.

"Is it because I lost it with a suspect? Are you going to make me sorry I told you?"

"No! It's not that. I think…I trust you more because you did tell me. I'm not a very violent person, but after Lucy told me what she went through, I understand how you felt. You might be her little brother, but I'll bet you always felt protective of her, didn't you?"

He stayed quiet for a minute, scanning her face. Then, as if accepting that she intended to keep her distance, he clasped his hands behind his head again. "I guess I did. The age difference wasn't much, and I was bigger and stronger than her by the time I was four or five."

"I'll bet that annoyed her."

A smile tweaked his lips. "You'd win that

bet. My size advantage kept her from getting too bossy." Lines deepened on his forehead even as the smile disappeared. "She was confident in her own way, but uncomfortable with new people or in crowds. She didn't know how to deal with it if a guy came on too strong." Gaze intense, he said, "When she told me she wanted to come down here for a visit, I wondered—" His lips compressed.

"You wondered what?"

"She talked about the Amish. What a peaceful people they are. She sounded so...wistful."

The way he said that, Nadia wondered if he'd ever used that word before.

"You know she'd be accepted among them only if her conversion was genuine, don't you? That is what you're worried about, right?"

"I guess so. Not that it would be so bad. It's her motives I don't like. Are the Amish in general more peaceful than the rest of us? Sure. Becoming Amish wouldn't come with a guarantee, though. They struggle, like everyone else. And plenty of crimes are committed against them." He lowered his hands and let his head fall back. "It's probably all in my imagination anyway. Except for this quilting thing, I haven't seen any sign—"

"She's gone to lunch several times with Hannah and Jacob," Nadia blurted.

He stared at her. "Jacob?"

"Hannah's brother." Oh, why had she opened her big mouth? She felt as if she'd betrayed Lucy. "He and their dad have the custom cabinet shop on my block."

"I've seen him," Ben said slowly, his eyebrows drawn together. "He has a beard. Doesn't that mean he's married?"

"Or was married. An Amish man doesn't shave his beard off even if his wife dies. Jacob is a widower."

He groaned. "Has Lucy said anything to you about it?"

"I'm not sure I'd tell you if she had, but…no. It just seemed friendly to me, except, well, *I've* never had lunch with him. Although," she added in fairness, "that's probably because Hannah is usually covering for me when I take a lunch break, and vice versa." She shook her head. "I can't imagine. If Jacob is thinking of remarrying, he wouldn't even look at a woman outside the faith."

"But she might look at him."

Nadia shook her head again, now that she'd had a minute to think about it. "I don't believe it. She hasn't been…secretive, or, I don't know, blushing or too eager."

"I hope you're right." Ben gazed at the television, but not as if he really saw it. "Let me use your bathroom, and then I think you should go to bed."

The change of subject was so abrupt, she guessed he wanted to be alone.

"Okay." He had the right idea. She could be tempted so easily. Besides, the idea of stretching out in bed brought on a wave of exhaustion.

She brushed her teeth, washed her face and braided her hair, then took a pillow and blanket from the linen closet for him.

When Ben saw the blanket in her arms, he said, "You do know it's probably ninety degrees up here."

"Well...just in case." If he stripped down to shorts, he might feel cool before morning.

If she got up early and came out here...

His hand grazed hers as he accepted the armful of bedding. Their eyes met, and she knew she was blushing. Was he remembering how little she wore to bed the night the money was stolen?

She rushed into speech. "I'll turn on my air conditioner. If I leave the bedroom door open, it ought to help a little out here, too."

"Thank you." He dropped pillow and blanket on the sofa and rose to his feet. "Did you take another pain pill?"

"They're in the kitchen. I will on the way to bed."

"Sleep tight." Ben's voice was low and husky, as tangible as a touch. Except he touched her, too, running his knuckles softly over her cheek. "Nothing will get by me."

"I know." She tried to smile, felt her lips tremble. "I didn't thank you for staying with me in the hospital."

Both of them were talking quietly now, as if they were trying not to wake someone else, only that wasn't it at all. It was more as if... She didn't know, just that she wanted to step forward and wrap her arms around his waist, let herself lay her head on his shoulder. But if she did that, she would want more, and so would he, and she needed to trust him absolutely before she let that *more* happen.

Ben's hand dropped to his side and she backed away, not wanting to tear her gaze from his. His tender expression warmed her deep inside. When she bumped into the other end table and had to grab the lamp to keep it from falling, Nadia knew her cheeks had heated again.

She turned and fled to the kitchen, and then to her bedroom.

However good it felt to lie down, she heard every quiet movement he made, even with the air conditioner rattling. Not until the last light went out did she close her eyes and relax toward sleep. She prayed Lucy wasn't lying rigidly awake because Ben was here instead of in his own house.

Tonight, he was protecting her.

BEN KNEW THAT stopping by to have a few words with the two creeps who'd written those letters to the editor was not wise for a police chief who had enemies on the city council. His internal debate lasted a whole thirty seconds or so. He wouldn't let his anger show, but they needed to know that vilifying an innocent woman wasn't acceptable.

The easiest to track down, Kyle Crandall owned a well-drilling and service business. Ben had never met him, but hadn't liked what he'd heard. Crandall was evidently a hard man to work for. Even with jobs scarce around here, employees tended not to stay long.

A white van ahead of him on the street turned into the parking lot in front of the business. Pulling in next to it, Ben saw Crandall Pump & Well Service emblazoned on the side. The solid, middle-aged man who got out wore a blue shirt with what Ben guessed was the business name embroidered on the pocket. Instead of continuing on in, he waited until Ben reached him.

"I'm Crandall," he said tersely. "What can I do for you?"

"Chief Slater." Ben held out a hand, reluctantly accepted for a quick shake. "I read your letter to the editor in yesterday's paper."

Crandall's expression and voice hardened. "And?"

"You seemed so certain of Ms. Markovic's guilt, I hoped you could share what you know with me," Ben said. "Since apparently you've uncovered something we haven't."

Angry color tinted leathery skin. "I didn't say anything that everybody else isn't, too. I just had the guts to speak out."

"Have you ever met Ms. Markovic?"

Crandall snorted. "You mean, when I was buying some flowery material to sew a new apron?"

"That's a no, then?"

"No, I haven't. Doesn't mean I haven't heard enough," he snapped.

"Care to name your sources?"

"No, I don't."

"In other words," Ben said, as if just reaching a surprising conclusion, "you accused her of a felony offense based on common gossip."

The color deepened. "In my experience, that many people aren't wrong."

"That so? What about Nazi Germany? McCarthyism?" *Wasting my breath*, he thought. He shook his head, losing patience. "I'm here to tell you that investigators, myself included, looked hard at her and are confident that Ms. Markovic was a victim, not a suspect in that crime. Maybe you should have called the department before you jumped to your conclusion."

Neither the bull-like stance nor the glare altered. *I'm making an enemy here*, Ben knew, and didn't care.

He dropped all pretense of friendliness. "You're aware that someone lay in wait for Ms. Markovic Monday evening and shot her."

Crandall was smart enough to look a little wary. "I read about it in the *Herald*."

"I need to ask you where you were Monday evening."

"*What?* You're accusing *me*?"

Ben let his eyebrows rise. "Accusing? Of course not. But the opinion you expressed in print of Ms. Markovic was…extreme. I'd go so far as to call it hateful. I've been a police officer for a long time, Mr. Crandall. Coincidences make me itchy. You had to have turned in that letter to the editor at the latest on Tuesday. Maybe you wrote it over the weekend, or on Monday. Monday night, someone tried to kill her. The attack had nothing to do with the theft…unless the man who attempted murder was riled into doing so by violent outrage. Which you felt."

Oh, yeah, the guy was vibrating with outrage right this minute. Didn't much like having the tables turned on him.

"Expressing an opinion is not a crime in this country, last I heard."

"No, it is not. Unless that same person took his outrage a step further."

"You can't pin this on me!"

Ben had long since learned how to sound unemotional but inflexible. "Mr. Crandall, all I'm asking is for your whereabouts at the time in question."

His glare felt like standing too close to a bonfire. "I was home, of course! With my wife. Feel free to ask her."

"I may do that." Ben inclined his head. "You have a good day, Mr. Crandall. I would advise you to check your facts in the future before you express an opinion publicly again."

He heard sputtering behind him as he walked back to his car and got in. Ben didn't look at the jackass again as he backed out and drove away.

Number two: Jay Bradshaw, long-haul trucker.

"YOU ASKED HIM *THAT*?" Nadia looked at Ben in shock.

"You heard me." He took a bite out of his burger, almost enjoying the attention they were drawing.

The Cozy Home Café was a classic diner—rotating stools lining a long counter, booths with padded, red vinyl–covered benches along three walls and tables filling the remaining space. Ben ate lunch here often, considering it an excellent place to shake hands and exchange a few words with citizens of his town. Keep his finger on the pulse. The good food was a bonus.

Today, he'd decided to make a statement. His hand had rested lightly on Nadia's back as they walked in. Fortunately, the corner booth had been empty, allowing him to see the entire restaurant including the entrance. This being the busiest time of day, he was really hoping Dave Rutledge decided to have lunch here today.

Nadia was still sputtering. "But…you can't really think either of those men shot me."

He shrugged. "Why not? They both expressed rage at your very existence. Could be one of them is just unhinged enough to decide to do something about that."

Shivering, she cast a surreptitious peek at the other diners. "You're scaring me."

Ben reached across the table for her hand, enclosing cold fingers in his. "I'm sorry. No, I really don't think either of them is anything but an intolerant, loudmouth know-it-all with anger management problems. I decided to shake them a little bit, that's all."

"Did it work?"

His grin probably wasn't very nice. "Oh, yeah. Especially Bradshaw. He didn't have even a wife for an alibi. I left him quaking."

The set of Nadia's mouth became prim. "What if one of them complains about you?"

"I say I had to look at the two of them as suspects, given their open dislike of you."

"You shouldn't have done it." A smile bloomed. "But thank you."

Ben laughed, then nodded at her plate. "Eat."

She picked up her BLT, then sneaked another look around. "Is everyone staring because of all the talk about me?"

"Nope, they're staring at us. Because the big, bad police chief appears to be romantically involved with that woman they read about in the newspaper."

Nadia made an inarticulate sound and dropped her sandwich. "I shouldn't have come! You could be putting your job at risk."

"Nadia." He held her gaze. "You are *not* a suspect. Repeat after me. Not a suspect. I have every right to be romantically involved with the beautiful businesswoman who was just the subject of an assault. In fact, I *am* romantically involved with her." He paused. "Or so I'd like to think."

They stared at each other. No cop should let this happen, but he lost all awareness of the people around them. Only she mattered. What if she said—

"Yes." Her smile and those glorious eyes both reflected her tangled feelings, but she hadn't said no. "Any man willing to sleep in a chair for two nights running and then on a sofa at least two feet too short for him so that he can protect a woman almost has to have romantic feelings for her, doesn't he?"

He could feel his heartbeat in a way he usually didn't. "Well, he'd do it for his sister or mother, but not any other woman. But she has something to say about it, too, you know."

This time, she answered with a tremulous smile. "She… *I* may be a little nervous, but you make me feel things I haven't in a long time. Or—" Nadia shook her head, deciding not to finish.

Or ever? Was that what had nearly slipped out? He hoped so. Because she was a first for him, too.

A cheerful voice intruded. "You need a refill, Chief?" Their waitress poised a coffeepot over his cup.

And he hadn't even seen her coming.

"Thanks," he said.

The waitress smiled at Nadia. "You need anything else, hon?"

"I'm good, thanks."

Once she moved on, Nadia wrinkled her nose at him. "I think we ought to talk about something else."

Ben grimaced. "I think so, too." He'd intended to make a statement by taking her out to lunch, but not the kind of statement he would if he kissed her passionately in front of half the town.

He didn't want to discuss his investigation—either of them—here and now, either. He had other stuff going on at work, too, of course, but couldn't take the chance of being overheard. Family, he decided. That was something two people who'd gone out together could talk about.

"Your parents know what's going on?" he asked.

"More or less." Nadia didn't look thrilled with the topic. "The money part, and I did say some people seem to think I must have stolen it. I haven't told them about the shooting yet."

"You think they'd be on the first flight out here if they knew."

"Yes, and what could they do? What if they got caught in the cross fire?" She made another face. "Literally."

"This isn't good timing for a visit," Ben agreed. "Put them off if you can."

"I will. If nothing else happens, I might not have to tell them about the shooting."

He gave her a quizzical look. "Do you ever plan to go clothes shopping with your mother again? Swimming with anyone in your family?"

She had refused to wear the sling today, but held her arm carefully to her side and wasn't using her left hand even to pick up a drink.

"Oh," she said after a minute. "Well, crud."

Ben laughed, if softly. Apparently Nadia hadn't given much thought to the recent scar. She was something new to him: a beautiful woman who didn't seem to waste a lot of thought on her appearance. She kept makeup to a minimum, wore pretty clothes that weren't obviously trendy, and never posed or paid attention to whether people were looking at her or not. Except right now, of course, when every single person in the place had definitely noticed her.

Speaking of… "Incoming," he murmured. He didn't know the woman, which meant he hadn't interviewed her post auction. Didn't mean she wasn't a former customer who'd turned her back on Nadia.

But Nadia's face relaxed and she smiled. "Audrey. Have you gotten started on that Pine Tree quilt?"

"I managed to get the pieces cut out, and then my daughter's appendix burst. I have the kids daytimes. Not complaining, but...how do young mothers ever manage to get a thing done?"

Laughing, Nadia said, "You should know. You had three of your own."

The plump woman didn't look old enough to have grandkids. Her laugh merry, she said, "Too many years ago! I don't remember."

They chatted for another minute, her friendliness extending to Ben, before she excused herself. She'd left her husband waiting by the door, although he'd found someone to talk to, too. She concluded with, "Glad to see you out and about."

"I hope your daughter recovers quickly."

The happy chuckle trailed behind the woman.

"A customer," Ben said.

"Yes, and really nice. I inherited her from Mrs. Jefferson, so to speak, but Audrey tells me I have a better selection."

"Dessert?" Ben asked. "The pies are really good."

"I'd better not, but go ahead." Her lips curved. "I might steal a bite or two from you."

Grinning, he lifted a hand to summon the waitress.

Hearing Nadia's ringtone sobered him for no good reason.

She had to twist in her seat to delve into her purse with her right hand. After taking out the phone, she lifted her gaze to Ben, letting him see her apprehension. "It's the shop phone. Hannah *hates* making calls."

Then she answered with a "Hannah?"

Eavesdropping, Ben could make out only enough to know that her Amish assistant was agitated. She spoke unusually fluent English, reflecting her exposure to *Englischers* first at her father's business and now at Nadia's. At the moment, her accent had deteriorated, and he caught a few German words thrown in among the English.

"Yes, I'm with Ben. I'll come back right away. You shouldn't have to deal with this. Why don't you lock the door and turn the sign to Closed?"

The waitress was bearing down on them. He said quietly, "Just the check, please."

Nadia dropped her phone in her purse. Her face was as close to expressionless as she could make it, but he knew her well enough to see the turbulence in her eyes. "I have to go."

"I gathered. Let me pay the bill."

"I could walk—"

"Don't be ridiculous."

He waited until he'd paid and escorted Nadia out to the car before he asked what was wrong.

"A demonstration is being staged in front of my shop." Bitterness edged her voice. "Hannah says they have signs. And it would appear a TV station has sent a reporter and cameraman. They tried to come into the shop, but she shooed them out."

"Amish don't want to be photographed. Anyone local would know that."

"But news must come first." Her clutch on the seat belt revealed white knuckles. "This will never end."

Rage had swept him first, but now he felt sick. How could he let her go?

He braked at the corner, where they could see the scene in front of her shop. Unbelievably enough, eight or nine people blocked the sidewalk, each carrying a sign. And damned if that wasn't a TV camera.

The icing on the cake was seeing that bastard Rutledge scribbling in a notebook as he talked to one of the demonstrators.

CHAPTER SIXTEEN

NO ONE AMONG the demonstrators had yet noticed Ben's approaching SUV. "I want to commit mass murder," he said grimly.

"You could accidentally swerve onto the sidewalk." Nadia had never said anything so awful in her life, but she was too mad to care.

"I can't tell you how tempted I am." He rolled his shoulders. "I'll park in back."

"I'll look cowardly."

"Unless Hannah told them, they can't know whether you're there or not. Once you have a chance to think about what to say, you can step out front long enough to make a dignified statement. If we go in the front, you'll be mobbed. I don't want to take that risk."

The alley proved to be empty, no scout for the opposition posted there to yell when he spotted her. Even so, she hurried to the back door, surprised when Ben managed to lock his SUV and get there as fast as she did.

They slipped in, stopping at the far end of the hall where they could see through the store to one of the large front windows. Hannah came to them, her face pink with dismay, her *kapp* askew with one tie dangling down her back, one down her ample front.

"That Allison Edgerton is there. After you were so nice to her! And Jodi Knowles! *Ach*, understand them I do not!"

Chest so tight, she didn't know how to try a breath, Nadia still managed to pat Hannah's arm. "I'm lucky to have you."

Ben kept his hand on Nadia's lower back. "Are any customers trapped here in the store?" he asked.

"Only Lucy. Staying out of sight in back, but upset."

Seeing Ben's dark face tighten, Nadia added another layer of dread onto everything she already felt. This was what he'd feared when he tried to order his sister to stay away. How could he help but blame her?

Not my first worry.

"Can you see who else is out front?" she asked.

"Allison's husband is with her," Ben said. "Son of a—" He swallowed the rest with a glance at Hannah. "I'm surprised they were willing to go so far. Edgerton raises harness horses. He's got to know the Amish support you. This can't be good for his business."

Nadia craned her neck to see past him. "Did I tell you she confronted me in the grocery store?"

"No." His jaw muscles bulged. "It's mostly women out there."

Nadia recognized several more, women who had shopped here and showed off their quilts to her and volunteered to work at the auction. They had to feel betrayed by her to do something like this, but she was shaken again by such ready condemnation.

"Your father and Jacob were out on the sidewalk, looking to see what's going on," Ben commented.

Riveted on the action, Nadia hadn't noticed them.

Nodding, Hannah said, "*Daad* called, worried, uh-huh. I think he sent Jacob to tell other people."

What, and start a counterdemonstration?

What if the two sides came to blows? Wouldn't that be a spectacle for the five o'clock news? But no—the Amish believed in turning the other cheek. Any blows would be one-sided.

Ben turned his broad back to the scene outside, his gaze on her penetrating. "You saw that Rutledge is out there."

"Jerk."

A smile flickered in his eyes, as if he found her puny insult to be funny. She might have said worse if not for Hannah. She'd never done a lot of swearing, and she restrained even that much out of deference for Hannah and her other Amish friends and customers.

She took a deep breath. "What should I say?"

The three of them hastily came up with a brief statement. Nadia closed her eyes, ran through it a couple of times in her head and nodded.

"I need to get it over with." She tried to convince herself they'd go away once she'd spoken and then thought, *Yeah, right*. They'd apologize and slink away? Only if the real thief was caught would any of these people concede they had been wrong, and maybe not even then. And, considering the weeks that had gone by since the money was stolen, Nadia knew it was unrealistic for her to hold on to any hope that would happen.

"There's *Daad* and Jacob," Hannah said suddenly. "And Amos, too. He works with them."

Nadia peeked again, to find herself looking at the backs of the three Amish men. They had arrayed themselves in front of the store, facing the protesters.

"Oh, no," she exclaimed. "They'll be on television!"

She dashed forward, aware that Ben was sticking close to her. When she flung open the door, she saw that more Amish were hurrying down the street. Men and women both.

The distinctive clip-clop of hooves and whir of steel tire rims on pavement had her looking the other way. A black buggy approached, and another came around the corner behind it.

Were they coming to defend her, even though doing so would place them in a position so uncomfortable to people of their faith? Tears burned the backs of her eyes, but Nadia refused to let them give her away. She stopped where she was, a couple of feet outside the door, Ben a solid presence at her back.

The small group of protesters drew into a tighter clump, their heads turning uneasily. The basilisk stares of the two Yoder men as well as their employee were enough to give anyone the willies. All three stood with their feet planted apart, their arms crossed, the brims of their hats shading their faces. And now they were joined by several other men, who ranged themselves with their backs to the window and wall on the other side of her doorway. A wall of defenders, she thought in astonishment.

The women…they hurried forward, calling, "Nadia, *was der schinner is letz*?" What in the world is wrong? "What is this crazy thing happening?"

A stout, middle-aged woman who had been at the quilting frolic on Monday tucked her arm through Nadia's while the others encircled her. Only a couple of them even looked familiar.

The first buggy stopped at the curb, the horse snorting as if in disgust. The second one advanced as if the driver was blind to the television cameraman, who had positioned himself in the street. He had to scramble back, and was suddenly cut off from the scene in front of the store.

More people were rushing down the street now, some Amish, some not. And two more buggies had appeared. Word must have spread like wildfire.

Likely, they were here for Hannah and her family; most had never set foot inside her store. But they had been told of an injustice, and came. Nadia hoped their bishops wouldn't disapprove.

The cameraman reappeared around the front of the horse that had cut him off, scuttling as if he expected to be trampled or bitten. Too bad the harness horses were too well trained to do any such thing, Nadia thought vengefully.

Ben bent his head, his warm breath tickling her ear. "They're off balance. Do it."

She squared her shoulders and raised her voice. "Excuse me! I have something to say."

The Amish women who had been exclaiming to each other fell silent. And, oh—she did know many of the latest arrivals, other merchants from a several-block radius, two customers who must have been shopping or eating at the café.

She focused on the protesters, looking from face to face, reading the signs they held.

DON'T SUPPORT A THIEF!
BOYCOTT THIS STORE!

HER KIND ISN'T WANTED IN BYRUM.

The last bothered her the most. It was carried by a woman who had taken one of the first classes Nadia offered, and been delighted by the start she'd made on a quilt that would be far more complex than she had ever attempted before.

Not acknowledging by word or glance the reporters or camera, Nadia said, "I loved this town when I came, when I opened A Stitch in Time. People were so welcoming. I had never lived anyplace where so many of the women shared my love of fabric arts and quilting in particular. I was unbelievably moved that so many of you gave generously of your time and skill to raise money for neighbors, even for strangers, who are so desperately in need." She was quiet for a minute, holding gazes, seeing the angry color in people's cheeks, the defiance in their eyes. At least they were listening. Traffic two blocks away could be heard; the jingle as a horse shook his head could be heard, the silence was so complete.

"That evening was one of the happiest of my life. The most satisfying. I would *never* have stolen that money." She had to swallow before she could get another word out. Ben's hand on her back helped. She let herself lean into it, just a little. She had intended to keep her statement shorter, but now she was talking to these people, saying everything that had been eating at her. "I wanted to build a life here in Byrum. To make friends, help quilters sell their extraordinary work to a wider market, to someday know I belonged. I have been stunned at how quickly people I thought I knew turned against me." Once again, she looked from face to face. Some would no longer meet her eyes. "I don't even understand it. Because I was the last person known to have the auction proceeds, the police had to look at me. I understood—" *lie, lie* "—and allowed a search of my building and car so that they could rule me out as quickly as possible. Chief Slater has made it clear that he does not consider me a suspect in the disappearance of the money." Her vision had become blurry, and she realized in panic that she was crying. But she had to finish.

"I have never in my life committed a crime. I have never shoplifted, or shorted a customer on change or cut a fabric length a little short. I keep promises. This—" she gestured at the signs and the people who held them "—hurts. I didn't do anything to deserve this. I hope…" She had to breathe for a moment, summon the will to finish. "I hope you'll search your hearts before you attack another person the way you have me."

With that, she turned and hurried inside, ignoring shouted questions. And applause. To her astonishment, many of the bystanders were clapping, for her. Was the camera panning the crowd? She felt sure Mr. Rutledge would say as little about her supporters in tomorrow morning's article as he thought he could get away with.

Nadia kept going, holding her head high but wanting only to reach the back room, to be out of sight. Behind her, she heard Ben's deep, firm voice saying, "I'd like to make a statement as well."

TWENTY MINUTES LATER, having also answered questions, he found Nadia in the back room sitting beside Lucy. The two women held hands, their eyes red and puffy and their faces splotchy. Hannah and several of the other Amish women hovered. All looked at him when he walked into the room.

"They've cleared out," he said. "Or should I say, they've run for their rat holes."

Nadia shook her head. "They'll hate me even more. I should have been more diplomatic. I could have said I understood why they were angry—"

He cut her off with a "No. There's nothing understandable about their race to judgment. You hadn't given a one of them any reason to think you'd do something that crummy. To the contrary."

Her bloodshot eyes didn't waver. "I hadn't given *you* any reason to think I'd do something like that, either."

The sting silenced Ben for a moment. "I thought we'd gotten past that. I didn't know you."

"I…" Nadia averted her gaze, then met his again. "I'm sorry. That just…came out."

Very aware of their audience, he nodded. Inside…he was shaken to realize that she might have forgiven him on the surface, but still harbored anger. *You really thought it was that easy?* he asked himself.

"To get back to the point, understanding was the last damn thing you had any reason to offer. Puzzlement, hurt, those will get better results."

Nadia gave a forlorn sniff and looked around. "Having so many people come running to the rescue helps more than anything I said."

Ben smiled at the group still here. "You're right."

"I just wish there hadn't been cameras here."

One of the women said, "You don't need to worry about us! *Gott* will understand. We don't have the televisions, so we won't see our faces there."

Hannah's father, who had unexpectedly followed Ben in, spoke up. "They know we ask them not to take their pictures of us. We cannot let cameras scare us from helping our friends."

Nadia burst into tears. With so many women to fuss over her, Ben kept his distance. Roy Yoder chuckled.

"Nadia must become used to having friends,

ain't so? I think Ruth Graber would have hit me over the head with an iron skillet if I had done nothing today."

Ben found himself smiling, too. "If she could have reached as high as your head."

Roy's laugh became heartier. "*Ja, ja!* Ruth is only so high." He held a hand a belt level. "But me, I would have bent over for her."

"Fierce, is she?"

"I would say so. She and Katie-Ann Chupp, they say Nadia is a good woman who tries to do right by people. None of us want her to close her store and move away."

"No," Ben said huskily. "None of us do."

He would have liked to stay, but knew there might be fallout in his town he would have to deal with. He exchanged a quiet word with his sister, bent to kiss Nadia's cheek and whispered, "You did good," and then went out the back.

One of Ben's least favorite city council members, Maurice Abbott, called not an hour after he reached his office.

"I understand you held a press conference to answer questions about an ongoing investigation," he said sharply.

"A press conference? No, I didn't. Did I answer questions when they were raised? Yes."

"Was that wise? How can you publicly proclaim Ms. Markovic isn't a suspect in the crime when you haven't identified anyone who *is*? Did this unknown person really waltz into a locked building, go straight to the money and vanish without a sound or a clue left behind? Or do you think it's a ghost?"

Ben would have smiled at the sarcasm if he liked Abbott better. "I feel confident in saying Ms. Markovic was the victim and is not a suspect," he said. And how many times would he have to repeat that? "As for the waltzing, she had not replaced the locks from the former owner. You may recall that Mrs. Jefferson was murdered by an individual who very likely had a key."

Abbott grumbled about him leaping to call a mere fall down the stairs murder. He explained again about the laws of gravity, about force and trajectory. This repetition was really beginning to annoy Ben. He also reminded the city councilman that the medical examiner had felt the severity of fractures suggested an accelerated fall. "Now, a gymnast with a springboard might have managed to hit the wall where she did, but you tell me how an elderly woman taking a tumble did."

Abbott didn't have a comeback, but complained that Ben shouldn't have made a statement without discussing it with the city council.

"It's part of the job," he said, forcing himself to sound a lot more patient than he felt. "That job is to enforce the law and provide justice when possible. Impartiality is essential, as is my ability to act for the good for the citizens of this city rather than for individual city council members." He was tempted to ask what he'd recommend if a member of the city government were to break a law, but refrained.

Maurice went away, but Ben didn't kid himself the guy was satisfied.

He hadn't realized that a police chief had to be a politician, but the calls kept coming. In addition, a car versus buggy accident was reported, the car driven by a fourteen-year-old joyriding with three friends. The buggy was damaged but horse and driver unscathed. None of the kids had been wearing seat belts, however. All were carried in screaming ambulances to the hospital. One was currently listed in critical condition, another in serious condition.

Ben wasn't able to get away, so at five o'clock he went downstairs to turn on the only television in the station, kept on a rolling cart in the bull pen.

The demonstration in front of A Stitch in Time and the surprising counterdemonstration led by peace-loving and reserved Amish was on the news at the top of the hour. The segment began with a recap of the theft, followed by a couple of harsh comments given by Allison Edgerton and a woman identified as Sandy Houser. But the arrival of not just Amish, but also store customers and other merchants was televised, and well-edited clips from Nadia's statement were aired. An angry reaction from another woman following the statement was kept brief, and the segment concluded with Colleen Hoefling, whom he hadn't seen arrive, stoutly defending Nadia.

Ben thought the station had been fair, and noticed that the cameraman had done his best to show the Amish slightly unfocused only in the background or in profile.

He called Nadia, who said, "Yes, I watched it. It wasn't as bad as I expected. Am I wrong in thinking the reporter came down on my side?"

"No, I think she did. Rutledge, now…"

She huffed. "I used to deceive myself that journalists tried for fair and accurate."

Ben laughed. "I suspect some—most—do. Unfortunately, Rutledge owns the *Henness Herald*, which gives him complete freedom to indulge his every nasty bias and desire to increase circulation by stirring the pot whenever he can."

"Do you know, I ran a weekly advertisement in his paper? Never again."

"Not many options," he pointed out.

"I'll go with the weekly. And I can do handouts, post on bulletin boards. Anything but the *Herald*. Maybe I should talk to other merchants, try to start a rebellion."

Ben laughed, imagining Rutledge's reaction.

Hearing her temper and determination let him release some tension. She didn't sound like someone planning to close her store tomorrow morning. Ben hoped she had paid attention to the proportion today of demonstrators versus supporters. While many of the supporters wouldn't be customers of hers, the small group of women waving those signs wouldn't be any big loss to her business, either.

Well aware she'd lost a lot of other customers who hadn't turned out today, Ben grimaced. Not only customers—Nadia had lost her sense of security, probably hard-won after the hideous shooting she had survived in Colorado. To have someone break into her place? To be shot again? It was a wonder she hadn't already upped and gone.

Having people turn against her would have stolen her assurance as well. Would she ever be able to trust the same way again?

Ben's inbox was still piled high, he hadn't answered all his emails, he ought to check on how the injured kids at the hospital were doing—but what he wanted was to go home. Lucy intended to invite Nadia home with her for dinner, at least.

So, to hell with it. This was Saturday. He was entitled to time off, and for once, he would be selfish. He had been trying to make himself delegate more anyway; his first two years here, he had concentrated on training, and maybe it was time to believe his efforts had been effective.

He powered down his computer, verified that

he had his cell phone and started for the door. Of course, that was the moment his desk phone rang. If it was an outside call—

Of course, it wasn't. If one of his officers or the dispatcher needed him, he had no choice but to answer.

"Chief?" It was Denise Small, the evening dispatcher. "Jim Wilcox is here to see you."

Surprised, he asked, "Did he say what he wants?"

"No, sir. He looks upset, though."

"Okay, I'll be right down."

Strange, Ben thought, leaving his office. For Wilcox to show up at the station twice in as many weeks…

Ben's feet quit moving. Did Jim Wilcox ever *keep* a key to a lock he installed for someone? He had a solid reputation, so that seemed unlikely, but, damn, it would be easy for him to do. And what if canvassing hadn't turned up a witness to the packet of credit card slips being shoved through the Wilcox Lock and Key mail slot because nobody *had* shoved it through?

What if he'd had it all along?

Don't jump to conclusions, Ben ordered himself. Why would Wilcox be here now if he'd committed a crime of that magnitude? The last thing he'd want would be to draw attention to himself.

Ben almost had himself talked out of his suspicion when he stepped into the waiting room and saw the man's face—and the brown paper sack with handles on the seat beside him.

CHAPTER SEVENTEEN

WITHOUT SAYING A WORD, Jim stood, picked up the sack and followed Ben into the same room they had used the last time. He set the sack on the table and dropped into a nearby chair.

Then he made a raw sound and buried his face in his hands.

Ben lifted the gray metal box from the bag, discovering it had some heft. The latch should have required a key, but sprang open with a touch. Inside, bills of every denomination were neatly piled in the slots sized for them on a tray. When he lifted the tray, he found rolls of coins in the bottom, ready to go to the bank, as well as the hundred-dollar bills, rubber-banded.

Exultant for Nadia's sake but regretful, too, Ben sat and waited until Wilcox wiped his cheeks with his forearm and lifted his head.

"I'm sorry. So sorry I—" He choked and shook his head.

"Is the money all here?"

"Yes. I needed it real bad, but...I couldn't do it. I kept thinking we won't need it because things will turn around, and even though I knew that wouldn't happen, I still—" His Adam's apple bobbed. "I've never done anything like this before. It's not me."

Ben had seen torment before, but not for this reason. He couldn't afford to sympathize, however, not yet. "Why did you take it?"

The story poured out. Jim's nine-year-old daughter, Maddie, had leukemia. "People have been real nice." His face contorted. "Only nobody knew that business has been down, and they didn't think about what it meant when Pam had to quit her job because Maddie is in and out of the hospital and needs one of us with her. We… I dropped our health insurance almost two years ago. Stupid when you have kids, but we just weren't making it. And then Maddie got sick, and I borrowed everything I could, but we're about to lose our house and probably the business. I don't know if they'll keep treating her if I can't pay for it."

Instinctively revolting against the possibility that local hospital administrators could be that inhumane, Ben said, "I can't imagine." Except, shit, he read about things like that happening all the time.

Wilcox shrugged hopelessly. "Maybe, but what if the chemo doesn't work and she needs a bone marrow transplant?" Despair made his voice thin. "What then?"

Ben shook his head, understanding on a level he didn't want to. Working as a new patrol officer, he'd had to arrest homeless people for shoplifting even though he knew hunger made them desperate. Sometimes, he could manage to justify what he was required to do, but there were occasions when he couldn't. When children were involved, he helped as much as he could personally afford, quietly and asking not to be credited. But he could never do enough. The problems were too big for a single man on a cop's income.

This one certainly was.

Now he made himself push ahead, asking how long in advance Jim had planned the heist, how he'd known Nadia had the money.

Maybe a week in advance, he'd started thinking about it, Jim admitted. Not really believing he would do something like that, but imagining what he could do with all that money.

"Pam went over for an hour or so to watch the auction. She came home talking about how much those quilts were selling for." Alarm flashed across his face. "She doesn't have any part in this! You wouldn't—"

Lock up a sick girl's mother *and* father? No, he wouldn't. Even if the evidence came to suggest that Pam had conspired with her husband, Ben would do his best to suppress it. That, he could do.

"Does she know about this?"

Once again, Jim's face crumpled and he shook his head. He kept his gaze fixed on the table.

"You have to know we never would have suspected you. Why did you change your mind and return the money?"

Voice thick with tears and emotion, the locksmith said, "I felt so bad every time I even looked at it. I had it stashed out in the garage, where Pam wouldn't find it. I, uh, went to the bank and got the rolls to hold the coins."

Ben nodded. He had guessed that volunteer cashiers at the auction hadn't had time to do anything but drop coins into the metal box.

"I'd heard talk, and I read the newspaper article Wednesday. It was all eating at me. Then today, I turned on the news. I saw what happened at Ms. Markovic's place. The ugly things said." He raised pain-filled eyes to Ben. "I should have brought it back the minute I realized she was being blamed." He swallowed, his Adam's apple prominent. "No, I shouldn't have even thought about taking it. Will you tell her how sorry I am?"

"I will." Ben squeezed the back of his neck. It was to Wilcox's credit that, after watching the news, he hadn't hesitated. He had come straight to the station. "Jim, you knew she was home when you went in to her apartment."

Wilcox stared uncomprehendingly at him.

"You got lucky that she'd set the money box down in plain sight. You must have expected to have to search. Open cupboards, drawers. She could have put it in her closet." He paused. "You planned in advance. You must have realized there was a possibility Ms. Markovic would wake up while you were there in her apartment. What did you intend to do if that happened?"

"You think I'd have…?" The chair scraped as the man half stood. "I'd have run away! I wouldn't hurt anybody!"

"You might not have wanted to. But she could have switched on her bedside lamp and *seen* you. Recognized you."

Sinking into his seat, Wilcox just shook his head and kept shaking it. "I would never," he mumbled. "Never."

Was he a sucker to believe the guy? Ben asked himself.

He let another pause develop before he asked, "Jim, how did you come to have a key?"

"To the box? I didn't, but they're not hard to…" Comprehension dawned. "The building, you mean."

"Yes."

"Edith Jefferson asked me to keep one. She didn't like the idea of having a hideout key. Like she said, where would she put it? Tape it under a

Dumpster? She wanted to know there was someone she could call."

"Her niece had one, too, I understand."

"Yes, but…Mrs. Jefferson said she didn't want
to get thrown into a nursing home just because
she had an absentminded moment. I told her it's
not that easy to get someone committed, and she
said she knew that, she just didn't want that niece
of hers rolling her eyes."

"You ever done anything like that before? I
mean, keeping a copy of the key?"

He looked puzzled. "Sure, I have half a dozen
on hooks at my shop. I'm careful with 'em.
They're color-coded, not labeled with names or
anything like that. They're all older folks worrying about the same thing."

"Did you ever think about letting yourself into
any of those homes?"

For an instant, Jim looked offended before
he sagged. "No. I wouldn't. They're…people I
know."

Ben made his voice hard. "And you didn't
know Ms. Markovic."

Shame stark on his face, he said, "It's not
that. I convinced myself that money was raised
for people who had been wiped out, and that
my family qualified. And I know that's no excuse. You don't have to tell me. I've just been so
scared. Felt so hopeless."

"Did you ever use Mrs. Jefferson's key before?"

"You mean, did she ever lose hers? No." He almost smiled. "I reminded her once that I had a copy, and she had forgotten."

"Whoever killed her seems to have had a key, Jim."

His face froze. "I would never… You can't think…?" He stiffened, but the starch didn't last long. Speaking dully, he said, "I guess I can't blame you."

Ben sighed. No, he didn't believe Jim Wilcox had murdered Mrs. Jefferson. This was a man under horrendous stress who had just returned the money he had stolen because he was too honest to use it, and too decent to see an innocent woman blamed for his crime.

And no, he wouldn't have hurt that same woman so he could make a clean getaway.

Finally, Ben said, "I can't let this go, Jim." If Wilcox had brought it back the next day, before the crime became so public… Water under the bridge. "If I don't lock you up right now, can I trust you not to leave town?"

Appearing bewildered, Wilcox bobbed his head. "I wouldn't leave Pam and the kids. Except…I guess I'll have to when—" A sheen in his eyes, he made Ben think of an animal waiting for slaughter.

"I think we can keep you from going to jail,"

Ben said gently. "That you brought the money back makes all the difference." He drew a breath, hating what he had to say. "Jim, you are under arrest."

THE SIGHT OF BEN always startled Nadia in a way she didn't understand. She'd never reacted to a man like this, been so conscious of how he moved, every flex of his muscles, the sharpness of his cheekbones and the brooding depths of his eyes. Her heart took the little jump that she expected, but when he walked into his own kitchen, she saw something on his face that had the beat continuing hard and fast.

"Ben?"

"I have the money," he said. "It was returned by the man who took it."

"Returned?" She could hardly comprehend it. "All of it?"

"I haven't counted yet. He says it's all there."

Lucy, too, had turned from the stove to gape at him. He nodded past her. "Something is boiling over."

"Oh!" Lucy spun back and lifted a pan lid before adjusting the burner heat. "Dinner will be ready in about five minutes. I put the noodles in when I heard your car."

"Okay." His gaze hadn't left Nadia. "Let me go change out of my uniform and I'll tell you all about it."

"Wait! Who?"

"I'd rather tell you the whole story at once."

What could she do but nod? He left the kitchen and his footsteps sounded on the stairs, slow, heavy.

Nadia didn't move, staring at the empty doorway he had gone through. "Did he really say he has the money?"

Lucy hugged her. "He did."

"I'm stunned."

"I can hardly *wait* to see all those people eat humble pie."

"Some of them won't, you know. They'll just…avoid me. Or even insist Ben isn't telling everything he knows. That I *had* to be involved."

"They've been awful to you. They deserve some comeuppance."

Nadia gave herself a shake. "Let me finish making the salad."

Ben returned just as Lucy dumped the noodles into the strainer. Seeing him in worn jeans that hugged long thigh muscles, a faded blue T-shirt and athletic shoes, Nadia stopped in the middle of the kitchen with the salad bowl in her hands, unable to look away from him.

She told herself not to be an idiot. He had left the room. Now he was back. Only…she liked him even better when he was less official. Although *liked* might not be quite the right word.

His mouth quirking, he took the bowl out

of her hands and carried it to the dining room table himself.

Nadia rolled her eyes at herself and went to the refrigerator for the dressing.

The minute they sat down, Ben began serving himself with noodles and Stroganoff. He reached for the bowl of green beans, but went still.

"It was Jim Wilcox."

"Jim…" Nadia knew her mouth had fallen open. "The *locksmith*?"

"Yeah."

"But…" She floundered. "He was so nice. Except…" It was like building with Lego blocks. Pieces snapped into place. "He brought back the checks and credit card slips, too. And…he told me he'd replaced the locks for Mrs. Jefferson." Indignation rose. "He kept a key?"

"I think he is nice." Ben repeated what Wilcox had told him. "He asked me to tell you how sorry he is."

Her shoulders slumped. "He's another Leonard Hixson."

"Yes."

Ben finished dishing up, then began to eat, but obviously kept an eye on her. Lucy urged her to eat, too, and Nadia did, although she didn't really taste anything that went in her mouth.

She couldn't seem to wrap her mind around this alternate reality. The thief wasn't a monster, he was a kind, anxious man with a gravely ill child. Instead of taking lascivious notice of her scantily clad body, he had probably averted his eyes, horrified to have to enter her bedroom.

In fact, she remembered his distress when they discussed the theft, him saying he hoped she hadn't been hurt or frightened. He had even said he was sorry—which she now realized hadn't been sympathy; it was an apology.

"How did he know I had the money?" she asked at last.

"He hid in front and saw you come out with the box."

"I couldn't have been more obvious if I'd tried, could I?"

"I'm afraid not." Ben's expression was sympathetic, but also cautious, as if he half expected her to melt down.

Still stunned, Nadia grappled with the idea of Jim Wilcox violating his deepest values to steal the money, but unable in the end to use any of it. And confessing to the police chief, rather than thinking of a way to return the money anonymously.

"You can't arrest him" was what came out of her mouth.

"I already did." Deep furrows carved Ben's forehead. "He committed a crime. Whatever his motivations, what he did was wrong. He left *you* hanging out to dry."

Lucy stirred beside her, making Nadia aware how quiet she'd been.

"Don't I have the right to choose not to press charges?" she asked.

"Not for something like this." There was no give in Ben's voice. "Sorry."

"But—"

"The money he took wasn't yours. He stole from a lot of people. Including the folks the money was intended for."

"Like Leonard Hixson," she said slowly.

"Exactly."

"He'll go to prison."

Ben shook his head. "I doubt it, considering he returned what he took. I'll push for him to get community service, some supervision. He's not going to be a repeat offender."

Nadia wanted to feel relief, but Ben's expression didn't let her.

"No matter how easy the judge is on him, Jim likely will lose his livelihood. A man convicted of stealing? And using a key he kept to a lock he'd installed? He says Mrs. Jefferson asked him to hold on to it, but she's not here to call him a liar. Who will trust him again?"

Nadia pressed a hand to her chest, trying to quell a deep-down ache. She reminded herself that this was the man responsible for everything rotten that had happened to her since the morning after the auction...but she still felt sorry for him.

"He could get something for it if he sells the business. And…he and his family could move." Like she had known she would have to do.

Ben couldn't have read her mind, but he said, "A felony on his record will follow along wherever he goes."

"You're making all the arguments I should be!"

"That's because I don't like what I had to do." Anger infused his voice. "But how could I justify not arresting him to other people who did something stupid and impulsive and faced trial because of it?"

Nadia absorbed that. "The hospital wouldn't really stop treatment, would they?"

He sighed. "I doubt they can, but are they obligated to provide a treatment beyond what they're already doing? I don't know. No matter what, Jim's daughter is old enough to see what taking care of her has done to her family. That will be hard to live with."

"You couldn't have claimed the money was found on the police station doorstep?"

"It's too late, Nadia. I booked him." He gusted out another sigh. "I thought about it, but two things stopped me. I doubt I'd have gotten away with it. The dispatcher saw him come in carrying something. Other people might have seen him going into the police station or sitting in the waiting room." The full force of all that intensity was zeroed in on her.

She nodded.

His expression hardened. "And doing that wouldn't remove the shadow over you, Nadia. In fact, it might convince our local citizenry that you surrendered the money because of their pressure. Can't you see the Edgertons feeling smug because *they* got results?"

Of course, he was right, and that would really grate. Nadia sat silent, coming to terms with those consequences. Even so... "I could have moved away. Business has bounced back some, but not enough. I may still have to move."

"No," Ben said, implacable.

At the same moment his sister cried, "No! You can't do that!"

Nadia reached for this new friend's hand and squeezed. "If...if I'd been given the choice, I'd have done that rather than see his life ruined."

"Fortunately—" and Ben sounded grim "—the choice wasn't yours."

Was she relieved? She couldn't help it. Ben had a lot to do with that. To move and know she'd likely never see him again? Never find out whether this tension and yearning would take them anywhere important? But she pictured Jim Wilcox's kind, friendly face, and imagined him sitting beside his daughter's hospital bed, holding her hand.

"I understand why you had to arrest him, but I wish there was something we could do to help."

Lucy sat up straighter. "Maybe there is."

Her brother groaned.

She turned a narrowed-eye look on him. "We're really excited about our crowd-funding plan. Nadia has been out of the loop because of her hospital stay, but the photos that woman at the *Herald* produced are awesome. Colleen has a friend who is designing the appeal. There's no saying we couldn't do one for the Wilcoxes, too."

"Put pictures of his sick kid out there? Talk about how he was driven to steal money to pay for her treatment?"

"No!"

"Ben's right," Nadia interjected. "Putting their story out there could be insensitive. Do we label him as the man who can't take care of his family, and then couldn't even go through with the crime he committed for them?"

"So we let him crash and burn?" Lucy fired back.

Very aware of Ben watching their exchange, Nadia said, "All I'm saying is, we need to think about this."

Then they both looked at him. "What will happen next?" Nadia asked hesitantly.

He talked about the next steps and his belief that a plea bargain would prevent a trial and lead to minimal consequences beyond the fact that everyone in the community would know what he had done. "We need that for your sake."

Nadia's stomach was tied in knots, but she could only nod. If Ben had tried to cover up Jim Wilcox's role, he could well have lost his job. He'd said enough about the city council members who didn't like him to make her feel sure they would have seized the opportunity. And... he was thinking about *her*. Protecting *her*. She couldn't forget his vehement reaction to the suggestion she might still have to sell out and move.

So she met those espresso dark eyes and said, "Thank you. And now I should be getting home."

His expression darkened. "You could stay."

"I didn't bring a change of clothes, or a toothbrush, or... Besides, I bet you don't have an extra bed, do you?"

"You can have mine. I'll bunk down on the couch."

She shook her head. "That's silly when I have a perfectly good bed of my own not fifteen minutes away. Lucy said you'd drive me."

He wasn't happy about it, but he gave in. Lucy declined Nadia's offer to help clear the table and load the dishwasher, electing to stay behind. Nadia and she hugged, Lucy whispering, "Maybe we can talk to the others about how we can help him," before she stepped back.

With daylight lingering Nadia was able to look

around as Ben drove. She felt odd—as if she was seeing the town anew.

Byrum wasn't a beautiful town, but it had a solid, settled feel. She liked that a mall hadn't torn the heart out of downtown, that small businesses dominated. Despite some fast-food restaurants on the outskirts, the old-fashioned diners thrived. People knew what to expect from each other. For the Wilcoxes, that was probably a source of comfort.

Until things went very wrong. In her case, she had been a logical culprit because residents *hadn't* known her forever and ever. That hurt, especially when she thought back to her rosy belief going into the auction that she'd made so many friends, that maybe she would be more than the newcomer now.

Would they all turn on Jim Wilcox now? Drive him out of business because he'd proved himself untrustworthy, even though his returning the money proved that he *could* be trusted? Or would they rally around, because they really did know him and cared?

They were halfway to her apartment when Ben said, "Don't move away."

Startled by his demand, coming out of the blue—or had he been having similar thoughts?—Nadia turned to look at him. He kept his gaze on the road ahead, although she had no doubt he was aware of her scrutiny.

"I don't know. I can't think right now."

He was quiet for a good minute. Then, steering his SUV into her alley, he said, "Okay. We'll put off that discussion. Unless you're trying to think of a way to tell me it's not my business."

Without knowing it, she'd made this decision.

"I'm not." She grasped his hand, then made herself let it go so he could park.

He ordered her to stay put and did a look around before permitting her to cross the open alley to the back door of her building.

"It's still light out here," she protested.

"Sun still up or not, it's evening, which means the alley is deserted."

That not only silenced her, she took an uneasy glance to each side before unlocking the door. Somehow, Nadia wasn't surprised when he followed her in. Still, she said, "Isn't Lucy expecting—"

Ben backed her into a wall, cupped her face in his big hands and kissed her.

The strap of Nadia's purse slid from her shoulder, and she distantly heard a *clunk*. Pressed between his hard body and the wall, all she could do was respond to a kiss of blazing urgency.

CHAPTER EIGHTEEN

HE'D ALL BUT knocked her into a wall. His hands were shaking.

Out of control.

Nadia hadn't given any signal suggesting she was ready for more, but the certainty in her voice when she talked about moving away had slammed into him like a hammer blow. And knowing she would have sacrificed the dream that had brought her to Byrum for the sake of a sick little girl and her family—yeah, that hit him hard, too. She could still *care* about a man who had sneaked into her home to steal the money she'd worked so hard to raise, who had let her take the blame.

Any doubts Ben had had that he was in love with her had been erased tonight during dinner. If she asked him to back off—he'd do it, of course he would, but stopping now wouldn't be easy. If she'd been wearing a skirt, he would have lifted her and slid his fingers beneath the elastic of her panties. Stroked her, found out how wet she was, how ready—

The vivid picture of himself taking her right here, against the wall, clanged an alarm in his head. This would be their first time, not how he wanted it to be even if her eagerness matched his.

Eager? Desperate was more like it.

With a groan that rumbled up from his chest, he tore his mouth from hers and gulped for air, then rested his forehead against hers. "I want you," he said gutturally. His hips rocked without permission from above. He should be striving for romance, but had lost his vocabulary.

She made a little sound and tried to align her lips to his again.

Taking a deep breath, Ben made himself lift his head and look at her. Really look. What he saw was stunning vulnerability. Her mouth was swollen, her cheeks pink—with a blush, and maybe from the scrape of his evening beard. Dazed and dreamy eyes had his heart lurching.

"I'm sorry," he whispered.

A tiny smile curved her lips. "I think I'm insulted."

"I'm not sorry I kissed you. Just…that I was pushing."

One hand hadn't made it up to his neck. She flattened it now on his chest, then began slow circles. When her fingertips found his nipple, his body jerked.

"I'm not sorry you kissed me, either," Nadia murmured. "I'm sorry you stopped."

He squeezed her hip, loving the lush flesh, even as he confessed bluntly, "I've reached my limit if we're not going upstairs."

"I... I'd like that, if..."

He didn't give her a chance to say if what. Instead he kissed her, hard and hungry, before hustling her to the door that opened to the staircase. When they got there, she stared at it for a moment as if her comprehension wasn't any sharper than his, then said, "Um, my keys."

Well, crap—where was her purse? Ben spotted it on the floor down the hall, and remembered hearing when she dropped it. Highly motivated, he moved fast.

Nadia snatched her bag from him and had the door open within seconds. Following on her heels, he locked behind them, then pursued her up the stairs. She wore thin, wrinkled linen pants that still let him drink in the sexiest ass he'd ever seen. Just a little jiggle. With the view, he would have happily climbed ten flights of stairs.

Or not. Getting there soon, and to a bed, would be better.

In her apartment, she cast a shy look over her shoulder, removed her shoes, let her purse fall to the sofa and walked straight through to her bedroom. Beside her bed, she stalled, as if unsure what she should do.

Ben gently turned her to face him. Brain hazed, desire so sharp it hurt, he could have laid her back, ripped off those pants and buried himself in her.

Instead, he found the self-control to look into her beautiful eyes and stroke her cheeks with his knuckles. This wasn't just sex, he reminded himself. It was love, even if she didn't know it yet.

Unless he was deluding himself, but he didn't think so.

THE TENDERNESS IN Ben's touch, in his eyes, settled Nadia's nerves. This wasn't wrong, or too soon, or any of the things she'd been fearing. He wouldn't turn on her again. She didn't believe that. There'd been so many times already when he had stood at her back, a hand resting on her as if to say, *I'm here.* She had no doubt he'd been staring down her opponents at the same time. And, while she might never get over her reaction to the sight of a gun, she knew Ben would never use the one he carried for anything but the right reasons.

All her doubts evaporated. All Nadia could think was how much she'd been wanting to touch him. To see his bare chest. To explore his fascinating body.

She skimmed her fingertips over his rough jaw, then down his neck, corded with tension. When she reached for the hem of his shirt and tugged, Ben bent and let her yank it over his head.

A throaty sound of pleasure escaped her, heat-ing his eyes. Nadia splayed her hands on that beautiful chest, testing the texture of his hair— springy and surprisingly soft—the play of muscles that tightened and jumped at her touch, the hard layer of muscles protecting his belly. All Ben did was watch with burning eyes as she explored, pressing nibbling little kisses to his chest as her hands moved on to his back. More lean, powerful muscles, pads protecting his spine, the sharp edges of his shoulder blades.

"You have the most beautiful body," she whispered.

"Not like yours."

Ben groaned, his hands a blur as he stripped off her shirt. Unfortunately, trying to lift both arms to help pulled a groan from her, a pained one.

"I forgot," he whispered. "How could I forget?" He made her turn so he could check the white gauze in back, too. "No bleeding," he said, as if to himself.

"No, it's a little sore, that's all." More than a little, but Nadia's awareness of that kind of pain was very distant right now. If he decided he needed to back off, she didn't know what she'd do. Cry? Clobber him?

At last, he cupped her breasts in his hands, his thumbs sliding over the white cotton of her bra, unerringly finding nipples that budded at his touch. His expression now was the furthest thing from worried.

Her fingers flexed involuntarily on his back even as she looked down at herself. "I wish I'd worn something prettier for you. But it's so hot, and—"

"I'm more interested in what's underneath." His voice was all gravel, as if he was on the edge of control. And yes his hands had a faint tremor, but that didn't prevent him from unfastening her bra with a single flick of those fingers. He swept it away, and then stared.

Nobody had ever looked at her that way, with wonder and desire that slashed color across his cheeks. She whimpered, and finally grabbed one of his hands and put it on her breast. And then he was kneading both, and his mouth had captured hers again. He kissed her as if starved for her, as if he'd never get enough. His tongue thrust in erotic mimicry of what he wanted to do to her—what he *intended* to do.

They all but fell on the bed, although he took their weight on his shoulder. Always protective. The frame creaked. He tore his mouth away so he could kiss and suckle her breasts until her hips rose and fell in desperate need. She wanted him inside her; she wanted to be inside his skin. She melted even as she grabbed him, probably clawed him, wriggled until his thigh pressed between her legs and she could push up against him.

"Please, please, please." That had to be her chanting the plea. Being embarrassed never occurred to her.

Ben reared up and fumbled with the button at her waist even as she struggled with his. He ripped her pants down, panties going with them, before she could get her fingers on his zipper.

On his feet, he backed away from the bed, dark eyes eating her up, and sat on the rocker by the window long enough to untie his athletic shoes, kick them off and send his socks flying.

Nadia couldn't just lie here anymore. She rose to her knees. "Come closer."

The hot Missouri sun had nothing on his blistering gaze. He took the step that brought him to the bedside. While she bit her lip and worked carefully at his zipper, Ben took his wallet from his back pocket and removed a couple of packets. In a sensible corner of her mind, she thought, *Oh, thank goodness.* She was on birth control, but still had always insisted on a condom, too. But tonight, if he hadn't brought one...she wouldn't have given a second thought to her usual caution.

The instant she had the zipper down, Ben shed his jeans and navy knit boxers.

It was Nadia's turn to stare. When she reached out and ran a fingertip down his penis, it jerked and Ben made a pained sound.

He also stepped back again. "I'm on the edge,"

he said hoarsely. "Let me—" Now his hands really were shaking, but he got the condom on.

The next thing she knew, she was flat on her back, Ben's weight pressing her into the mattress. Her legs parted to accept him, and she answered his ravenous kiss with her own hunger. On the edge or not, he took his time, stroking, kneading, until his fingers slid between her legs and he stoked her liquid fire. And finally, finally, he was there, pushing inside, still holding back as he watched her face.

"Yes," she said, trying to pull him deeper. He responded by driving deep, pulling back, doing it again, until they found a rhythm so *right*, it had her clutching him and making incoherent noises, while Ben's chest vibrated with a groan that seemed to go on forever. He never looked away from her face. Nadia imploded with shocking speed, him right behind her, teeth gritted, head bowed back.

Somehow he kept his weight on his elbows. The stunned expression on his face matched what she felt.

SHE MUST HAVE been drowsing, but Nadia roused when Ben got up and went to the living room. Voice low, he talked briefly to someone. Lucy, of course. Who would now know he was spending the night in Nadia's bed.

The idea was a little embarrassing, but she sus-

pected Lucy had already been very aware that
something was going on between her and Ben.
She had maybe even encouraged it.

When he slipped back into bed and found
Nadia awake, he made love to her again, starting
slow and sweet, discovering what pleased her,
letting her indulge herself as she learned what
pleased him, too. But slow became intense, even
frantic, driving them both to pleasure and a sense
of closeness that was completely new to her.

And always, always, he remained conscious
of her wounds and protected her.

When she awakened the next time, sunlight
poured in. The temperature was already rising in
the room. Not that she and Ben had ever pulled a
cover over themselves. He was still sound asleep.

Nadia didn't move for a long time, savoring
the beat of his heart beneath her hand, the curve
of his shoulder providing a pillow for her head,
the utter relaxation on a face too often taut and
guarded. But temptation beckoned, and she let
her hand stray. Not more than a minute passed
before his dark lashes lifted and a smile tugged
at his mouth.

"You're an early bird," he said in a voice still
roughened by sleep.

"I don't actually think it's early." She hadn't
looked at the clock yet, but the angle of the sun
suggested they had slept in. And why not? It was
Sunday. She'd hardly have to see a soul until

Tuesday morning, by which time everyone in Henness County who followed the news or belonged to a gossip network would know who had taken the money and why—and that it had been returned. That *she* hadn't had anything to do with it. She let herself feel giddy, uncomplicated relief, if only for right now.

This time, she teased and played until Ben's entire body vibrated and he flipped her to her back. And then he swore.

"I only had two condoms."

"Don't stop." She lifted her hips until he was nudging her again. "You can't."

"Nadia." He sounded desperate.

"It's okay." Forming words was almost beyond her. "I'm on birth control."

He grabbed her hips and plunged deep. Morning laziness became raw need.

By the time she lay panting atop him, Nadia wished they never had to leave this bed. She suspected Ben felt the same. His hands roved with astonishing tenderness, as if she was the same miracle to him that he was to her.

But finally he sighed. "It may be Sunday, but I have things I need to do."

They took turns showering. To shave, Ben used a small, plastic razor she offered, muttering a curse or two as he nicked himself. Both dressed; Nadia scrambled eggs while he made toast and poured the coffee.

Once they were finished, she asked what he could accomplish on a Sunday.

"Count the money and be sure it really is all there. Let the prosecuting attorney know. Give the mayor a heads-up. Prepare a statement, although I may not issue it until Monday. Depends on how successful I am talking to people today."

"Will you let me know about the money? And...when you'll be making a statement?"

Ben's face softened and he reached across the table for her hand. "I will. If you don't object, once we count the money, I'll put it back in a locker until tomorrow."

Nadia shuddered. No, she didn't want it here in her apartment ever again.

"I'll return it to you tomorrow morning," Ben added.

That made her twitch. "Maybe it would be better if you took it right to the aid organization."

"You're not opening on Mondays anymore, are you? Once I confirm the money is all there, you can give the good news to Bill Jarvis and have him meet us tomorrow morning at whatever bank they're using."

"Yes." She relaxed. Except... "Should we wait until you've made the statement?"

"Maybe." He frowned. "That might be better. I don't want a garbled story getting out."

With a lingering kiss and caution to be careful, Ben took off.

Now alone, Nadia wished she wasn't, that she, too, had somewhere she needed to be. Instead… what *was* she going to do today, besides wonder how her detractors would react to the news?

Quilt, she decided. She wasn't far from done with the one in the frame downstairs. She might even finish it today.

She did work, but also found herself glancing at the clock with absurd regularity, frustrated by how slowly the minute hand moved. A tiny jerk forward now and again wasn't nearly enough.

When her phone rang after a seeming eternity, she pounced on it. "Ben?"

"Are you home? If so, do you mind if I come by?"

"Yes. Hurry!"

His chuckle warmed her.

When he pulled up in front, Nadia unlocked the door and had it open by the time he crossed the sidewalk. He had driven his own SUV, but wore a crisp blue uniform with badge.

"You went home and changed," she said in surprise.

"I didn't think I should wear jeans and a T-shirt that spent the night on the floor when I met with His Honor. Besides, I rarely appear at the station in civvies."

Nadia took a deep breath. "Was the money all there?"

"Every penny, plus a few."

"What?"

"Someone miscounted. You have an extra eleven dollars and sixty-seven cents. We counted twice."

"Come on in back. I've been quilting."

She resumed her seat, but didn't reach for her thimble or needle. She just waited as he pulled up a chair.

"Those weren't easy conversations," Ben said. "Both the mayor and the prosecuting attorney have known Jim for years."

She only nodded.

"Neither had heard about Jim's daughter, though," Ben continued. "He tripped over his pride. If he'd been more open about what was happening, I'm guessing the community would have come together for the family. They were both more sympathetic than I am to Jim for not coming forward sooner. *And* planning the theft well in advance. Impulse, that's easier to forgive."

"He did bring the money back."

Ben's mouth twisted. "That's damned unusual— I'll give you that."

"Do you think the prosecutor will go easy on him?"

"No question. I called Jim, told him he needs to find an attorney, and he said he already has. His wife pushed him. So I'll be out of this soon.

Bob and I sat down together and roughed out a statement."

Bob? Oh. The mayor. Bob Finzel. She'd seen his name in the paper often enough.

"I'll announce that an arrest has been made because the man who took it deeply regrets his actions and returned every penny. I have to name him." Ben's regret colored his voice. "I'll say that we can't condone his criminal behavior, but do feel he redeemed himself in bringing back the money and is unlikely to offend again. That Ms. Markovic, whose reputation has suffered from unwarranted suspicion and accusation, is relieved to have her name cleared but wouldn't have pressed charges if given a choice. She's deeply concerned for Mr. Wilcox's daughter, undergoing treatment for childhood leukemia." He paused. "I'll delete that part if you'd prefer."

"No, I like it."

"And in conclusion—" he deepened his voice and gave her a wry grin "—we're very pleased to be able to hand over the money to the aid organization for which it was intended, etcetera, etcetera."

"So…it's over, for everyone but Jim and his family." She felt oddly numb.

"Yeah."

"If only he were Amish."

Ben grunted. "Hospital bills would be paid,

church members would be sitting with his daughter, babysitting his son, providing meals so his wife didn't have to cook, and he'd never have fallen behind on his mortgage."

Nadia frowned, thinking. "He must have a church."

"Yeah, and I'm sure a collection will be taken up for his family, but the total will be a drop in the bucket. In a community this size, people would have to dig deep in their pockets to cover the kind of medical bills showing up in his mailbox. A lot of those people will be thinking about how tight their budgets are and how *they're* still paying for insurance, so why didn't he?"

Maybe no jail time wasn't that big a favor, Nadia realized, depressed. It was like throwing a drowning man a life ring with no attached rope. He might not go under right away, but nobody would pull him in, either.

"Can I tell people now?"

Ben glanced at his watch. "The press conference is scheduled for one o'clock. So yes, I don't see any reason you can't contact anyone you please." He raised his eyebrows. "Say, Allison Edgerton, or Julie Baird."

"Neither of them deserves a minute of my time. I was mostly thinking of Colleen, and then I can drive out to see Hannah and— Oh, shoot, it's Sunday. Is it church Sunday?"

He frowned. "I've lost track."

Nadia touched his hand. "Thank you. For caring about me and still doing your best for him."

"Even cops can be decent human beings, you know."

He didn't sound offended, but she jumped to her feet and kissed him anyway. "I know," she said softly. "I even know the negotiator and SWAT officers in Colorado Springs thought they were doing the right thing. I shouldn't blame them."

When she straightened, he grabbed her hands. "We have to make hard decisions too often," he said, eyes intent. "It's not always about whether to shoot or not. In law enforcement, the most minor actions or inactions can have deadly consequences."

Was that a warning? Maybe it was one she needed to hear, if they were to be involved. She couldn't let her own experiences color her reaction when he told her about something that happened. Or when some small-minded or embittered person did.

"I need to go." He grimaced as he got to his feet. "Gotta do my favorite part of the job."

"Come on," she teased. "Most people love to see themselves on television."

Ben grunted his opinion of that. "You going to stay here?"

"I think so. I don't want to intrude even if the Amish don't have church today. But I will call Colleen and some of the other women who have been so nice."

He tugged her into his arms. "You need to do some prep, too. The minute I step away from the podium, your phone will start ringing, so prepare a short statement of your own, then stick to it."

"Oh, no."

He grinned. "Oh, yes. News outlets will all want a comment from you."

She made a face. "Do I have to talk to Dave Rutledge?"

Ben chuckled and kissed her cheek. "Console yourself that he's having to eat his words. Be *extra* sweet."

"Oh, fun."

"And be careful." All trace of his amusement was gone. "Don't open the door to anyone but a good friend. I'd rather you don't drive out to the Yoders or anywhere else, not yet. We still don't know what was behind the shooting."

"If it had to do with the money—"

"You'd be safe after word gets out."

She searched his face. "But you don't think I will be."

"No. Spitting on you, that's one thing. Being willing to kill, that's different."

Her stomach took a big swoop, or maybe it was her heart. This morning's giddy relief? Premature.
Somebody wants to kill me.
And she couldn't afford to forget that.

CHAPTER NINETEEN

PROVING THE EFFECTIVENESS of the Amish grapevine, Hannah dashed into the shop Tuesday morning and exclaimed, "I am so glad for you! You must be relieved, *ja*?"

Nadia looked up from the fabric bolt she was returning to a row. "You already know?" Then she laughed. "Of course you do. And yes, I'm relieved. But also…sad."

Hannah nodded. "Mr. Wilcox has done work for many of us, too. So kind, he is. People are always saying he doesn't ask enough money, not when he has to drive so far out into the country."

"He put my new locks in, too." Nadia hesitated. "And the locks for Mrs. Jefferson, of course. You know he kept a key? That's how he got in to take the money."

"It's true, he brought it all back?"

"And a few extra dollars. Either a cashier miscounted, or somebody made a small, last minute donation at the auction. Ben—Chief Slater—and I met Bill Jarvis yesterday at the bank. The money is safely deposited, and he can start distributing it."

"*Gut*. Good. But sad, too. To think of his little girl so sick."

"Yes. Ben thinks no one will trust him again, after he stole, so I don't know what he and his family will do."

"That should not be," Hannah insisted.

"No." Nadia told her what Ben said, about Jim's pride keeping him from letting people know he needed help. "He and his wife were having trouble keeping up with bills, so he quit paying for medical insurance."

"I hear all the time that people pay for insurance, but it doesn't always take care of them."

"That's true, but mostly for people who didn't read carefully what the insurance would pay out for and what it wouldn't. Like all those farmers, who thought their homeowners' insurance would rebuild their houses, but their policies didn't cover tornado damage." Nadia went to the front door and flipped the sign to Open. "It will be interesting to see who stops by today." She wouldn't be surprised if nobody who had shunned her ever offered an apology. Doing so would be awkward, uncomfortable on both sides. Avoiding her would be easier.

And truthfully, Nadia hadn't decided how she'd respond to anyone who *did* apologize. If she were Amish, of course, that wouldn't even be a question. Forgiveness would come naturally, intrinsic to her faith.

So if she admired their willingness to offer genuine forgiveness without hesitation, shouldn't she do the same? Or was holding on to anger more satisfying?

She was a teeny bit disturbed to discover she wasn't sure, which meant she wasn't as good a person as she'd like to think she was.

The bell on the door tinkled, and she braced herself. *Don't make me have to decide now.*

Jennifer Bronske walked in.

Nadia glanced at Hannah, who smiled gently at her, as if it hadn't occurred to her that Nadia's response to people like Jennifer would be anything but generous.

Of course, Jennifer might have no intention of apologizing.

Nadia managed a pleasant smile. "Jennifer." Oh, how she wanted to say, *What a surprise to see you.* But snide was not the way to regain friends and customers.

Jennifer came directly to her, stopping on the other side of the counter. "I know how inadequate this is, but I'm here to tell you how sorry I am that I jumped to conclusions. I owe you that much."

Nadia's anger quivered and dissolved. She shook her head. "You don't owe me anything. You felt betrayed. I understood that. I won't deny that it hurt to have so many women I'd started to believe might be friends decide I had to be guilty. But there are plenty of con artists out there, and I could have been one of them. You really hadn't known me long." She smiled weakly. "At least you didn't join the demonstration out front."

Usually composed, Jennifer flushed with hot color. She held herself stiffly. "After that man spit on you and you handed me the money from the quilt, I saw your expression. I...think I knew then. I almost said I was sorry, but..." Her one-shouldered shrug spoke of hesitation and doubts.

"I appreciate you saying this." Nadia tried to project sincerity. "I know it's hard to do. As far as I'm concerned, the whole episode is forgotten." From somewhere inside, she found the ability to offer a warm smile. "I'll hope to see you in here again. In fact, I'd love it if you'd consider teaching a class on appliqué techniques sometime. I don't know anyone who does it better. You may have noticed that the idea of doing teeny, tiny leaves or cherries on a tree, or, heaven forbid, a bird's beak gives me hives."

Jennifer actually laughed. "I had noticed. Not many people seem to enjoy that kind of finicky handwork. If you think there are enough to fill a class, I'd be glad to teach one."

"Excellent! I'm putting together a schedule for August. Or if you have a vacation planned, we could do it in September."

"Either would be fine. Just give me a call when you have dates that might work. Now, if you'll excuse me." She gave Hannah a vague smile, Nadia a still embarrassed one, and left.

The moment the door closed behind her, Nadia sighed. "I really had to bite my tongue."

"Forgiveness is never easy." Seeing Nadia's expression, Hannah chuckled. "No, not even for us! We get mad, too, you know. I have had to pretend once or twice." The humor in her eyes suggested that was an understatement. "But I know I *should* forgive," she went on, "so I say the right words, and one day I know I mean them."

"That makes me feel a little better." Nadia wrinkled her nose. "Jennifer was a good one to start with, because she didn't do or say anything that bad."

"Not like that Allison."

"Julie Baird, too," Nadia admitted. "She didn't say anything terrible, either, but we'd spent a lot of time together planning the auction. And yet, the very second I told her about the money disappearing, I could tell she blamed me. She didn't even hesitate. That really stung. I don't think I'd have lasted if it hadn't been for people like you and Katie-Ann and Ruth and Colleen."

In the course of the day, three other women came into the store to apologize. Having already accepted one graciously gave Nadia a template for responding to more apologies. Ellen Shaw's was her favorite. She marched in looking militant to say, "You were so dignified that day, and I was such a bitch." Nadia wouldn't have guessed the word was in Ellen's vocabulary. Ellen even had the guts to ask if she could bring quilts again for Nadia to sell. Of course, Nadia agreed. Aside from appreciating the apology, there was the old saying about not cutting off your nose to spite your face.

The smile was cracking by the time Ben arrived to take her to his house for dinner again.

He kissed her softly. "The worst is over."

"Maybe."

Neither of them talked about the other threat she still faced, the one that had her scared to carry a bag of trash out to the Dumpster or drive alone anywhere. How long could she go on this way? What if two weeks from now, a month from now, nothing else had happened? The shot might have been fired by someone mad about the auction money…or the person who hated her might be really patient.

Nadia always came back to the *why*. Had she done something offensive? Seen something she shouldn't have? But what? Thinking about it made her head ache.

Midafternoon Wednesday, Colleen burst in, excited because within twenty-four hours of the crowdfunding appeal going up, donations had begun pouring in. "It's amazing!" she crowed. "Two separate people gave five thousand dollars each! I don't know how fast the response tails off, but if it lasts even for a week or two, we might be able to give the Hixsons a good start on rebuilding."

"Would it be possible to organize a community barn raising?" Nadia asked. "Well, and house raising, too? Not having to pay contractors would save a bunch."

Hannah's face lit. "I'll talk to *Daad* and Jacob. If they agree, we can go to the bishop and ask for the members of our church district to join in. I think that not so many *Englischers* know *how* to build a barn. They might need our help."

Colleen hugged her. "They will, because you're right. But I'll bet a lot of the other farmers within a several-county radius would come, too. They may need the same help someday."

"And then we could post photos of what the donations have accomplished, along with an appeal for another family who lost their home, too," Nadia suggested.

Ben stopped by in the middle of their excited plotting, shook his head and said, "I guess I don't need to worry about you being alone here," and left.

Just seeing him, even for a few minutes at a time, lifted her spirits.

BEN DIDN'T LIKE his constant awareness of the danger to Nadia. Back at the station, he propped his feet on his desk. His phone momentarily silent, he brooded. When would the next strike come?

Living here, he'd seen tornadoes from a distance. This felt too much like that. He imagined one approaching, the sky a sickening yellowish green, the dark, spinning monster's path unpredictable. Worse, he put himself in Leonard Hixson's head, when he bellowed his son's name over and over, finally realizing the boy wouldn't make it to shelter. Closing and latching that door, listening to the roar, offering up house, barn, anything the monster wanted, if only it would pass by the terrified kid and his dog.

Ben rubbed both hands over his face. Every time his damn phone rang lately, he expected the caller to be either Nadia or a first responder, letting him know she'd been attacked again. If she died…

He couldn't let himself think that way. She was being careful, not being stupid enough to be rebellious. Unless she was slipping out when he was unaware, she hadn't yet stepped out of her building alone. She should be safe there. Daytime, the risk of being seen and recognized would be too great for a gunman to, say, walk right into the fabric store and gun her down. The streets were busy, A Stitch in Time surrounded by other businesses.

Breaking in at night…that would be harder,

but not impossible. It wouldn't happen quietly, though. The chair she was still bracing beneath the doorknob at the foot of the stairs was low-tech, but it would be a surprise to an intruder, and probably a noisy one. She'd have time to call for help, maybe blockade herself in the bedroom.

In the next days, he took to stopping by her store often, making his visits at unpredictable intervals, even on days when they planned to get together for dinner. That was just about every night. Lucy usually cooked. Either he'd pick Nadia up, or he and Lucy would bring the meal to her place. Those times, he didn't even get a serious good-night kiss, but he liked to see the growing friendship between the two women. They both needed the connection. What he didn't like was leaving Nadia alone. So far, she had stubbornly refused to stay at his house, either putting him out of his bed or sleeping with him across the hall from his sister's room.

This morning, Lucy had displayed her finished quilt for him. These past weeks, he'd become enough of a connoisseur to see that the stitches weren't as tiny as Nadia was putting in the quilt in the frame at the back of her shop, or on some of the quilts displayed on the walls there, but they weren't far off. Lucy pointed out her mistakes, then told him she intended to start another one right away. Not bed-size yet, but her third quilt would be. The firm way she said that was just another sign of her growing confidence.

She hadn't said a word about when she intended to leave, and that made him uneasy. Just yesterday, he had asked Nadia if she'd seen Lucy with Jacob Yoder again.

Her hesitation was answer enough.

He had growled, *That's what I thought.*

She had been cutting out fabric at the time, but the rotary cutter went still. Nadia didn't look at him. *You'd rather she wasn't hanging out here so much, wouldn't you?*

His *Don't be ridiculous* was probably too brusque, and not a 100 percent honest. What if somebody came after Nadia again, and Lucy was injured, too? Or instead? Or was so traumatized, all the progress she'd made was erased?

But he had to believe that Nadia was safer when somebody was with her. Alone, that was when she became vulnerable.

Identifying the would-be killer was the only way to ensure her safety. His investigation into the shooting had gone dead in the water, which made him more than a little unhappy. All he had to go on was a dyed blond hair that might or might not be from the shooter, and a whopping big diamond that logic said could have lain there beneath the Dumpster for days and had nothing to do with the assailant. Ben just didn't believe it. Given the value of the earring, it didn't make sense that the woman who'd lost it wouldn't be searching. Plus, wasn't an alley an unlikely place to have an earring happen to fall off? Nobody who lived or worked on the block had claimed it. The alley didn't see much foot traffic. Why would it, when the nearby street had wide sidewalks, crosswalks and attractive shop windows?

Now, a woman crouched in the narrow space between Dumpster and car bumper, sighting in the dark down the barrel of a rifle, shooting, maybe losing her balance when she scrambled away...*she* could have jarred the earring loose with the butt of the rifle or even her shoulder.

Women were less likely than men to use a gun even when they did kill. That said, plenty of women around here were as handy with a hunting rifle as their husbands, brothers and fathers were.

He grumbled under his breath. This was getting him nowhere. He'd grill Nadia again this evening. Somewhere in her head was the answer. Sooner or later, he'd ask the right question.

"I SAW A Square-in-Square pattern that I really liked," Lucy said, taking the rinsed casserole dish from Nadia and drying it. "I love the idea of using colors in new ways, but this time I want to leave open blocks so I can experiment with fancier hand quilting."

"That sounds like a good idea, but I can't picture the pattern." Nadia let the water drain from the sink and dried her hands. "Was it in one of my books?"

"Uh-huh. I think I can put my hands right on it."

"Why don't we go look for it right now?" With her hip, Nadia nudged Ben, who hadn't seemed crushed when his offer to help clean up had been rebuffed. "Unless your brother is itching to get home."

Sitting at the table, he looked up from his phone. "No hurry." His gaze drifted over her in a way that warmed her skin as it went. The impact when his eyes met hers had her wishing this was one of the evenings when he drove her home and stayed for a couple of hours—or all night. "Shades drawn down there?" he asked.

Dose of reality, thank you. "Yes, I let down the ones in front every day when I close now. And I never raise the blinds in the back room." The alley view wouldn't exactly enhance the colorful, feminine world she had created in her store.

"Okay." He smiled at his sister. "I'll stay here, if you'll forgive me for not coming along to share my opinion."

She kissed his cheek. "I think I can live without it. Do you remember what you said when I showed you the fabrics I chose for the first quilt?"

He was smart enough to look wary. "Ah...no."

"Direct quote—'Those don't really go together, do they?'"

Nadia laughed. "Remind me never to consult him."

Downstairs, Lucy began in front by browsing the books for sale, some displayed face out, some spine out. "I know it was a hardback. Country something…" Her face cleared. "Wait, it might have been in back."

Nadia had a good selection of books available for sale, but she kept the larger library in the back room, available for customers and students to browse or even borrow. She could think of at least a couple of books with *country* in the title that were out here, however, so she scanned for them as Lucy turned on the light in the back room and started for the shelves.

The explosive *crack* of a gunshot and the sound of shattering glass came at the same time.

"Lucy!" Nadia screamed.

Furniture scraped on the floor, as if Lucy had stumbled against it. Then came the thud of a falling body. Within seconds, Ben thundered down the stairs.

Horror filled her. Once the light came on in here, Lucy must have appeared as a dark silhouette through the filmy blinds. Nadia bent low and started into the back room.

Crack.

Something splintered behind her even as she

fell to her hands and knees. She crawled toward Lucy, who lay unmoving on the floor, an overturned chair half on top of her.

THE FIRST GUNSHOT acted like a starter's pistol. Ben tore down the stairs and sprinted for the back door, even though he desperately wanted to go to Nadia and Lucy. But Lucy and he had come separately, him straight from work, and since he'd parked in front, the shooter might not know he was here at all.

He'd have given a lot to be wearing a vest, but turned the dead bolt and flung open the door anyway. He went through fast, gun in his hand, leaping to the side off the concrete pad.

"Police! Put your weapon down. Now!"

A scrape of gravel, a metallic clatter and running footsteps.

He wouldn't shoot somebody in the back. But if that had been a rifle, and he thought it was, he had the advantage now. He sprinted after the dark figure.

THIS WAS WORSE than being shot herself. It felt like a nightmare, as if the monster who still haunted her dreams was pacing just out of sight and would appear any moment to make sure none of them had moved, that they were really dead.

No, no, no. This was different. *He* was dead

and hadn't come back. *It's Lucy. No children. No staring eyes.*

But it shouldn't be Lucy. *I was the target*, she thought, even as she carefully rolled the other woman enough to see the bloody front of her shirt. Bone white, Lucy's face had a familiar slackness to it, a lock of hair hanging over her open mouth. She looked dead.

No, she was breathing. *Not dead.*

Having heard Ben go out the back door and start yelling, Nadia strained to hear more. *Don't let him be shot, too, please, not him. I can't bear it.* She tore open Lucy's shirt, finding a wound high on her shoulder.

Then she sank back on her heels. Why was Lucy unconscious? Shock? No, smoothing back her hair, Nadia saw more blood. A bullet graze? But looking around, she spotted the smear of blood on the edge of the table, which along with the chair had been pushed askew. Lucy had hit it as she went down, knocked herself unconscious. Oh, thank God.

She crawled back toward the doorway. She had to get to the store phone to call 911.

Another gunshot rang out from the alley, farther away, and Nadia's heart skipped a beat. Ben!

ALMOST TO THE CORNER, the dark figure slowed enough to swing the rifle around and take a shot.

It went wild, of course. Ben used the chance to gain ground. His longer legs ate up the distance.

He launched himself and they crashed down, skidding on gravel and pavement. The minute he gripped one wrist, he knew this was a woman. She fought wildly, with wiry strength, bucking and screaming, but she'd come down atop her rifle, and Ben used his weight and greater size to keep her flat.

He managed to holster his gun with one hand. But, damn it, he didn't carry cuffs. He hoped like hell somebody had called 911, because he'd left his phone on the table upstairs.

He tried not to think about Nadia or Lucy.

At last he got his hand on the woman's other arm. He yanked both behind her and pushed himself up, one knee planted on her back. "Fighting won't get you anywhere," he growled. "You are under arrest."

Distant siren.

The streetlight was adequate for him to see that she wore a black hooded sweatshirt. The back of his hand had brushed her breast during the struggle, verifying that he was holding a woman captive, not a small man or teenager. The *why* was still a mystery—but his gut told him that once he could free a hand to yank off the hood, he'd see bleached-blond hair.

He recited her Miranda rights even as he prayed she hadn't succeeded in killing either of the women he loved.

CHAPTER TWENTY

"CORINNE BISSETT." SITTING in a small waiting room at the hospital, Nadia gaped at Ben, who had just joined her. "But…that's the woman I bought the building from."

"Mrs. Jefferson's heir," he agreed. He had a secure hold on her hand, which he needed. His fear for her and Lucy had settled to a simmer, but whatever his eyes told him, he needed the contact to help him believe Nadia, at least, was safe. Unhurt.

Lucy had been taken right into surgery, but she had regained consciousness by the time the ambulance reached the hospital. That helped when he called his parents to tell them their already fragile daughter had been shot. They were catching a red-eye to Saint Louis and would be here by morning. He wasn't thrilled, but understood.

"I have to see her myself," his mother had declared, anxiety threading her voice.

Now he and Nadia were waiting while the surgeon dug out the bullet.

Her expression held only perplexity. "That doesn't make any sense."

"I have to believe it has something to do with her aunt's death." The theft hadn't, as it turned out, but these attempts on Nadia's life...no other possibility made sense.

Nadia's forehead stayed crinkled. "But...I never even met her when I was buying the building. And that was months after the murder."

"Did she ever stop by to say hello?" he asked.

Nadia shook her head, but her expression changed. "Actually, I did finally meet her by chance...oh, not that long ago. I told you, didn't I?"

"No." He could all but hear the *ping*. "When?"

Her forehead crinkled. "I think it was the week after the auction. I mentioned Allison Edgerton cornering me at the store, right?" When he nodded, she said, "Apparently Corinne was right behind me and overheard. She commiserated and——" Her voice slowed. "Well, I recognized her."

"From?"

"She and I had met, oh, months before I even considered Byrum. I'd flown to Missouri to check out half a dozen possible towns. In a couple places, fabric stores were up for sale, and in the others——" She shook her head. "It doesn't matter. That day at the grocery store, it took me a minute to recognize her, because her hair wasn't blond the first time I saw her, but then it came to me. We were in Trenton. This café was really full, and she was nice enough to tell me I could sit at her table. We chatted while we ate, just, 'oh, are you a tourist' kind of stuff. You know."

But they'd talked long enough for Nadia to recognize Corinne…how much later?

"When was this?" he asked.

"It was over a year ago."

She had confirmed what his intuition was telling him. Corinne's alibi for her aunt's death had always bothered him. A woman who, from all reports, rarely traveled, just happening to visit the Big Apple the weekend her aunt was murdered. But her friends had insisted she was with them, and the airline had confirmed her flights.

Seeing his expression, Nadia said, "I kept a, well, sort of a diary. Notes about possibilities I spotted online, my trips to scout them out—that kind of thing. I'd have to look at it to tell you exactly when I was in Trenton."

Had Corinne *driven* back and forth from New York? Or, now that he knew where to look, would he be able to prove she'd taken a bus or train to get home for a day or two? Trenton made a nice stopover—just far enough away from Byrum, she'd be unlikely to run into anyone she knew, but also an easy drive. Into town, push aunt down the stairs, confirm she was dead, out of town.

"You think…?" Nadia said.

"I do think."

"So…if we hadn't happened to meet in the store that day…"

Ben shook his head. "You'd have met another time. This isn't that big a town. She had a shock running into you and finding out that, of all people in the world, *you* were the one who bought her aunt's building and business. But I imagine it was the theft that sent her into panic mode. I was investigating you, asking a lot of questions. I'd made it plain I wouldn't give up on her aunt's death. Because you bought that building, there was a connection. She had to know that if you mentioned her even in passing, I'd jump on it."

"That's it, then." Nadia sounded numb now. "She tried to kill me, an almost complete stranger, on the chance that I might blow her alibi."

"I'm afraid so."

Misery apparent, Nadia pulled back a little, even tugging at her hand, but he didn't let go.

"I'm sorry. I mean, about Lucy. You were right. She *should* have stayed away from me."

This was probably the strangest of times for him to feel a smile forming, but he couldn't seem to stop it. "You know what she said to me, when they were wheeling her from the ER to surgery?"

Eyes big and luminous, Nadia shook her head. She'd hung back when he walked beside his sister down the hall to the elevator. Ignoring the orderly pushing the bed, Lucy had grabbed his hand. Her eyes had been doing whirligigs—Ben guessed they'd already given her a painkiller—but she had still managed to project fierce determination.

"Lucy told me not to dare blame you. She also said—" his voice thickened "—that she was glad you hadn't gotten shot again."

He didn't tell Nadia that the last thing his sister had mumbled was, "Only fair to spread it around."

"I still feel—"

"Don't." Ben pulled until she was leaning against him, her head resting on his chest. With the wooden arm of the chair denting his ribs and probably hers, too, the embrace wouldn't last long. But he had to hold her. He'd have lifted her onto his lap if the chance of someone walking in on them hadn't been so good.

Nadia said something he didn't catch. He rubbed his cheek against her already disordered hair. "What?"

"She's the best friend I've made here. I wish she didn't have to go home."

That let him ease his grip. He nuzzled her temple. "I kind of doubt she has any intention of leaving Byrum."

Nadia lifted her head. "But you don't want her to stay."

"I'd love to have her live here. My fear is that the

Amish were the draw for her, and that she might make some decisions for the wrong reasons."

"I really don't think…"

"I don't, either." He smiled at her. "Quit worrying."

Her eyes shimmered, and for a moment he was afraid she'd cry, but instead she said, "It wouldn't be the end of the world if she and Jacob hooked up, would it?"

Ben laughed. "Do you think that's how he'd put it? *Hey, babe, wanna hook up?*"

Nadia giggled—just as Ben heard a soft footfall. The graying surgeon in his green scrubs, face mask pushed below his chin, stepped into the small room.

"Lucy is in recovery," he said briskly. "We had no difficulty getting the bullet out, and the damage is less than we feared. I'll be surprised if she isn't ready to go home tomorrow, the next day at the latest. Oh—I saved the bullet for you."

The bullets from Nadia's shooting were already in the evidence room. Ben had no doubt that they would match up with the Marlin Model 336 hunting rifle Corinne had carried. The shell casings she hadn't had a chance to pick up tonight might well have her fingerprints on them, too.

"Thanks," he said huskily. "When can we see her?"

"I'd suggest tomorrow morning. Sleep is what she needs."

Ben hesitated, but finally nodded. He felt drained himself. "You have my number."

"Yes." The surgeon nodded at both of them and strode away.

After a moment, Nadia said, "I'm glad we didn't have the same surgeon. He'd be really wondering about us right now."

Ben's chuckle left him feeling loose. "He'd figure it was all in the family."

Her eyes widened in what he was afraid was shock. Did that mean she wasn't ready for what he had in mind?

As they walked out to the car, he called his parents, getting his father this time, who in his usual way received the good news with a long silence. Call over, Ben said to Nadia, "I asked for your window to be boarded up—"

"Déjà vu," she muttered.

His mouth quirked. "—but I'd like it if you'd come home with me tonight."

"Yes. Please." And Nadia tucked her hand in his.

Emotion swelled in him, complex, painful and good. Since he'd started his freshman year in college, an eighteen-year-old boy who didn't yet know his big sister would be brutally raped a year later, he wouldn't have used the word *happy* to describe himself. *Happy*, he discovered now,

was no longer the same, simplistic concept…
but, damn, it was powerful.

NADIA SHOWERED IMMEDIATELY, frantic to wash the
blood off herself. The sharp scent made her want
to gag. Ben had promised to find her something
to wear. Toweling herself dry, she discovered his
idea of *something* was one of his T-shirts. Period.
She considered putting her panties back on beneath the soft knit T and decided not to bother.
She felt sure he'd have her out of them in no time.

She emerged from the bathroom to find him
waiting in the hall, leaning against the wall. The
sight of him in nothing but low-slung sweatpants
made her whole body cramp with longing.

Ben made a rough sound in his throat and
straightened. Nadia walked right into his arms,
her head against his shoulder.

"When I heard that gunshot…" His voice
broke. "I was so scared. Not knowing which of
you had been shot, how bad you were hurt—"

"If you hadn't gone after her, we still wouldn't
know who and why. I'd still be in danger."

"I know." His arms tightened. "But it killed
me to leave you two to cope on your own."

Eyes burning, Nadia nodded. She thought she
knew what he was telling her, but believing, that
was something else. He wasn't the kind of man
she had ever imagined herself loving, and especially not after her terrible exposure to violence.

But there had been something between them from the beginning. The search of her shop and apartment would have been humiliating under any circumstances. She'd have been angry. But the hurt that seemed to tear her open...that had been because it was *Ben* who suspected her, *Ben* who was callous enough not to care what he was putting her through.

She had believed she could never forgive him.

And yet, here they were.

He let out a long, ragged breath. Nadia lifted her head to meet his eyes.

A muscle twitched in his cheek. "You know I'm in love with you." Just like that, he had bared himself.

The uncertainty Nadia saw on his face shook her. Still, she heard herself saying, "We haven't known each other that long," but knew perfectly well that she was pushing back against herself as much as him. Even so, she laid an open hand on his scratchy jaw.

"That's true." As always, those dark eyes saw deep, increasing her unsettling sense of vulnerability. "When we met at the auction, you flipped a switch in me," he said huskily. "But I could see I scared you, so I tried to convince myself to give you some time before I stopped by at your store." He mocked himself with a twisted smile. "I might have lasted a whole week."

"You're so intense." She wasn't sure how else

to explain her reaction. "I looked at you and *knew* you were fully capable of exploding into violence." Eyes stinging again, she pressed a kiss to his throat. "The next morning, you made me feel safe instead."

He lifted one hand to her nape. The other traveled down her back. It was a second before she realized he was gathering the fabric of the T-shirt. By the time she did, his big hand had found bare flesh and squeezed her butt.

"Until I blew it," he murmured.

"Yes." But her thoughts blurred. Her skin felt sensitized, hot. She was exquisitely conscious of his growing arousal.

"I had to investigate you."

"I know." She squirmed against him.

"Nadia. Will you look at me?"

She went completely still for an instant, then tipped up her chin.

"If you decide not to stay in Byrum, I won't, either." His jaw tightened. "No, I don't plan to turn into a stalker. But…I want to be with you."

Struck speechless, Nadia gaped at him.

His eyes burned. "I need to know how you feel about me. And I mean it. Anywhere you want to go."

Some chances in life, you had to take.

"I want to stay. At least…to see how it goes. And if the atmosphere stays too ugly for me to feel at home, I hope we'll make a decision together about where we should go." She took a deep breath for courage, even as his expression changed. "I love you, too."

For what had to be ten seconds, he only stared at her, as if he really had thought she might reject him, or say, Hey, you're moving too fast. The next thing she knew, he swept her up and carried her into his bedroom.

Passion exploded between them, the lovemaking frantic, hungry, fast. She had barely come back to herself when he started moving inside her again, and this time tenderness tempered the urgency.

His heartbeat in her ear, beneath her hand, Nadia had never slept better.

"I WISH PEOPLE would quit apologizing!" Nadia exclaimed two weeks later. "It's horribly awkward, and I'm afraid they're ending up so embarrassed they'll slink around avoiding me forevermore."

Ben laughed at both the sentiment and her choice of words. "You don't feel even a *little* secret pleasure when they're groveling?"

She tried to frown at him, but the effort wasn't convincing. Finally she sighed. "Okay, sometimes."

Lucy appeared from the kitchen with a basket of cookies from the Hadburg Café. She'd gone earlier today to scope out the shopping in a smaller town, she had told them. If she'd explained what stores she'd visited or what she'd bought, Ben had tuned her out. The cookies were a bonus, though. "Julie Baird," she said now, taking her seat.

"No." He looked at Nadia. "Really?"

"Really." She made a face. "She even did it graciously."

Lucy rolled her eyes. "Because in her egocentricity she had no doubt you'd accept even more graciously and all would be forgiven and forgotten."

Ben reached for a cookie. Oatmeal raisin. "Kills the idea of *forevermore*."

She made a face. "Unfortunately."

"She told us how much she admired the online campaign for the Hixsons and other people." Which had, to date, brought in over $90,000 dollars and was still going strong. Lucy gave a small, feminine snort. "She was sure she could help."

"What did you say?" Ben asked Nadia.

"I told her that I'm not really involved in the effort—" which she wasn't, since Colleen, Lucy and Rebecca Byler had run with it "—but that I'd let Colleen know she was interested in case they ever felt they needed more input."

"A polite 'thanks, but no thanks.'" He took a big bite of cookie.

"She couldn't hide her surprise." Lucy's smile brimmed with satisfaction. "With luck, she won' be back."

"I don't think she was ever really interested in quilting." Nadia took a cookie, too. "What she does enjoy is being in charge. She'll find some other cause."

Ben said, "I saw Jim Wilcox today when I stopped by the hospital to check on the motorcyclist who hit the overpass embankment."

Both women nodded. In a town this size, everyone would hear about a serious accident within a matter of hours, even if they never turned on a television or radio.

"How was he?" Lucy asked. "The guy on the motorcycle, not Jim."

"Hasn't regained consciousness. Doctor is still hopeful, though."

His sister nodded.

"Jim and I crossed paths in the parking lot. He was stunned. Maybe this isn't news to you two, but Bishop Josiah and Roy Yoder—" He stopped. "Did you know he's a minister along with running the cabinetmaking business?"

Nadia nodded as Lucy said, "Hannah has said so."

"Anyway, they sat Jim down and said they have agreed among themselves to take care of the hospital and doctor bills for his little girl, just as they would for a member of their faith. He has dealt fairly with them, the bishop said, and should not have to face such a burden alone."

"Oh, thank God." Tears shimmered in Nadia's eyes. "Hannah said her father agreed to talk to the others, but I hadn't heard what they'd decided. That has to be a staggering amount of money!"

Ben grimaced in agreement. "Jim was surprised to find they had a good idea of how much it would amount to. I reminded him that the Amish undergo extensive surgeries and medical procedures, too. They're not naive. After telling me, Jim, ah, broke down and cried, and I'm guessing it wasn't for the first time."

"His own church members are pitching in, too," Lucy contributed. "Colleen attends the same church. They're taking meals to the family, and have raised over ten thousand so far to help with bills. Maybe now he can use that money for the mortgage or whatever else he's behind on."

Ben chased the last of the cookie with coffee. "His problems aren't over, but he has a chance now."

"Him and the Hixsons." Nadia used her napkin to dab at her eyes. "I don't know why I keep crying. It's just…"

When she failed to come up with an explanation, he filled it in for her. "Happy endings get to you." For that instant, he'd almost forgotten his sister was in the room. It was Nadia he saw with her perplexity and joy.

Her face lit. "Yes!"

There *were* happy endings all around them. People were too often small-minded, selfish, even mean. But he was learning that they were also capable of coming together, of forgiveness and sacrifice, which made him feel better about staying on in Byrum.

The barn raising at Leonard Hixson's place was scheduled for next Friday and Saturday. Unless something came up at work, Ben intended to help at least one of the two days. He knew both Lucy and Nadia were involved in planning and preparing meals to feed the volunteers, in the way of the Amish who used work frolics as a social gathering, too.

The Hixsons had already moved back to their property, thanks to the donation of an old manufactured home. They planned to stay in it for the time being, and use the donated funds to buy the equipment dairy farming required.

The decision had been made to get the Hixsons back on their feet before moving on to raising money for another family. Their loss was the greatest. Some of the other victims had received insurance payouts, and a number of organizations were contributing to the rebuilding.

While Ben's parents were here, they'd driven out to survey the tornado damage. Before leaving three days ago, his dad told them he had kicked in $10,000 to the Hixson dairy farm fund.

"So, I have an announcement," Lucy said suddenly.

The other two looked at her.

"I got a job. I'm going to be working for Hannah's dad, in the cabinet shop. They've gotten busier and busier, and want someone to take over billing, answering phones, greeting people who come in. After Hannah went to work for Nadia, they thought they could do without her, but they're having trouble keeping up."

Ben was careful to hide his conflicted feelings about a job that would have her working closely with an unmarried Amish man she already counted as a friend. She'd have every right to slap him down if he so much as mentioned his concern, however. She was definitely an adult.

And, he reminded himself, happier than she'd been in a lot of years.

Nadia beat him with her congratulations, but he added his.

"I had an idea." It was Nadia his sister was now looking at. "If you're moving in here with Ben, I wondered if you'd rent your apartment to me."

Now, *that* was a great idea. Nadia had been hovering on the fence, keeping most of her stuff at the apartment even though she'd been spending some nights here, him some nights there.

She blinked a couple of times, then turned her gaze on him. "Ben?"

Why did she sound as if she wasn't sure what he wanted?

He took her hand in his. "I want to go to bed with you every night, wake up beside you every morning." He paused. This wasn't the usual way to do this, but why not? "I want us to start planning a wedding."

The tiny gasp from his sister was easily ignored. He stayed focused on Nadia, who had gone completely still. She might not even be breathing, but she searched his face with those haunting eyes.

After a moment, she gave a small nod, as if she'd seen everything she needed to. "Yes." Her smile felt like the sunrise, glorious and hopeful. "I love you."

"I love you, too," he said, voice scratchy. Didn't matter how many times he told her that. Every time, his rib cage constricted his breathing.

Then Nadia smiled at Lucy. "I would love to have you in the apartment."

His sister's delight tightened the squeeze around Ben's chest.

He wouldn't cry, but happy endings got to him, too. Something about himself he'd never known.

Not minding Lucy's presence, he pulled Nadia from her chair and kissed her.

* * * * *

*If you enjoyed this story by
Janice Kay Johnson,
you'll also love her most recent books:*

*PLAIN REFUGE
A MOTHER'S CLAIM
BECAUSE OF A GIRL
THE BABY HE WANTED*

*Watch for her next book
coming in October 2017.*

All available at Harlequin.com.

Get 2 Free Books,
Plus 2 Free Gifts—
just for trying the Reader Service!

Get 2 Free Books,
Plus 2 Free Gifts—
just for trying the Reader Service!

HARLEQUIN *Presents*

Get 2 Free Books,
Plus 2 Free Gifts—
just for trying the Reader Service!

HARLEQUIN
HEARTWARMING™

YES! Please send me 2 FREE Harlequin® Heartwarming™ Larger-Print novels and my 2 FREE mystery gifts (gifts worth about $10 retail). After receiving them, if I don't wish to receive any more books, I can return the shipping statement marked "cancel." If I don't cancel, I will receive 4 brand-new larger-print novels every month and be billed just $5.49 per book in the U.S. or $6.24 per book in Canada. That's a savings of at least 19% off the cover price. It's quite a bargain! Shipping and handling is just 50¢ per book in the U.S. and 75¢ per book in Canada.* I understand that accepting the 2 free books and gifts places me under no obligation to buy anything. I can always return a shipment and cancel at any time. Even if I never buy another book, the 2 free books and gifts are mine to keep forever.

161/361 IDN GLQL

Name	(PLEASE PRINT)	
Address		Apt. #
City	State/Prov.	Zip/Postal Code

Signature (if under 18, a parent or guardian must sign)

Mail to the **Reader Service:**
IN U.S.A.: P.O. Box 1867, Buffalo, NY 14240-1867
IN CANADA: P.O. Box 611, Fort Erie, Ontario L2A 9Z9

Want to try two free books from another line?
Call 1-800-873-8635 today or visit www.ReaderService.com.

* Terms and prices subject to change without notice. Prices do not include applicable taxes. Sales tax applicable in N.Y. Canadian residents will be charged applicable taxes. Offer not valid in Quebec. This offer is limited to one order per household. Books received may not be as shown. Not valid for current subscribers to Harlequin Heartwarming Larger-Print books. All orders subject to credit approval. Credit or debit balances in a customer's account(s) may be offset by any other outstanding balance owed by or to the customer. Please allow 4 to 6 weeks for delivery. Offer available while quantities last.

Your Privacy—The Reader Service is committed to protecting your privacy. Our Privacy Policy is available online at www.ReaderService.com or upon request from the Reader Service.

We make a portion of our mailing list available to reputable third parties that offer products we believe may interest you. If you prefer that we not exchange your name with third parties, or if you wish to clarify or modify your communication preferences, please visit us at www.ReaderService.com/consumerschoice or write to us at Reader Service Preference Service, P.O. Box 9062, Buffalo, NY 14240-9062. Include your complete name and address.

HW17

Get 2 Free Books,

HARLEQUIN

INTRIGUE

Plus 2 Free Gifts—

just for trying the Reader Service!